D1348705

I2748930

Praise for award-winning author of
Silk, Swords and Surrender
Jeannie Lin

'Lin's politically and culturally rich story
is atypical, sensual, and filled with honour
and wit.'

—Publishers Weekly on
The Sword Dancer

'This is one bit of fancy and fearless footwork
that you won't want to miss.'

—Heroes and Heartbreakers on
A Dance with Danger

'Lin has a gift for bringing the wondrous and
colourful world of ancient China to readers.'

—RT Book Reviews on
My Fair Concubine

'The action never stops, the love story is strong
and the historical backdrop is fascinating. For
the adventurous reader…this is a treasure.'

—RT Book Reviews on
Butterfly Swords

Award-winning author **Jeannie Lin** started writing her first book while working as a high school science teacher in South Central Los Angeles. Her stories are inspired by a mix of historical research and *wuxia* adventure tales. Jeannie's groundbreaking historical romances set in Tang Dynasty China have received multiple awards, including the Golden Heart for her debut novel *Butterfly Swords*.

Books by Jeannie Lin

The Touch of Moonlight

The Taming of Mei Lin
is linked to *Butterfly Swords*

The Lady's Scandalous Night
is linked to *The Dragon and the Pearl*

An Illicit Temptation
is linked to *My Fair Concubine*

Capturing the Silken Thief
is linked to *The Lotus Palace*

Don't miss these full-length novels,
all available now!

SILK, SWORDS AND SURRENDER

Jeannie Lin

MILLS & BOON™

First published in Great Britain 2016
by Mills & Boon, an imprint of HarperCollins*Publishers*
1 London Bridge Street, London, SE1 9GF

Large Print edition 2017
SILK, SWORDS AND SURRENDER
© 2016 Harlequin Books S.A.
ISBN: 978-0-263-06747-7

The publisher acknowledges the copyright holder of the individual works as follows:

THE TOUCH OF MOONLIGHT © 2016 Chi Nguyen-Rettig

THE TAMING OF MEI LIN © 2010 Chi Nguyen-Rettig
First published as a Mills & Boon Historical Undone eBook

THE LADY'S SCANDALOUS NIGHT © 2011 Chi Nguyen-Rettig
First published as a Mills & Boon Historical Undone eBook

AN ILLICIT TEMPTATION © 2012 Chi Nguyen-Rettig
First published as a Mills & Boon Historical Undone eBook

CAPTURING THE SILKEN THIEF © 2012 Chi Nguyen-Rettig
First published as a Mills & Boon Historical *Undone!* eBook

Printed and bound in Great Britain
by CPI Antony Rowe, Chippenham, Wiltshire

CONTENTS

THE TOUCH OF
MOONLIGHT

Author Note

I started writing the earliest novella in this collection six years ago. I remember the joy of writing it—I had just sold my first novel, *Butterfly Swords*, and *The Taming of Mei Lin* was originally a story-within-a-story of that larger narrative.

When it was released I remember posting instructions on how to download it, since so many readers had never read an e-Book before. How times have changed! Six years in a writer's life isn't a great expanse of time, yet it feels as if publishing has lived a thousand lives.

During that time I've alternated between full-length novels and shorter works, expanding my Tang Dynasty world. With the shorter stories I was able to experiment with condensed timelines and building conflict quickly. I was able to explore ways of creating a vibrant world in fewer words while playing with multiple side stories and characters.

In this collection there are linked stories to *Butterfly Swords*, *The Dragon and the Pearl* and *My Fair Concubine*. *Capturing the Silken Thief* was written as a lead-in to the Lotus Palace series. And the new addition, *The Touch of Moonlight* presents a girl-next-door tale, Tang Dynasty style, to counterbalance the sword fights and high drama.

I loved writing these stories and I've always been proud of them. I've always hoped they would be gathered into a single collection for readers to enjoy and here they are! Dreams do come true.

You can find out more about these stories or contact me online at my website jeannielin.com. Let me know which story is your favourite.

Chapter One

Tang Dynasty China, 841 AD

A flock of young ladies hovered near the garden wall. The neighborhood girls were on their afternoon stroll, and a pleasant cloud of chatter and gossip surrounded them. Baozhen appreciated the familiar sight after nearly a year away from the city. He appreciated it enough to stop at the end of the lane to watch and listen.

He knew all these lovely sparrows, of course. Everyone knew everyone in this ward. The courtyard houses were packed closely together, with only their surrounding walls to provide privacy. Families lived in the residences from one generation to the next, sharing news big and small across the narrow alleyways between them.

Lian was among them, a face perhaps a little more familiar than the rest. She was merchant

Chen's daughter, and the Chen family were his closest neighbors. Lian had her eye to an opening in the garden wall while the other girls giggled around her. The odd thing was that Lian—sensible, serious Lian—was giggling along with the rest of them.

"Now, *this* is a sight these eyes have missed," he announced.

The ladies scattered like peach blossoms in the wind as he approached, only to regroup with a fresh round of giggling.

"Baozhen!"

"You're back."

"Did you bring me anything?"

The last voice was the quietest of them. "You're home early."

Little Lian was blushing when he looked at her. The last time he'd seen her had been on the day of his departure. She'd come out to her front gate to wish him a safe journey, wearing a blue robe the color of a clouded sky. Odd that he'd remember that now.

Her father had a formidable reputation in the East Market. He'd cleverly negotiated lucrative deals with foreign traders from the northwest and had a reputation for being able to procure anything. Chen was a serious businessman, with no tolerance for fools, and his daughter was the same. Lian *never* blushed. Baozhen simply had to see what was on the other side of that wall.

"What could have everyone so distracted that they'd forget to greet an old friend?" he accused lightly as he went to the aperture.

"Oh, just the new object of our admiration," one of the girls teased. "You've been away for so long we've all but forgotten you."

A chorus of voices agreed. They really were pretty little songbirds and, as always, he appreciated the attention. He had grown up with them. There was always some infatuation or another among them. It was with curiosity rather than jealousy that he searched out the figure through the wall.

"Liu Jinhai?"

More giggling.

Jinhai was flamboyantly dressed as usual. His father dealt in textiles, and Jinhai never gave up an opportunity to display his wardrobe. He was probably on his way to the drinking house. Baozhen might even join him later.

"I'm wounded." Baozhen grinned as he faced them. "For a couple of bolts of pretty silk you've forgotten me."

"No!" they cooed.

"Never."

"He's not as handsome as you."

One girl took his right side and another quickly swept in to take his left. Lian remained apart, looking upon the theatrics somewhat impatiently.

"When did you return?" she asked.

"Yesterday evening. I was actually coming to pay your family a visit for tea."

As entertaining as the cooing and flattery was, Baozhen shifted into conversation with his neighbor and the others took the hint. They flitted away to other diversions.

His family managed several transport routes to the cities of the southern provinces. This last trip had taken longer than usual as it had been time for him to learn the routes and meet their many business associates.

"I had heard you wouldn't be back for another month at least."

Lian seemed subdued, and much less enthusiastic than the others about his return. Something else seemed to occupy her thoughts.

"I missed being in the city," he said.

They fell into easy step beside one another, making their way down to the lane where their families resided. Lian was looking straight ahead and he took the opportunity to scrutinize her a little more closely. She seemed somehow...*different* walking beside him. Something about the way she carried herself.

Baozhen broke into a smile. "I missed you, as well," he added as an afterthought.

She didn't show any response to the casual flirtation. Instead she smoothed her fingers through her hair, tucking the left side neatly behind her ear, and continued inquiring about his journey and the state of his father's business.

He should have known better. This was the child with the dirty knees who'd run wild through the alleyways in pigtails. The girl he'd teased for being bony and the one who'd thrown crab apples at his head whenever he'd done so. They were too familiar for any tantalizing innuendoes between them.

And he hadn't really missed Lian while he'd been away. Well, he hadn't exactly thought of her much, but now that she was here beside him maybe he had missed her. Was it possible not to know how much you'd missed someone until you saw them again?

"Is Liu Jinhai an acquaintance of yours?" She was looking away again, occupied with straightening her sleeves.

Baozhen frowned. "You could say."

"Hmm." She made a soft, noncommittal sound

beneath her breath that he would spend the rest of the day trying to interpret.

He went on talking about Hangzhou. The lushness of the forests and the great West Lake. Hadn't Lian been excited that he was going to these faraway places? When she'd bade him farewell, the way she'd regarded him, with eyes shining and full of wonder, had made his chest puff out. She was only the skinny neighbor girl, but she was still female, and female admiration was not something to be shrugged aside.

But Lian was barely paying attention to him now that she wasn't so skinny anymore. Her eyes had taken on that faraway look again and her cheeks were tinged pink.

"Baozhen." She interrupted his tale without remorse. "We're longtime friends, aren't we?"

Lian's midnight-dark eyes were finally fixed on him and he was reminded of another time when she had approached him so directly. An unexpected knot formed in his throat.

"Of course," he said casually, with a smile that he found he had to force. He who was so careless with his smiles. Who was notorious for them.

"Can you introduce me to him?"

"To who?"

She blinked away from his gaze, batting silken

lashes that were longer than he remembered. Heaven, everything was different from what he remembered.

"You know who," she said impatiently. "Liu Jin-hai."

Baozhen barked out a laugh, and Lian didn't have anything to throw at his head besides a poisoned look. His skin was a shade darker, turned copper by his travels in the sun, and he did appear more worldly—though that was likely her imagination. She could see his boyish behavior hadn't changed.

"Did you just remember an old joke?" she asked, glowering. "Because I haven't said anything funny."

"Since when do your attentions follow the whims of that flock of songbirds?"

"I don't pay any attention to what the others are fawning over," she protested. "For instance, now that you're back they'll likely return to swooning over you. I find Liu Jinhai interesting, that's all."

Baozhen stopped short, forcing her to halt and turn back to him. "Interesting?" he challenged with a quirk of his mouth.

She lifted her chin stubbornly. "Yes."

His eyes creased at the corners as he regarded her. That was twice he'd paused to look her over.

Lian glowed inside with triumph. Finally Baozhen was the one who was confused and trying to figure her out.

She had known him for as long as she could remember. Their families lived side by side, with only an alleyway separating them. When the neighborhood girls had started gossiping, and calling Baozhen handsome, Lian had stared at him, eyes squinted, trying to figure out what they were talking about.

He was six years her elder, and infamous throughout the ward. Even Ming-ha, her older cousin, had been infatuated with him at one point. Lian had caught them kissing once, behind the shrubbery in the garden. Lian alone had seemed immune to Baozhen's charms—until three years ago. Since then it had been torture to maintain her veneer of indifference. It was torture to continue to be overlooked every single day.

Now, for the first time, Baozhen was actually paying attention to her. All it had taken was the mention of another man's name. She should have guessed as much. Men were like rams, battering their hard heads together.

"Liu Jinhai is a no-good wastrel," Baozhen began. "He drinks. He frequents gambling dens and cavorts with song girls. Completely unsuitable for you."

Lian listened to the litany, each denouncement adding to her good mood. "The same things can be said of you. Every single one."

"I'm not suitable for you either."

He tapped the tip of her nose with a finger and graced her with one of his smiles. It was a bright flash that tickled her insides and weakened her knees. Baozhen had a way of doing that without any effort at all. He made her feel important, as if all that radiance shone only on her, but she knew that wasn't true. He had that effect on everyone.

Lian didn't give him the satisfaction of swatting his hand away. It would play into his view of her as a young and impetuous brat, and she was tired of playing that game.

"I don't need your opinion of him," she insisted. "All I want is an introduction."

"I can't stand by and watch a dear friend be devoured by a wolf. Why, you're practically like a little sister to me."

Oh, she didn't like *that* at all. "No matter, then," she said with a wave, and continued toward home. "I'm sure there are countless places where I can run into Liu Jinhai while I'm alone and in distress..."

Baozhen caught up to her in several long strides. "All right, I surrender. I'll introduce you to your precious prince if only to keep you out of trouble. I never knew you could be such a she-demon when you wanted something."

Chapter Two

"You can't go looking like that," Baozhen declared.

Apparently her family had immediately welcomed him into the fold. He was roaming about their courtyard once again as if he lived there.

"You're going to be late," she told him.

He paid no attention to her reprimand. Instead he frowned as he looked her over. She had taken care to dress in a light summer robe with many eye-catching colors. The outer layer was a hand-painted gauze which revealed the barest hint of her arms through its sheerness. The morning air was cool in the garden, with a slight breeze rustling the cypress trees. A flood of heat swept through her as Baozhen's gaze lingered at the lowered neckline.

"Too obvious," he declared. "Any man seeing a woman like this would know that she's interested."

"So?"

"A lady should be a bit more subtle. *Yin* is the essence of darkness and secrets, after all."

Lian stood her ground. "Of course. It's so much better to be so subtle and secretive that I'm never noticed at all. Not even when someone has known me for years and years."

Baozhen's scowl deepened as he considered her words. A look of displeasure creased his brow, but within moments it had been smoothed out to his usual careless look. The one that so easily charmed the world.

"There are other ways of being noticed," he drawled.

The low suggestiveness in his tone took her off-balance and she scrambled to recover. "What are you doing here, anyway? Cousin Ming-ha and I were just headed out to the park."

They were supposed to "accidentally" meet Liu Jinhai in an hour.

"I came to bring you your gift." He produced a parcel from the fold of his sleeve. "I saw this in Suzhou. It made me think of you."

The package was wrapped in plain sackcloth. Despite its humble appearance, the gesture warmed her, and a little shiver of excitement ran down her spine as she loosened the twine. Baozhen folded his hands behind his back and hovered to watch.

She held up the polished hardwood frame wrapped with red cord. "A slingshot?"

He beamed proudly. "You used to be quite dangerous with one of those."

When she was twelve. "What did you get Mingha?" she demanded.

"A bottle of perfume," he replied with a shrug.

Her cousin warranted a gift that was pretty and feminine, to match her pretty and feminine self, while Lian received a child's toy. She could feel the heat rising in her cheeks. Baozhen really was insufferable.

"You don't like it?" he asked, hurt.

"No, it's wonderful. *Perfect*," she said through her teeth.

"You're upset." He was following her through the garden. Still smiling. "I can bring you another gift if you'd like."

She turned on him. "You didn't speak to Liu Jinhai at all, did you?"

"Of course I did. I have nothing to fear from him."

His smile widened. That devastating smile. It confused her so.

"You'll get your chance encounter, but—looking as made-up as you do—I'm thinking you're hoping for a little bit more than an introduction."

She realized he was gradually backing her into the corner of the garden, behind the pruned cypress. Now he was back he was obviously looking for more conquests to add to his collection. Her hand shot out to brace against his chest, where she collided against a solid wall of muscle.

"Scoundrel."

The scoundrel laughed. "It's just a kiss, Lian."

She couldn't help the way her stomach fluttered, nor how her heart pounded. He ventured a step closer, but she held firm. She knew Baozhen too well. He had no control over his effect on women and had come to accept their adoration as a matter of course. It took no effort for him to make her feel these things. He did it without knowledge and without care, taking no responsibility for her hope, her excitement or her pain.

He was blissfully ignorant while her spirits soared or plummeted at his whim.

She gave him a little shove, though it did little to move him. "Maybe it's not you I want a kiss from."

"You asked me for one once."

She froze.

Any gentleman would have conveniently forgotten her request. She had been young and had foolishly gathered her courage to ask for a kiss.

Baozhen had been older and more experienced. He had refused her. Even worse.

"You laughed at me." The sharp, piercing embarrassment came back to her. She had shrunk inside to nothing more than a wisp of smoke and disappeared into her room for days.

Baozhen looked stricken. "I didn't laugh at you." He paused, as if trying to recall. "Or I didn't mean to, if that's what happened. You surprised me. It was just that you were—"

He struggled for words, his smooth charm failing him. He seemed earnest in his uncertainty and she let down her guard.

"Perhaps I was waiting for a better time," he said, but his tone was more gentle than beguiling.

A small crack formed in her resistance. He backed her farther behind the cover of the shrubbery and this time she let him. She let him because it was Baozhen, and it had hurt so much when he'd rejected her. She had been fifteen years old and foolish, and now she was eighteen and not so foolish—but she still very much wanted that kiss.

He didn't put his arms around her. Instead he rested his hands over her shoulders as he bent to her, holding her carefully, as if she were made of porcelain. She couldn't breathe. Baozhen was so close and she had imagined this for so long, in so many different ways. She could feel the sigh of his breath against her lips, and then his mouth was on hers.

His lips were softer and warmer than she'd imagined—but in no more than a heartbeat he was gone.

She was left blinking up at him. *That was all?* Baozhen straightened abruptly, and for a moment they simply stood there. The tingle of the maddeningly brief touch had already faded. She didn't even have any time to consider returning his kiss.

"I'll see you at the park." Baozhen wasn't smiling or teasing, or really doing anything but staring at her oddly.

"Until then," she said, her voice dull.

She stood clutching that ridiculous slingshot to her breast as he turned to go. Someone as adept as Baozhen couldn't even flirt with her properly. She truly was as hopeless as she had always feared.

Baozhen had just arrived at the park when he saw the yellow-pink flash of Lian's summer robe through the green. She was at the far end, strolling along beside her cousin. Within moments she caught his eye but quickly looked away, pretending to be absorbed with something Ming-ha was saying.

"I thought we were going to the tea house," Jinhai said from behind him.

Usually he found Liu Jinhai to be an agreeable companion. They had similar interests and he was good-humored and unpretentious. Today, Baozhen found him unbearable.

"In a while. There's something we must do first," Baozhen said, resigned.

The two ladies glided along the pebbled walkway, making an unerring path toward them.

Conveniently, it was Ming-ha who called out. "Why, it's Baozhen!"

Lian came up beside her, her robe catching the breeze just enough to tease them with a glimpse of the rounded curves beneath the delicate material.

Baozhen stepped out in front of them. "What a surprise. This pleasant morning has become more enjoyable."

"Ah, now I see…" Jinhai's murmur came low and amused from behind him.

Baozhen suppressed a scowl and positioned himself squarely at the lead, to greet Lian and her cousin. Ming-ha was the taller of the two. Her features were slender and elongated and he had been thoroughly fascinated with her once for half a summer, in the way of a boy just beyond childhood.

It was Lian who had his complete attention now.

She was softer in the face, with eyes that were keen like a cat's. After such a long time away, he had decided he *did* find Lian pretty. This morning had confirmed it. Why else would he have been so compelled to kiss her? Now, every time he saw her, he couldn't look away. His senses demanded to be constantly fed with this new discovery.

"It's been too long, Miss Lian," he said with an overflow of meaning.

"Nonsense, Baozhen. We live next to each other. We see each other too often, one might say."

Lian had drawn a red tint over her lips since they'd parted. The little fox. She also had a fan in her hands, which she wasn't using at all to her advantage. It was supposed to be an excuse to bring attention to shapely hands and bared wrists, but instead she was waving it in short, impatient movements while trying to glance around him.

"Your friend, here, is another matter," she said pointedly. "I don't believe we've ever met."

Her directness was refreshing—except that it was directed at *the wrong man*. Baozhen could sense Jinhai similarly trying to weave around him to make an introduction. Any man would, the way Lian was dressed and painted like a newly ripened peach, ready to be plucked.

"Liu Jinhai's father is a textile merchant in the

East Market," Baozhen offered rather magnani-mously. "And this is Miss Chen Lian."

"Miss Lian." Jinhai executed a rather courtly-looking bow.

Baozhen noted with displeasure how Jinhai im-mediately adopted the more intimate form of ad-dress. He also had nothing good to say about the way Lian's eyes fluttered downward. She echoed Jinhai's name between her lips with a sweet mur-mur that set Baozhen's pulse into a dangerous fer-vor.

"Miss Lian's family lives in the courtyard beside ours. We're very close," he added.

"Our *families* are very close," Lian corrected, flashing him the eye.

Jinhai had managed to maneuver around him to stand beside her. He granted her a smile that was full of even white teeth. "You must have interest-ing stories to tell about this fool."

"I do…but only if one wants to hear about Guo Baozhen. Do you?"

"On second thought, I don't. Not really."

They shared a laugh. How charming.

Baozhen was preparing to insert himself back into the conversation when dear Ming-ha chimed in. "Let's go see the fish pond."

She took his arm and held on tight before he could slip away.

"Let's all go together," he said, loud enough to interrupt Lian and Jinhai. Ming-ha's nails dug lightly into his forearm.

Jinhai gallantly took Lian's side as they circled the pond, remaining a respectful arm's length away—which was still too close in Baozhen's opinion.

"Our fathers often do business with each other," Jinhai was saying. "Mister Chen is a tough businessman, but always fair."

"My father speaks very highly of yours, as well," Lian replied. "Funny how our families know each other but we two have never met."

"I'm grateful that fate brought me to the park this morning, Miss Lian."

"I was having the same thought."

Baozhen snorted, causing both of them to turn to look at him. Lian lashed him with a glare. He replied with a smirk.

The two of them turned back to their conversation. Jinhai was being a gentleman, the dog. He was commenting on the beauty of nature and even stole a few verses from the poet Li Bai. Lian was nodding politely, offering a few meek words here and there.

Baozhen couldn't believe how bland the conversation was. It was nothing like the spirited exchanges he and Lian shared.

One turn around the carp pond later and Lian took her leave of Jinhai with a proper bow. Baozhen needn't have worried. Jinhai must have thoroughly bored her for Lian to give up so easily. He knew her temperament. She had no tolerance for coy little games.

He was beaming in triumph when she came to him to say farewell. He wouldn't tease her too much about this, he resolved.

She leaned in to take him into her confidence. "Thank you," she whispered softly.

The look she gave him was full of joy. Her smile brightened and the warmth of it radiated throughout her. Baozhen's own smile quickly faded.

Lian looked happy. Happier than he could remember ever seeing her. All for a few lines of stolen poetry from some peacock who barely knew her.

Chapter Three

Lian placed the pebble into the leather sling and took careful aim. She was perched on top of the gardener's ladder, which raised her high enough over the courtyard wall to see into the alleyway. She also had clear sight of the side entrance to the Guo residence. As soon as Baozhen appeared, she let the pebble fly. It flew past his ear and struck against the gate.

"Hey—"

She sighed. "I must be out of practice."

Baozhen brushed a hand over the front of his tunic to regain his composure.

He glanced up at her from the alleyway, showing off the strong cut of his jaw and that playful mouth. "Miss Lian, I see that you're in a blood-thirsty mood today."

Some of the successful merchants in the ward wore bright embroidered fabrics, as a show of their wealth, but Baozhen and his family favored muted, darker colors. He didn't need a bright banner to draw attention to himself.

"Have you heard?" she asked.

Baozhen responded with a raised eyebrow—a look that he thought made him endearing. Most of the neighborhood girls agreed.

"Liu Jinhai sent my family a gift of tea and lychees yesterday," she said smugly.

"Hmm...lychees. You must have really made an impression."

So at ease with himself. It wasn't a matter of pride or vanity for him. Everything came naturally to him.

"There's some creature hovering at your head, there," he remarked.

She couldn't help gloating. She touched a hand to the gilded hummingbird ornament. "It's a hairpin. Jinhai had it delivered to me personally."

"Let me guess: along with a few lines of poetry that he copied from somewhere?"

She sniffed, refusing to let him dim her glow. Baozhen disappeared momentarily into his house to re-emerge atop his wall. They were now face-to-face across the two compounds.

"So, only two days and Liu Jinhai is already

introducing himself to your parents and sending you gifts?"

"Nothing as impressive as a slingshot," she pointed out wickedly.

"I should have thought more carefully about arming you. I don't think you'll miss next time, and this handsome face is the only asset I have."

"Don't forget the mouth part of that face," she retorted.

He laughed at that, and a lazy warmth filled her. It was so wonderful, speaking with Baozhen like this. All his attention was focused on her and it didn't matter what they said. The only thing that mattered was spending time in his company.

"Now that you've shown yourself to be so highly sought after..." he began.

She preened accordingly.

"Are you certain you want to limit yourself to only one admirer? You should have an army of suitors pushing their way through the gates."

"Not everyone needs to surround themselves with a flock of admirers," Lian scoffed. "Some of us are only looking for one person to make us happy."

He frowned, confused.

"Liu Jinhai actually thinks I'm pretty," she added, a little too shyly.

"*I* think you're pretty," he replied, a little too easily.

"You call me 'alley cat.' Like all the scrawny strays prowling the streets."

"I'll have to come up with a better name. That one hardly suits you anymore."

He granted her a look that was far from brotherly and her toes curled with delight. He didn't even have to make an effort to coax every part of her into drawing toward him with longing.

"Are you going to the banquet tonight at the Ko mansion?" he asked.

Ko was the registrar, whose offices recorded and approved all the goods that flowed through the East Market. He was celebrating his son's civil appointment and had invited all the influential merchants and businessmen of the ward.

"Father and Mother will be attending," she said.

"And you?"

She shrugged airily. "I have a feeling I won't be well enough to go out this evening."

"Oh?" His eyebrow was raised again, but this time it wasn't in a charming fashion.

Baozhen took all the attention bestowed upon him for granted. He was used to having women sighing at his every word and he had become indifferent. She would be just another lovesick maiden if she fell prey to him.

"My family will be out all night drinking wine and playing the dice. I'm already feeling a bit tired," she declared, conspicuously adjusting the hummingbird pin. "It's best I stay home alone and rest."

"Lian…" he began in warning tones.

She took that opportunity to disappear down the ladder. Her heart skipped with excitement as her feet settled onto the ground. Baozhen's look of concern had been the last thing she saw before descending. And it had been very far from indifferent.

It was evening and the neighborhood had cleared. Everyone had gone to attend the registrar's gathering. Baozhen remained behind—only to find that Lian had already slipped away from home. He'd expected as much from the dreamy look in her eyes that morning. She was a smitten young girl, floating in a world of clouds. With cursed hummingbirds flitting about her.

Liu Jinhai could be a gentleman when he tried. He was capable of being smooth and charming and well-spoken. But he was a wolf at heart. Cads like Liu Jinhai and himself ran in the same pack.

It was all in good fun. Flirtation, secret meetings, stolen kisses in the dark—until someone got careless. Until some pretty, passionate flower like Lian, who believed in eternal love, came along and made them lose their heads. The wolves were prey as much as predator in this game.

Baozhen would have been wasting his breath to try to dissuade her. No one since the first dynasty had ever been talked out of a romantic liaison. Certainly not any love-stricken young girl.

It wasn't hard to figure out the location for their secret meeting. There were only a few places one could sneak away to in the ward. Baozhen returned to the public park. Sure enough, there was an orb lantern bobbing in the trees just beyond the carp pond.

"Were you expecting me?" he asked as he entered the circle of trees.

Lian jumped from her spot on the stone bench. To his relief, she was still alone.

"No," she said. "I wasn't."

He made himself a place beside her. "One wolf is as good as another."

"You're more of an old goat than a wolf," she complained.

Heaven help him, he liked her. He had always enjoyed her company, but now he was forced to admit it. She'd always laughed at him, at what everyone thought him to be. She'd teased him and challenged him as much as he'd tormented her. What they'd shared had become so much more than childish games, but he had never known it until now.

This was a more inconvenient discovery than his sudden realization that Lian was pretty. When Jinhai showed up, Baozhen would simply have to kill him. And with his bare hands, too, though Baozhen had never been violent by nature.

"So, Jinhai slipped you a note telling you to come here?"

She didn't answer. Instead she folded her hands in her lap and stared into the night.

"And when you saw it your heart began beating faster than it ever had. You read that letter again and again, keeping the precious paper hidden from everyone. Every time you thought of it you could hardly breathe, and tonight you couldn't come here fast enough. It's exciting to be desired like that."

He faced her and willed her to look at him. She finally did.

"You're probably a little frightened, as well."

"I never realized the likes of you put so much thought into what happens to their many admirers."

"I don't. I never did—" *Before.*

The word was left unspoken and it was his turn to stare into the night. The rising moon cast silver ripples across the pond and he was stricken by a sense of loneliness. Every new face, every kiss was a novelty, a new adventure, but they all faded away when the slightest wind blew. He'd known too many empty embraces.

"You really believe you and Liu Jinhai are meant to be?" he admonished her.

Baozhen knew what that was like. He'd once thought his first love would be his only love. The only love possible in his overflowing heart. It was everyone's rite of passage, but Lian was so sensible and Jinhai was such a… The scoundrel just wasn't enough for her, and Lian should be bright enough to see it.

"Oh, Baozhen, you sound so serious." She sighed.

"This *is* serious. We grew up together." This was exactly the sort of conversation he was not good at. The serious ones. "I'm older than you. There are things I know from experience."

Lian stiffened. "Are you saying you have a duty to protect me?"

"You have no real brothers."

She made an impatient sound. "You of all people should know. Perhaps Liu Jinhai is not my other half—the summer to my winter, the dragon to my phoenix." The lantern light gave her eyes a wicked gleam. "But at least he might like me enough to kiss me properly."

Properly?

The wolf instinct took over and a lightning streak of fire shot through him. He reached for her and pulled her against him roughly. Lian grabbed on to his shoulders to steady herself before his mouth descended.

She made a startled sound as his lips pressed against hers. The moment he felt her yielding against him a fever streaked through him. He had known Lian all her life. If she wanted to flirt and kiss someone just to satisfy her curiosity it should be him.

And he had no intention of keeping this kiss "proper."

The first touch of his lips stole everything from her. All strength drained from her limbs and every breath was surrendered to him. Baozhen was kissing her. *Kissing her.* But it was so much more than the brief meeting of lips he'd shown her in the courtyard. It was breath and body. The smell of him was so close. The roughness of his mouth was urging her own to yield, to open to him.

His arms tightened around her and his kiss was

relentless. Magnificently so. She could feel the heat of him as he surrounded her. Her own skin had come alive…her senses were awake and sharpened, demanding more.

When he broke the kiss, she was gasping for air. Her heart pounded as if she'd run a hundred *li*.

"Baozhen…" She murmured his name, her voice filled with wonder. He'd devastated her.

"Put your arms around me," he urged in a low voice.

Her hands gripped his upper arms, the crisp material of his tunic clenched in her fingers. Then she circled her arms around his neck as he pulled her fully onto his lap. His mouth captured hers again.

She sighed into the embrace. His palm traced a slow path down her spine before curving at her waist to pull her close. Their bodies molded together, soft against hard. If the first kiss had been meant to destroy her defenses, this second kiss was intended to savor the victory. Baozhen's touch was confident as he tantalized her. With each caress her body responded, becoming flushed and swollen with pleasure.

So many nights trying to imagine what it would be like to be kissed. Not by anyone, but by Baozhen. She'd wondered if she'd know how to kiss him back, or where to put her hands. All those doubts fled in his embrace. He held her and guided her. There was nothing to do but feel.

He coaxed her lips gently apart and a tiny shock rippled through her at the touch of his tongue inside her mouth. Every muscle within her tensed, but she gripped him tighter, exhilarated. He explored her with just the tip of his tongue, inviting her to taste him in the same way. Before long she'd grown bold, reaching for him with every part of her, her body pressing against him. He was broader, harder, stronger than she'd imagined. And she ached with a fever more intense than any she'd ever suffered. An ache gathered low in her belly, in the soft place between her thighs.

Baozhen lifted his head and continued to hold her cradled against him, though they no longer kissed. In the dim light his eyes looked black and endless. He was breathing hard and she could hear each labored exhalation. Down below she could feel him hardening, and it fascinated her. *This* was the way a man kissed a woman he burned for.

"Your reputation is well-deserved," she said in awe, barely able to find her voice.

"Don't say that."

He rested his forehead against hers. His skin was damp and flushed, though the night was cool around them. She didn't say anything. She was too happy to think of words.

They stayed that way, folded around each other, for what seemed like a long time. Was she brave enough to try to kiss *him* now? She definitely, definitely hoped there would be more of that.

"We should go."

Before Lian could gather her courage, Baozhen gently lifted her from him and back onto the bench.

The darkness hid her look of disappointment. She would have been content to stay there all night.

Baozhen held the lantern for her and they hardly spoke as they made their way back to their street. Lian couldn't help glancing at him as they walked side by side. Every inch of her had become awakened and newly aware. She searched his face for some small sign that things had changed between them—that she was something more to him than the plain, skinny girl who lived in the next house over.

Baozhen turned to her as they neared the front gate of her house. He slanted her a half-smile that held unspoken knowledge and a shiver of pleasure coursed through her. She didn't care if he'd given this sly look to a hundred other girls. He was looking at her that way now. Only her.

"No one is home yet," she ventured as they came

to a stop and he handed her the lantern. The light sputtered inside, the candle nearly spent. "They won't be back for hours."

She could see the walls of the Guo residence just beyond her house, and the thought of watching Baozhen disappear inside them tonight left a hollow feeling in her chest.

He ran his thumb over his mouth, swiping at the color that lingered there from the tint on her lips. There was something so masculine and assured about the gesture.

"That's a foolish thing to tell me," he admonished.

Heat rose up the back of her neck. How silly of her! She should have left him gracefully and then waited for Baozhen to come to her—but there had been so many times when she'd waited and watched from afar, hoping he'd turn away from his newest beauty just to notice her. Give her one little look.

Here she was once again—overeager and naive before him.

"Farewell, then," she mumbled.

Hastily, she ducked through the gate without looking back. She couldn't wait to disappear into her room and bury herself beneath her quilt.

A moment later she heard the sound of footsteps behind her and her heart leapt.

Lian. Foolish little Lian.

Baozhen followed her through the garden, appreciating the tapering of her waist and the slight sway of her hips beneath the thin robe she wore. He was discovering all those things very quickly. That she had a waist and hips, and a luscious mouth and breasts, and all the parts a woman held in her arsenal to bring a man to his knees. His blood pumped so hard he could barely think.

Lian was the most dangerous sort of woman. She was impetuous and passionate and she lacked any fear of him. She was also too innocent to know how this game was played, and too bold to play it with caution. If Jinhai had come to the park tonight, as Lian had intended, would it be a different wolf now following her irresistibly to her chamber?

Foolish Baozhen.

The courtyard was silent as Lian opened her door. She used the candle from the lantern to light the oil lamp inside, and Baozhen found himself for the first time in Lian's sleeping quarters. He noticed how her hand trembled as she set the candle down.

He approached her slowly. "What did you think would happen here, Lian?"

Her chin lifted and her eyes met his, though he could see her gaze wavering slightly and the slight blush in her cheeks. She was trying so hard to be worldly.

"I thought we would kiss some more."

"And did you really think that would be all?"

He was close enough to detect her perfume. She smelled of springtime and innocence, which was seductive in its own way. Her mouth was still flushed from his attentions.

"You know better than to invite a wolf into your home."

"I'm not a fool," she insisted. "And I didn't invite any wolf. I invited you."

"And if Jinhai had come tonight?" A flash of anger streaked through him, but he countered it with a smile.

"I don't see Liu Jinhai here."

"Indeed…"

He reached for the damned hummingbird pin and tossed it into the corner in one motion. Despite her bold words he saw her pulse jump as he lowered his hand to her cheek.

He caressed her with just the tips of his fingers,

murmuring close to her ear. "You shouldn't have asked me in, Lian."

This wasn't just another pretty girl. This was *Lian*—his neighbor, a friend. The little brat who'd grown up into a beautiful and willful woman. He had to be careful and not let things go too far.

Baozhen drew her against him and her lips parted instinctively, as if she'd been waiting for him. The shortness of her breath as he kissed her told him everything. She wanted the danger...this small step into the unknown. This taste of passion that she was pursuing with complete recklessness.

He trailed a caress along her arm and along the underside of her breast. For a moment he hoped she'd shriek in outrage and demand that he leave. Instead she pressed closer, and he knew without a doubt that her once thin and sharp angles had been transformed into soft, pleasing curves. Entranced, he cradled her breast in his palm, stroking his thumb lightly over the rounded nipple. He could feel it tightening to a hard peak beneath the silk robe.

A shudder ran through her and he caught her as her knees weakened. She wound her arms around his neck and did something too seductive to resist.

She spoke his name.

The sound of it on her lips was sultry and decadent. It was a bedroom voice that promised abandon. He stroked her other breast out of greed, just to feel the eager response of her flesh. His own sex thickened within his trousers.

Lian didn't protest when he backed her onto her bed, nor when he worked the edges of her robe open. The bodice hidden underneath was a tantalizing flash of red, embroidered with a lush orchid pattern. The garment fit snugly over her torso, accentuating the swell of her breasts.

"You shouldn't be letting me do this," he taunted lightly as he lay down alongside her.

"Then you shouldn't be doing it," she countered, but it came out as a sensuous purr that nearly undid him.

He reminded himself that there would be no release for him tonight, but that didn't prevent him from easing the edge of her bodice downward. His mouth closed around one pink bud and his tongue circled it hungrily. She writhed against him, making him burn. Her fingers tangled into his hair to hold him to her.

A rush of power and possessiveness filled his chest. He was drunk with the taste of her skin. Lian was his tonight for the taking, if he so desired.

To his surprise, Lian began fumbling at his clothes, trying to disrobe him. He shouldn't have been so shocked. He had never known her to be shy—at least not with him. Her movements, though eager, were unpracticed, and that was what saved her. This wasn't some carefree and nameless dancer or song girl beside him. This was Lian, and she wasn't meant to be used for a night of pleasure.

He took hold of her hands just as she managed to open his tunic. With a wicked grin he guided them over her head. Her wrists were slender enough for him to pin them beneath one hand.

"If you move, I'll stop," he warned.

Her eyes were fixed on him and her pupils were wide and black with desire. Her breasts rose and fell rapidly, half-exposed. She had no idea what would happen next, but he could see how much she wanted to find out. His hold on her would have been easy to break, yet she lay back…waiting. Waiting for him to show her.

With his free hand he reached for her skirt, sliding the silk up over her knees. She continued to watch him, her breath coming faster now as she willed him to continue. Her legs were nicely shaped and her skin glowed in the lantern light. Baozhen slipped his hand beneath the robe, but he didn't touch her yet. If she denied him then there was a small chance he could still be a gentleman about it.

There was no denial.

Lian closed her eyes as his hand settled on her thigh and followed the shape of it upward. She bit her lower lip in anticipation just before he reached her sex. His own heart stopped the moment his fingers touched against warm, willing flesh. His mind clouded with a thick fog. She was already damp. *Heaven and earth.* Elation surged through him.

In slow circles he deepened the caress, gradually initiating her to a man's touch. He was rewarded when her knees parted instinctively and her hips arched against his hand. Her head was thrown back and her cheeks suffused with color. The look on her face was indescribable. He moved just the tip of his finger over her most sensitive spot and she whimpered and moaned perfectly for him.

He wanted more of this. So much more. Women were so beautiful, with all their hidden looks and mysteries waiting to be uncovered. And Lian was the most beautiful creature of them all. He quickened his strokes to intensify her enjoyment.

His erection had become painful, and the sight of Lian pinned beneath him only made it worse. He'd become a slave to her responses, to her small cries and the sensual churning of her hips. His singular purpose was to bring her to climax and take pleasure from being the one to bring it to her.

He closed his eyes and rested his forehead against hers, letting the sounds of her arousal guide him.

Lian was crying out shamelessly, but soon any sense of embarrassment faded in the wake of the most devastating pleasure she had ever known. She and the neighborhood girls had always speculated what exactly it was that happened between a man and woman, but she had never known it could be like this.

This was not romance or poetry, a flight of sparrows or a fall of spring rain. This was tawdry and base and she was rendered helpless against it. There was nothing she wanted more than Baozhen's touch on her, inside her. She was completely at his mercy and she'd die if he stopped.

He seemed to know. He ground his body against her while he stroked her with wicked skill. His touch was lightning-quick, like the beat of a hummingbird's wings. She gasped for air, her mind whirling as she fought for some way to tell him she needed more.

Baozhen had trapped her hands to keep her still, but it was no longer needed. She was ensnared by this rapture that consumed her. Her heart was beating so fast it would surely burst. He was whispering heated words into her ear. Love words. Gutter words. The blood was rushing so furiously through her head that she couldn't make them out. She only knew that Baozhen was there—holding her, touching her.

He relaxed his hold on her wrists to twine his fingers with hers. "Soon," he gritted out, and she wasn't certain whether it was a command, a question, a promise.

A sob caught in her throat as the pleasure intensified to a nearly unbearable throb. She had never cried in front of Baozhen, but she was suddenly filled with desperate longing. She wanted without knowing what it was she wanted.

A short but endless time passed, and then her entire body and soul tightened to a single, blinding point. A flood of nameless emotion swept through her. She shuddered, lost between heaven and earth, filled with light and sensation.

When she found herself again Baozhen was reaching for her. He kissed her lightly on her cheek, her lips, the tip of her chin. Each affectionate gesture seemed wholly innocent after the lightning storm she'd just experienced.

But while her limbs were waxen and languid, Baozhen remained taut beside her. She'd thought he'd joke now, and say something to lighten the mood, but his expression was strained.

She didn't have any experience in the bedchamber, but she knew enough to understand that this was not the end of things. His tunic was open, exposing a patch of sun-warmed skin and lean muscle, solid from labor and riding. It was enough to show her that Baozhen was as beautiful beneath his clothes as he was on the outside.

Pushing all hesitation aside, Lian reached for his trousers. Baozhen moved to stop her, but she refused to be denied. The knot at his waist fell open. She slipped her hand inside, running it along the flat of his stomach and downward to find him. Baozhen tried to push her away, but all the while his hips shifted restlessly toward her.

"No," he choked out. "Lian, wait. You're very beautiful...it's very difficult to stop when—"

He was nearly incoherent before falling silent. Her questing fingers had encircled the male part of him. The skin was heated and incredibly smooth. Another mystery uncovered—and not at all what she had expected. Now he changed, becoming as hard as jade when she touched him. She could barely breathe.

"Baozhen," she implored as she pushed the trousers down around his hips. "Please."

He made one last feeble attempt to remove her

hands, but his body was insinuating itself into her grasp, begging for her.

"It was you I was waiting for tonight," she confessed. "It was always you."

She didn't know if he'd heard her, but he lowered her back onto the bed with sudden resolve and pushed her robe up around her hips. She was exposed scandalously below the waist, but there was no time for embarrassment to set in before Baozhen covered her with the length and breadth of his body.

He took only a moment to center himself, his fingers touching her down below briefly, before she felt the blunt press of his member between her legs. She looked up at his dark expression as he cupped a hand to the back of her neck, gripping lightly. His breath fanned hot against her cheek as he pushed into her.

The air rushed out of her in one sharp exhalation. The sensation was indescribable. Overwhelming. A moment of fear gripped her as he continued to fill her. She didn't know what to do other than drape her arms over his shoulders. Her limbs became weak as the feeling of being invaded and stretched increased, sending unknown shocks through every part of her. Above her, Baozhen's brow furrowed sharply, but he didn't stop. She dug her nails into his back.

"Lian—" He spoke her name brokenly as he finally settled deep within her.

They were hip to hip, as close as two people could be. He remained still for a string of heartbeats before his body lifted. She thought it might be over—until he slid back in, shuddering with the movement.

She whimpered softly as he continued to move, his thrusts increasing in speed and forming a rhythm. His fingers tangled into her hair, a rough reassurance, and his mouth touched against her throat. Her body began to open for him, to accept these new sensations.

Before she could decipher what it was she was feeling—pleasure or pain—Baozhen's muscles suddenly constricted. With a groan that came from deep within his chest he sank down onto her and laid his head against her shoulder: an odd position, considering he was much larger than her. He buried his face into her hair.

The enormity of what had just happened began to sink into her. They were on her bed, their clothes hastily shoved aside. The boy she had always wanted, now a man, was there in her arms. Baozhen shifted some of his weight from her and she became aware of the soreness where their bodies had been joined. She didn't know what to think. The experience had been both confusing and exhilarating. Now everything was so…*strange.*

Baozhen lifted himself onto one elbow so he could see her. "I didn't expect any of this."

His voice even sounded odd, and unlike him. Heavy and uncertain.

"What happens now?" she asked.

Absently, he brushed a strand of hair from her eyes and then sat up. His movements were slow and deliberate and his expression showed he was lost in deep thought. He smoothed her skirt carefully back down over her legs before righting his own clothes. The silence became oppressive, and Lian couldn't think of anything to do but watch and wait.

He moved to the edge of the bed, then paused to turn back to her. "What do you want me to do, Lian?"

She was at a loss. Why would he be asking her? He was more experienced than she was.

Before she could think of an answer the sound of voices in the courtyard stopped her heart. Baozhen straightened, his shoulders tensing.

"My parents!" she gasped.

Baozhen shot to his feet. His eyes darted to the door, the window, then back to her.

"Hide," she said frantically.

"Where?" There was no place in her tidy room for him to fit.

"Are you feeling better, daughter of mine?" Her mother's sing-song call came from just outside the door.

Lian was still struggling out of the bed when the door opened and there stood her mother, staring at Baozhen.

"Chen *Furen*," he addressed her formally, his voice rasping.

"Oh, dear heaven!" her mother wailed, rushing past him to the bed.

"Mother, Baozhen was only—"

Lian's words caught in her throat. Only…what?

Mother threw her arms around Lian and called for her father.

Baozhen looked sick as her father entered. Her father was tall, the cut and color of his robe severe, and he had his piercing glare fixed upon Baozhen. Her father was well-known as a force in the East Market and he appeared particularly imposing tonight.

"Mister Chen." Baozhen managed a small bow.

Lian tried to extract herself from her mother,

who was fluttering worriedly about her and cooing little assurances and endearments that were supposed to be soothing. Her father had never been violent, but she was certain Baozhen was about to be dragged away and flogged.

"Mister Chen," Baozhen repeated, and he swallowed. His infamous honeyed tongue was thick in his mouth. "I must say…please understand…I hold your daughter in the highest regard…"

Her father raised his hand, stopping Baozhen in his painful admission. Baozhen stiffened as her father approached, as if preparing for a strike, but her father only put his arm around him and turned him to face the door.

"How is your father, my son?"

"My fath—? He's well…sir."

Something really, *really* bad was about to happen. Her father never showed when he was angry. He just grew overly calm and controlled. He was very calm now.

"It has been a while since your parents have come for tea," her father was saying as he and Baozhen disappeared into the courtyard. "I think we shall see them tomorrow. The earlier the better."

Lian turned frantically to her mother. "Tell Father that Baozhen didn't do anything wrong."

"Shh." Mother ran her fingers through Lian's hair, smoothing it away from her face. "Mother and Father will take care of everything."

It occurred to Lian that her parents were home at an almost discourteously early time from the registrar's party, and that her mother didn't seem nearly as distressed as she had appeared only moments earlier. A sly smile even appeared on her lips as she pressed them to Lian's forehead affectionately.

Chapter Four

Everything happened quickly. Now that "the rice was cooked," as the expression went, there was no time to waste. The once-innocent Lian might be with child at that very moment. Honor was at stake. Both families could either lose face or celebrate a lavish union.

It was hardly a choice at all.

Within the week the necessary inquiries were made. The families were gathered. A fortune teller was consulted. Baozhen and his parents made a formal procession, bearing engagement gifts of tea and lychees, silk and jade. The parade marched all of twenty steps next door for the traditional tea.

Now Baozhen sat in the parlor of the Chen mansion with Lian directly across from him, eyes cast downward. The two of them remained dutiful and silent while their parents exchanged pleasantries. The entire time Baozhen watched the pink rising in her cheeks and thought of her flushed and glowing with her body tight around him.

He was still stunned. His body hadn't yet recovered from the pleasure of their joining or the shock of their discovery. Theirs was certainly not the first marriage to be negotiated on such terms, he told himself. And he had to marry someday.

"This is fate," his mother was saying to Lian's mother, who nodded sagely.

But throughout it all Lian refused to look at him. She kept her head bowed and her gaze averted, as if they were indeed strangers bound together by the whim of a matchmaker. As if she needed to impress upon him that she was demure and innocent and pliant. All of which he knew wasn't true. Well, except for her innocence—until he'd taken it in a moment's passion.

Baozhen knew he should be sorry, but it was hard to be sorry when his pulse refused to stop hammering at Lian's nearness. She sat just beyond arm's reach, yet she might as well have been on the other side of the empire. The sullen look on her face twisted his stomach into knots.

He finally caught up to her as the engagement party started to disband. He'd had to make an excuse about using the privy—a request which Lian's father had obliged with a knowing air. He found her at the far side of the garden, before she could slip away to the women's quarters.

"Lian." He took hold of her wrist when she turned to flee. "What's the matter?"

She looked ill as she regarded him. Was it possible she *was* with child? Would the symptoms already be evident?

Gently, he pulled her behind the shrubbery in the garden. Almost the exact spot where he'd attempted a kiss just days earlier. "I know this isn't what we expected, but we'll do what we must."

She looked up at him, her eyes wide and her face pale. "What's done is done," she said miserably.

Her words struck him square in the chest and he let her arm slip out of his grasp. His fingers had gone numb.

"You wanted Jinhai, didn't you?" he asked coldly. "Maybe you still do."

Her eyes flashed at him as she shot him a look like an arrow. This was the Lian he'd known all his life.

"I don't care a thing for him," she said bitterly.

"Then why do you look as if this were a funeral instead of an engagement?"

She was the one who had all but demanded he kiss her. He certainly hadn't protested—but neither had she. And her skin had been so soft and her lips so pink. And he hadn't been a virtuous man to begin with.

"Lian—"

The gray cloud in her eyes stopped him cold. Her expression was one of anguish. There was shame there, and regret.

"I didn't think it would go that far," she protested.

He hadn't meant for things to happen this way either. There was just something about being so close to Lian and the touch of moonlight on them that night.

"We've known each other for so long," he began gently. "This isn't the worst of fates."

He stepped toward her, ready to make promises. They would make the best of things. He would mend his ways. And he did, at the end of all things, care for her.

Lian shook her head fiercely. "No, Baozhen. You should know… You should know that Liu Jinhai and I haven't only just met."

Jinhai again. The sound of his name was starting to feel like a thorn in his eye. "What does that scoundrel have to do with anything?"

"We've met before," she went on, looking more tortured with each word. "Long before. And Jinhai *is* a scoundrel. Completely unsuitable for me and he knows it. But he was willing to play along."

Baozhen had held his hand out to her, but he let it drop now to his side, like a dead weight. "You care nothing for him?" he said dully, echoing her words.

She shook her head miserably.

"Then…?" He tried to piece together the fragments of the last week. Her sudden interest in one of his acquaintances…the rendezvous in the park…all the while taunting him—

"You little she-demon," he proclaimed.

Lian didn't deny it, but her expression was far from triumphant. "I never meant to trap you. I… I just wanted you to notice me."

With that, her shoulders slumped, and she appeared at once both small and uncertain. Nothing like the scheming creature he knew her to be. Now her look of regret made sense. Lian had been responsible for all of it—every single moment.

Wordlessly he stepped away from her, forgoing a farewell as he turned on his heel.

His mind was spinning.

He might have had a reputation for having three girls in the morning and four in the evening, but it was all talk. Lian's parents were known as the most skillful negotiators in the city and Lian was apparently as shrewd and clever as they were.

Baozhen might be a wolf, but he'd been completely ensnared by a fox.

Lian sat alone in an unfamiliar chamber, upon what was to be her bridal bed. She was still dressed in her embroidered wedding robes, though she had cast aside the ceremonial veil as soon as she had been led to the bed and left alone. The wedding banquet continued in the main part of the house, where Baozhen would be accepting good-natured toasts and fending off well-wishers before making his way to her.

The wedding procession hadn't had far to travel earlier that afternoon. Only the mere twenty paces that separated their households. And yet Lian felt as if she had traveled a thousand *li*. She had often visited the Guo household, but Baozhen's private chamber was unknown to her.

As the muted sounds of the evening banquet droned on she searched for signs of him. The furnishings were tidy, but not stringently so. A stack of books lay upon the desk. The fragrance of rosewood and cedar surrounded her, making her think of dark and distant forests and the remote places where Baozhen had traveled.

He had been beside her for the wedding ceremony, but she'd been prevented from seeing him by the red veil draped over her face. All she'd had to sustain her was the tug of his hand opposite hers upon the symbolic red ribbon that had joined them together. He'd been a silent, forbidding presence.

They hadn't spoken a word since she'd confessed her scheme to him after their engagement. Lian was beginning to worry. Neither of them had expected to be married so hastily, and his last words to her had been far from passionate.

"What do you want me to do?" he'd asked. The heat of desire had faded and there had been nothing left but a sense of duty weighing down his shoulders.

It didn't matter. What was done was done.

The minutes stretched into hours, during which Lian had nothing to do but sit there and try very hard not to think of how many girls her husband had kissed before her. Baozhen was staying away for too long. He had no business staying at the banquet and enjoying the festivities. Wasn't an eager groom supposed to extract himself from his guests in a timely manner?

Finally the door creaked open and she shot to her feet. Baozhen stopped just inside when he saw her, and closed the door behind him. He was dressed in a heavy robe of blue brocade and his hair was covered by a ceremonial cap. Her heart pounded. She hadn't realized how hungry she'd become over the last few weeks for the sight of him.

"Why were you away for so long?"

Lian cringed at the unintentional shrillness in her voice as he blinked at her in surprise. Her first words to her newly wed husband and they sounded like an accusation.

Her mistake was immediately evident. Rather than coming to her, Baozhen sank into the chair beside his writing desk. He leaned back to regard her, his shoulders tense.

"It was our wedding banquet," he replied.

His flat tone left a hollow feeling in her stomach.

"Wine was poured, and then more wine. Everyone wanted to give us their blessings."

"Have you had very much to drink?" she ventured.

He was in a peculiar mood.

His eyebrows lifted. "Are you worried that I won't be able to fulfill my duties as a husband?"

This was all wrong. They had always been able to speak openly, but now every word between them seemed forced.

"I suppose it doesn't matter, since the deed is already done," she said tightly.

His eyebrows rose slightly, but he said nothing.

She went to stand before him, stopping just as her robe brushed the tip of his slippers. Her heart lodged in her throat. "You're angry with me."

The line of his jaw flexed as he tilted his head down to her. So handsome. He had never appeared so far from her reach. It wounded her to see him so withdrawn, tonight of all nights.

"You can't be angry," she protested. "This is our wedding night. It would... It would be a bad omen to start out this way."

"You are *forbidding* me from being angry?" he asked incredulously.

Desperation grew within her. Her fingers twisted together as he continued to assess her, taking her apart with his eyes.

Was she going to be one of those shrewish, demanding wives? What sort of husband would he be?

"Tell me," he began slowly. "And no more games. Did you lure me into your bed, *Little Lian*?"

His emphasis on her childish nickname was sharp and devoid of affection. Her breath caught as his gaze pinned her in place. She had always known how Baozhen could disarm anyone with his easy charm, but now she saw he was twice as formidable when he wielded this iron stare.

"Yes," she said, fighting for her voice.

"Every step of the way?" he murmured.

"Yes."

Lian had never intended to force his hand, nor put him through such shame and dishonor. Her parents had been supposed to be gone late into the evening. She'd wanted Baozhen to burn for her. To choose her above all the other women who had ever caught his eye. Now he had no choice in the matter and he resented her.

"I didn't mean to trick you, but I refuse to apologize," she said stubbornly.

His hand shot out and caught her around the waist, making her tumble in a squirming heap into his lap. His arms closed around her, making escape impossible.

He willed her to meet his eyes. A smile lifted the corner of his mouth. "I've never been pursued so ruthlessly."

"You're not angry?"

"At first," he admitted. "But then I realized it was me you wanted all along. Me. I can't help but be flattered at inspiring such deviousness in you. Seducing me like that."

"You're shameless," she accused.

She braced a hand against his chest to push him away, only to find her fingers caught in his grip.

His smile faded, along with any trace of smugness, as he searched her face. For the first time there was no more taunting.

"No more childish games," he said.

Her reply was no more than a whisper. "I have only ever wanted you."

He pulled her close, his palm cradling the back of her neck. His mouth captured hers and her fingers curled into the front of his robe from the sheer pleasure of finally being in his embrace. He tasted of rice wine and the faint spice of cloves. She was floating, flying...

Without a word, he lifted her from his lap and led her to the bed. She sat perfectly still upon the edge while he extracted the pins from her hair, one after another. Each touch sent a tingle down her spine. She could hear Baozhen's breathing deepen as he tended to her. He smoothed the hair away from her face as it fell loose and her cheeks flushed hot at the stark intimacy of the moment. The near solemnity of it.

Baozhen touched her as if she were something precious.

Their first night together had been a fever. Tonight was a slow, simmering burn. She could feel each pulse of her heart as Baozhen bent to press his lips to her forehead. It was innocent—or rather a farewell to innocence. His next caress was at her earlobe, which he tugged at gently with his teeth, making her insides go soft and liquid.

"You were wrong, Little Lian…"

His voice was low, stroking her in hidden places.

"The deed is far from done. It will never be done between us."

His mouth rasped over the sensitive skin of her throat and her toes curled restlessly within her slippers. Their bodies were interconnected in so many wonderful and mysterious ways.

"Baozhen…" She called out his name breathlessly, encompassing a plea within it that had no words.

"My wife."

They kissed again. Any lingering questions faded like a morning mist. The moment was right between them.

She found the parting in his robe and her hands slipped inside to roam over skin and heated muscle. Baozhen didn't stop her this time when she loosened his belt and slid the cloth away from his shoulders. The shape of him filled her hands: broad shoulders, arms that were lean and strong. There wasn't any part of him that she didn't want to explore and caress.

"Lian…"

His mouth curved against hers and she could hear a touch of amusement.

"You really aren't afraid of anything."

They separated as he shrugged his arms free of the robe, baring himself down to his waist. He caught her watching him. His eyes were dark, lit only by an almost dangerous gleam. Though her face heated, she refused to look away.

When they had made love before it had been furtive and rushed. She had only caught a tantalizing glimpse of what Baozhen looked like beneath his clothes. Her gaze slipped to the evidence of his arousal, straining against his trousers. Her mouth went completely dry. She really was shameless.

"Don't stop there," Baozhen said, his voice thick with desire. He guided her hands to the ties at his waist. Then he embraced her again as she worked the knot free and found him, willing and waiting for her.

Her first intimate caress sent a shudder through him. When she closed her fingers gently around his sex, his hand tightened possessively in her hair. He sucked in a breath as she slid her hand along his length. She loved what her every touch did to him. Every muscle in him was steeled and his breath became shallow. The heat from his skin enclosed her.

This was what it had been like when she'd lain beneath him, helpless with pleasure, but there was pleasure in giving, as well. Her own sex dampened in anticipation.

She grew bolder, gripping him harder when she saw that it only excited him more.

Suddenly Baozhen brushed her hands aside. He kissed her roughly, thrusting his tongue inside her mouth. Her mind went dark with pleasure and she could feel his hands deftly working at her robe. His skill was undeniable. Before long she was sinking back onto the bed, with Baozhen stretched on top of her, skin to skin. His tongue stroked wickedly over hers and she could taste him, feel his weight on her, his hands anchoring her hips. He was everywhere.

She moaned against his mouth as he stroked his finger between her legs. He had learned what pleased her—was learning still as he parted her folds and deepened his touch, making her writhe and tremble. Her hips twisted against his hand and her cries took on the sound of distress, of desperation.

As the sensation within her began to rise to an

unbearable peak Baozhen once again gripped her hips. His head lifted and he met her eyes. His hair had slipped free of its knot and an errant lock fell over his face, giving him a wild look. They were discovering each other after so many years of growing up in close quarters.

There was a moment of stillness as Baozhen positioned himself. Lian's chest rose and fell rapidly. His ragged breath formed an irregular harmony against hers, as if they had been chasing one another and the hunt was finally done. Done, but not finished.

Baozhen kept his eyes on her face the entire time as he entered her, refusing to relinquish her gaze even when she moaned and clung to him. Her body resisted for only a moment, and then her back arched as the length of him filled her in an endless sensation of penetration and surrender.

He began to move slowly over her. A sheen of sweat formed on his brow as his body lifted and lowered. It was different from last time. Now that she knew what would happen she focused on the feel of Baozhen inside her and let it consume her.

His hips shifted by the barest angle, but it was the difference between heaven and earth. Her lips parted with a gasp as a flood of euphoria swept through her from head to toe.

"Like that?" His breath was hot against her ear as his thrusts sent wave after wave of pleasure through her.

Lian held on to his shoulders and buried her face against his neck as their bodies writhed together, seeking oblivion. It was almost there—just out of reach.

She wrapped her legs around him and Baozhen groaned, his thrusts becoming shorter, deeper.

Soon. Soon, please, soon.

Her vision blackened as climax took her and she squeezed her eyes shut to revel in it. Baozhen was right there with her, letting himself go as soon as he felt the pulse of her body around him, falling as hard and completely as she had.

Finally his muscles loosened and he sank on top of her. For a few moments his weight was welcome, but soon he started to feel heavy and she tried to squirm out from under him. With a chuckle, Baozhen rolled onto his back and took her with him, settling her into the crook of his arm. She drew a lazy pattern over his chest, feeling warm and sated.

"Do you think our parents always wanted us to be wed?" Lian asked after a short silence. She had been enjoying the sound of Baozhen's heartbeat against her ear.

"They must have gotten impatient waiting."

She poked at his ribs. "Waiting for *you*," she said ruefully.

Baozhen burst into laughter—a deep, rich laughter that filled the room.

"What is it?" she asked, but soon she was caught up in it, laughing as well.

She knew exactly what it was: chasing each other in the alleyway as children, Baozhen taunting her for being skinny, her aiming at him with her slingshot. All those moments…all those memories.

"I loved you from the first moment I saw you," he said.

"Liar." She settled back into the warm hollow of his shoulder now that he was no longer shaking with laughter. "You never noticed me."

"But I did—I always did."

She pouted a little. That wasn't how it had happened at all, but all the frustration and endless longing seemed far away with his arms around her. Baozhen had always been there. Their lives intertwined.

"I can't remember it any other way," he said tenderly.

She snuggled close and followed the drift of his voice into sleep. All her memories blended together until it seemed there was truth in what he said.

"That's how it was for me, as well," she conceded, smiling at the thought of how mercilessly he'd teased her and how she had once hated him with a passion. "From the very first moment."

* * * * *

THE TAMING OF MEI LIN

Sometimes it feels like it takes a village
to put a story to paper!

Special thanks to the emergency brainstorming crew:
Eileen Dreyer, Kimberly Killion, Patricia Rice
and Karyn Witmer-Gow. And also the
Tuesday critique group: Dawn Blankenship,
Amanda Berry, Kristi Lea and Shawntelle Madison.

I'm a lucky girl to be surrounded by
so many talented friends.

Author Note

In Chinese culture it's natural to speak of ancestors
as if they're still present, looking over your shoulder
to nod in approval at good decisions and frown over
disastrous ones. The role of family is inescapable,
ubiquitous and ever-present. Of course this is true for
all cultures. Our family histories inspire and guide us.

Ai Li, the heroine of *Butterfly Swords* for Mills &
Boon Historical Romance, constantly refers back to
her ancestors and the importance of family honour.
The Taming of Mei Lin takes place forty years before
Butterfly Swords and tells *that* love story—the family
story that's passed down for generations to come.
In order to create Ai Li's story of rebellion and
impossible love, I always had Mei Lin's adventure in
my head.

I was thrilled to be able to bring that story to life. *The
Taming of Mei Lin* explores the humble beginnings of
the Shen family, a line of warriors steeped in duty and
honour and, most importantly, love. Writing Mei Lin's
tale allowed me to explore the delicate ways that the
past affects the future. It was also an opportunity to tie
two love stories near and dear to my heart together.

Chapter One

Tang Dynasty China, 710 AD

Mei Lin could feel the strands of hair slipping from her knot, tickling against her neck. Uncle made her stand outside during the hottest part of the afternoon, even when there were no customers. She wiped her brow and looked over at Chang's tofu stand at the end of the street with envy. He at least had the shade of a tree to duck under.

If she planted a seed today, she reckoned she'd still be here selling noodles by the time the tree grew tall enough to provide shelter. And Uncle would still be growing fat, napping in the shade.

A tingle of awareness pricked against her neck. Out of the corner of her eye, she could see someone had stopped just beyond the line of the wooden benches. The stranger wore a gray robe, but that was the only thing plain about him. He had the high cheekbones of the people of the north and stood with his shoulders back, lean and tall. Unfortunately the town riffraff stood just behind him, grinning and poking at each other over some boyish joke only they found humorous. Mei Lin ignored them as she always did.

"Little Cho."

The boy came eagerly running at her call. Her little cousin was not yet corrupted by his father's laziness.

"Fetch the tea," she said and he went running to the stove.

She turned back to the intriguing man. He remained at the perimeter watching her. He had a pleasant expression and seemed particularly still, as if supremely comfortable in this heat and in this world. She stood there with sweat pouring down her back wishing her hair wouldn't keep falling over her face like it did. It was so rare that strangers came to their village.

He bowed. "Wu Mei Lin," he greeted formally.

Even rarer that strangers came who knew her name. The smile she was about to give him faded into a frown.

"Little Cho."

He had just returned with the teapot.

She blew a strand of hair away from her face impatiently. "Fetch my swords."

The boy scrambled away, nearly tripping over his feet in his excitement. She turned back to the stranger.

"This is why you came, isn't it?"

"When I learned of Lady Wu's skill, I couldn't help but come to pay my respects."

He insisted on using her family name in an overly polite fashion. The onlookers chortled. The hated Chen Wang was at the head of the pack. Wang tended to stay away from her after she'd given him a black eye that lasted for a week, but he couldn't resist the show.

"Well, then. Let's get started," she said.

Little Cho returned and handed over her short swords. She fixed her gaze onto the man before her. He had his weapons strapped to his side. She'd missed it in her initial fascination.

"I don't mean to presume," he began. "If the lady would like time to prepare—"

"There's no better time. Besides, the rabble will be expecting a performance."

She scowled at Wang and his lot as she brushed past. It kept her from having to look at *him*. Why did he have to be so tall and his manners so impeccable? And why was she so taken with this swordsman when it was obvious he was here to humiliate her, just like all the others?

"Little Cho, watch the shop," she called over her shoulder.

"But, Mei Lin!"

She ignored the boy's protest and kept walking. He shouldn't be watching street fights at his age, impressionable as he was. Uncle and Auntie Yin had enough to complain about without her being a bad influence on her little cousin.

The swordsman caught up with her easily, keeping an arm's length between them while they walked together down the dusty street. There was none of the posturing and swagger she'd come to expect from Zhou's lackeys. From outward appearances, they could have been joining one another for an afternoon stroll.

"Those are exquisite."

He was talking about the swords. Twin blades—short, light and quick. Many called them butterfly swords, but there was nothing delicate about them. They were ideal weapons for a woman fighting a larger opponent. Heaven forbid he'd look at her with the same interest.

She sniffed, but a thread of doubt worked loose inside her. He was the first to be interested in her skill rather than the novelty of this odd girl who dared to challenge men.

"You don't seem like one of Zhou's thugs," she said.

"Who is Zhou?"

He sounded earnest; she wanted to believe that he wasn't just another bragging oaf, here to put this stubborn woman in her place. She stole another glance at him. His black hair was pulled back and tied, highlighting his distinct features.

And he was handsome. She might as well admit it. Looking at him left her with the disturbing sense that she had lost something—something she desperately needed to find.

"You are not what I expected from what they told me."

He was looking at her face now. A rush of heat flooded her cheeks. "What did they say?"

"That you were the meanest shrew in the empire."

He smiled as he said it. His brown eyes were a shade lighter than what was common in this region. It reminded her of the golden wash of the sun over the mountains.

She knew then what she couldn't find: her usual confidence that the fight was already won.

They reached the center of town where the main

roads met at the market square. If Zhou hadn't sent this swordsman, then he must have come on his own to challenge her. It had been two months since Zhou made his outrageous proposal, which she had countered with an even more outrageous declaration.

Zhou was a lesser magistrate of the district. He had proposed marriage after catching a glimpse of her at the noodle stand while he was passing through. Uncle and Auntie Yin had been thrilled that someone wanted to take her off their hands, but Zhou already had a wife. Two wives, in fact! She would be little more than a bed warmer and glorified kitchen maid.

She had announced publicly she would marry no man unless he defeated her in a fight. Her uncle and aunt were mortified, but she wouldn't back down. Her parents had been poor, but proud people. It would offend their spirits to see their only daughter become some lecherous goat's mistress.

Zhou dismissed her challenge as the ramblings of a madwoman. She doubted he could lift a sword, but his henchmen continued to bully her whenever they came by. Over the last few weeks, several strangers had wandered into town to goad her into a fight. She suspected they had all been sent by the disgruntled official.

She'd defeated all the country thugs and village boys who'd tried to teach her a lesson. But this swordsman was different. If Zhou hadn't sent him, then he must have come on his own. Could news of her declaration have traveled beyond the dusty edge of town?

She turned to him. "Do you still want to do this, considering what a shrew I am?"

That half smile again. "I am not afraid."

More townsfolk had gathered to see crazy Mei Lin and another one of her displays of rebelliousness. There was a moment of sadness when she squared off across from him. She'd become a spectacle. The only marriage proposals she ever received were these stupid challenges from scoundrels trying to show her up. One of these days, some brute would defeat her. Someone a hundred times worse than Zhou. She'd done this to herself.

"What shall the terms be?" he asked as he paced to the other side of the square.

Still so composed, his every movement measured and graceful. She should have been paying attention to how he moved, not how captivating his eyes were.

"We're simple folk here. First blood should be good enough."

She raised her swords while her opponent drew

his weapon. The blade gleamed in the afternoon sun, the craftsmanship obvious to even an untrained eye. Even if she discounted the quality of the blade, she knew immediately this man was serious. There was a way a sword fits into the hands of a true practitioner, as if it were an extension of his body.

"You're not even going to ask my name?" he said.

"Why bother? You'll run from here in shame very soon."

"Wu Mei Lin, the honor would be all mine."

The way he spoke her name sent a shudder down her spine, despite the heat of the afternoon. Certainly he had come to see her out of curiosity, but could it be he was actually interested? He watched her so intently and his pleasant manners gave the impression he was actually enjoying the exchange. She wished they didn't have this duel between them to confuse her.

He bowed, blade pointed downward, very formal. Like this was a sacred ritual instead of a street brawl. She looked down at her swords and for a moment they felt strange in her hands, as if she didn't practice every morning and night with them.

Master always said she wouldn't know her limit until someone pushed her to it.

"Now?" the swordsman asked from afar.

She tossed her hair out of her face. "Now."

He waited, relaxed in his stance. She was nowhere near that patient. If she was to win this fight, she needed to know the extent of his skill, his level of intuition with the sword. She'd know all of that with the first cross of their blades. The touch of steel never lied.

She rushed forward and the swordsman never flinched. He lifted his sword and her first strike met against a solid wall of strength as the shorter blade clashed against the longer reach of his *jian*. The swordsman deflected in one fluid motion.

Disciplined. Small movements, no waste of energy.

She gave him no time to recover before snaking forward again, her swords seeking an opening through touch and tension. The cry of metal rang through the square and the crowd gasped. He was stronger than her, but there was guile beneath his force. His blade slipped past hers with a deft rotation of his wrist. He was testing her as well, exploring the boundaries between them.

They separated, but remained closer this time, dancing just outside contact range. Her heart pounded, cutting through the sluggish pulse of the afternoon. She was breathing hard, but so was he. His chest rose and fell as he watched her.

Wang laughed from the perimeter. "More than you expected, Shen Leung?"

A nervous flutter rose in her stomach at the sound of the name. It was a name they'd heard of even here in this small corner of the empire.

"Well, if I had known you were famous, I wouldn't have insulted you—" she taunted him "—quite as much."

Curse her wicked tongue. She couldn't stop herself with the energy of the battle flowing through her like this.

Shen Leung wasn't so easily distracted. He wiped his brow with his sleeve and circled her, his feet steady over the packed dirt of the marketplace. His presence filled the space with hardly any effort.

"Who is your master?" he asked.

"No one you know."

"He must have recognized your natural ability. Few swordmasters will train a woman."

The surge of pleasure at his words was dangerous. "What makes you think my master is a man?"

She attacked again. Talking wouldn't resolve this and she wanted to get a closer look at his sword work, even if it was going to be her defeat. Shen Leung was magnificent with the blade and he moved with a confidence that made her heart race. There was a joy in being pushed to the edge by a worthy opponent. She hadn't found such harmony since leaving her old home to come here.

"Stop being nice to her!" Wang shouted.

Shen Leung breathed through each movement. His eyes met hers. "I'm not."

Only she could hear the reply amidst the sword strike. His voice was husky with exertion and his skin glistened with a sheen of sweat.

"You're good," he said.

She parried and twisted his blade aside. "I don't need you to tell me."

He grinned and pushed her further until she had to fight for balance. She wasn't done yet. Boldly she ventured closer where his longer blade would be less effective. Most practitioners weren't comfortable there, but Shen Leung found her rhythm and flowed with her. The edge of his weapon broke through her guard. She leaped back, knowing it was too late.

But he missed.

The blade whistled past her ear. She stared at him in shock while he regained his stance and prepared for another advance.

She had him. It had nothing to do with skill. They were closely matched in training, but there was so much more that went into a fight. The honorable Shen Leung was unwilling to hurt her. He didn't realize it yet, but this battle was hers if she wanted it.

With her new confidence, she could see all the openings. A warrior had to be ruthless and strategic. That was what she had been taught. He became a series of targets in her eyes. All she needed to do was catch another moment of hesitation and she would break through.

And once she won…what then?

Someone else would come. Another one of Zhou's henchmen now that he was bent on revenge. Or maybe no one would ever defeat her or care to approach her with a serious marriage proposal. She'd have nothing but this speck of a town and the noodle stand. Shen Leung's arrival had broken through the clouds. She might never feel this way again about anyone.

They said he was a good man, a just and courageous one.

She decided then. She met his attack edge on edge, loosening her grip slightly with the impact of their blades, and the strength of his next attempt wrenched the hilt from her grasp. A collective murmur went through the crowd when her sword fell to the dirt. For a second, it almost seemed they had been cheering for her. Supporting the local madwoman.

Shen Leung's sword darted forward to stop just shy of her throat. She grew still beneath his gaze. He regarded her with admiration and something else, a fire she'd never seen before.

He rested the tip of the blade gently against her collarbone, almost like a caress. "Do I need to draw blood, my lady?" he asked softly.

He had already pierced her, deeper than he knew.

It was Wang who broke the standoff. "Claim your prize, Master Shen!"

"Prize?"

The blade fell back. The exertion of the battle began to sink into her along with the oppressive heat of the afternoon. She wanted to wipe the perspiration from her face, but she didn't dare move. She didn't dare breathe as she watched Shen Leung's reaction.

"Take your bride," Wang said. "From your battle we can see the wedding night will be quite an adventure."

His cronies hooted with laughter. She considered blackening both of Wang's eyes and perhaps breaking his nose, as well.

"Don't be ridiculous, Brother Wang." Shen

Leung looked embarrassed when he glanced back at her. "There will be no wedding."

Her chest squeezed tight. Heat rushed up her neck and flooded her face while he bowed once more. The noble swordsman didn't want her.

"Thank you for the match. Lady Wu is a formidable opponent." He turned to leave. The cronies chanted their congratulations and ushered him toward the tavern to celebrate.

Mei Lin was left alone, her sword fallen in the dust. The curious eyes of the townspeople bore into her while the cruel sun beat down upon her back.

Chapter Two

Shen Leung extracted himself from the tavern to taunting and cries of "One more round!" The chorus finally faded by the time he made his way to the shed behind merchant Wang's house. The storage area had been cleared and swept so that a cot could be laid out to serve as a bed. He unclasped his sword belt and managed to shrug out of his tunic before sinking onto the cot.

Among the many cities and villages he'd passed through, this place was truly remarkable. The people were generous, the wine strong. And the woman…

He closed his eyes and she was there. Mei Lin. Pretty, pretty Mei Lin and her deadly butterfly swords. The noodle shop wouldn't be open this late, otherwise he'd go there now and spend what little coin he had even though he wasn't hungry.

He'd stolen glances from the tavern to search the

stand throughout the evening, but she'd never returned. There had been such a quiet sorrow about
her after the duel was finished. He'd felt the echo
of it inside him. Every time he tried to make an
excuse to leave, he'd been dragged back by well-
wishers demanding stories of his travels.

Perhaps there would be time in the morning.
He'd visit the stand before he left and she'd be there
in the sunlight, as beguiling as she'd been when
he'd first seen her. She had such delightful skin.
The women of these southern regions were so soft
and curved and feminine. So different from the
harsh northern steppes. He pulled the quilt over
his shoulders and prepared to dream.

With a sharp crack, the door flew open. He
jerked awake and sat up so fast that the world
tilted. A wash of moonlight highlighted the form
in the doorway. He'd know that silhouette anywhere. That slender waist and graceful neck. His
eyes had already committed Mei Lin to memory.

"Shen Leung."

Tentatively she stepped forward. Her hair was
pulled up into a simple knot and her skin glowed
in the pale light. Elegant. Sweet. Tempting.

She blinked at him, then glanced away. The blanket had slipped from his shoulders and the stir of

the air against his skin reminded him that he was half-naked before this maiden. Blood gathered in his loins alarmingly.

"Mei Lin?" His voice came out thick and huskier than he had expected.

Her mouth pressed tight. It was then that he noticed the glint of the butterfly sword in her hand.

"Shen Leung, you are going to die tonight."

She lunged at him and his pulse jumped, survival instinct taking over. He flung his quilt at her and she stumbled, temporarily blinded. He scrambled for his sword. Mei Lin was pinpoint-precise with those blades and she might be aiming for something lower than his heart.

Her knee struck the edge of the cot and she struggled to regain balance. She ended up sprawled over his thighs and the wooden frame cracked beneath him. They crashed to the ground in a heap of arms and legs.

The shattered fragments of the cot dug into his back as he tried to catch his breath. The sword fell from her grasp, but that didn't stop Mei Lin. Her elbow struck his ribs when she reached for his throat. She didn't feel nearly as soft as she looked.

"Bastard!"

He caught her wrists. "Lady Wu—"

"Don't you talk to me."

Her knee jammed precariously close to his groin. He flipped her onto her back and anchored her down with his weight pressed over her. The glimpse he caught of her eyes promised murder.

"What has got into you?"

The sound of footsteps came running from the house. He shoved the door closed with his foot and clamped a hand over her mouth, using his free arm to pin her wrists to the floor.

"Master Shen? We heard a sound."

Voices hovered just outside while Mei Lin squirmed like a wild fox beneath him, her cries muffled by his hand.

"I'm fine. I just fell—"

He bit off a curse as the demon girl bit down hard.

"Are you all right?" the merchant asked.

"Yes! Please go back to bed, Master Wang."

He tried to shake his hand free of Mei Lin's teeth while still keeping her gagged. She only dug in deeper and glared at him. How had he ever imagined her to be sweet? He must have been bewitched.

The footsteps finally retreated and he pulled his hand free.

"I was trying to protect your reputation!"

She strained against his hold. "Why won't you marry me?"

"Marry you? Why would anyone want to marry you?" His hand throbbed mercilessly. "You're the meanest woman alive."

"Dog-faced...bastard."

"And the most foul-mouthed."

She started struggling again and he made sure to keep her pinned. He didn't trust what she'd do to him if she even had a hand free. Unfortunately his body was responding to being pressed so close to warm, feminine flesh and it wasn't at all thinking of self-preservation.

"If you didn't want to marry me, why did you bother with the fight?" she demanded.

"What does that have to do with anything?"

"Don't you know?" Some of the hostility drained from her. "Didn't they tell you about the challenge?"

She told him about the magistrate who tried to force her into marriage. "It was the only way I could think to escape," she said bitterly. "But it only made matters worse. When I realized that Zhou hadn't sent you, I thought..."

She looked away. He struggled with the right words, but couldn't find them. It angered him that an appointed official would abuse his power in such a way.

"It wasn't my intention to embarrass you," he said.

"I know that now."

Her voice broke at the last part and it was all he could do to keep from kissing her. They spoke in whispers, pressed close like lovers once he relaxed his hold. If she only knew how desirable he'd found her from the very first moment. The swordfight had been a welcome excuse to approach her.

Of course, the fools at the tavern hadn't told him the whole story. They'd piqued his curiosity by boasting about the girl with the butterfly swords and then goaded him into the duel. Now she'd been publicly humiliated and there was nothing he could do to set it right.

They were still lying among the wreckage of the sleeping cot with the quilt tangled between them. She went still and soft beneath him. He could feel her heart beating against his chest. The last dregs of wine still swam in his blood and he sank his head down over her shoulder. The day had brought a long journey, an unexpected duel, several rounds of drinking and then finally this wild tussle with a beautiful she-demon. The scent of her hair assailed him. Orange blossoms mixed with something mysterious and feminine.

"You smell nice," he said dully.

She said nothing. All he did was turn his face the slightest bit and his cheek brushed inadvertently against hers. Smooth, cool skin.

He inhaled. "You wore perfume to come and kill me?"

A ribbon of tension rippled through her, but nothing for him to be alarmed at. Yet. She took a long, shuddering breath before she spoke.

"I wasn't coming here to kill you at first."

"No?" He couldn't help himself. He burrowed into the space above her shoulder. His lips brushed her neck. Just enough to still be accidental. He hoped.

"I first thought I would…I came here to…" She let out a sigh, defeated. "I thought I would seduce you."

Fierce, hot lust slammed into him. He stiffened and hoped that the quilt was strategically wedged between them.

"But when I saw you, I realized I had no idea how to seduce a man. So I thought it would just be easier to kill you."

Laughter erupted out of him. "Mei Lin, there is no other woman like you."

"Stop it. Stop laughing at me." She was on the verge of tears. "You must understand that either you marry me or one of us must die. I won't be able to live with the shame otherwise."

"I've been in the highest courts of the land and no one would say such a thing."

"I'll be ridiculed!" She slapped the ground in frustration. "An outcast."

He fought the urge to take her in his arms. Instead, he straightened and moved away. His body was so heavy with arousal that he needed the distance or he wouldn't be able to trust himself. The headiness of the wine had faded, but her touch made him more drunk than any spirit.

Fumbling around in the dark, he found the oil lamp Wang had left behind and lit the dish before placing it between them on the floor. Mei Lin sat up and blinked at him through the halo of light. She scanned the wreckage around them, looking lost. Her hair had fallen loose in the struggle and it flowed over her shoulders like water.

Barely able to catch his breath, he sat back, painfully erect. If only he were in the wild plains of the north. If these were still his brash, younger days.

"So this man, Zhou. Is he making things difficult for you?"

"He's just an old goat," she muttered. "I don't want to waste my breath even talking about him."

"What are you doing offering yourself in an appalling contest like this? You're a remarkable woman, Mei Lin. Talented and—" He took a breath. "Beautiful."

She looked down at her feet, blushing furiously. "You say these things, yet you won't marry me."

"A woman such as Lady Wu doesn't need a worthless scoundrel like me."

"I'm not a lady," she sulked. "No one will ever want to marry me."

The teeth marks glared red against the heel of his palm. She was vicious one moment and demure the next. A confusing, enticing combination. He tried to be rational.

"Of course they will. What about that boy— Wang?"

Even before the words left his mouth, a rash of anger spiked through him at the thought of Mei Lin with any other man.

She scowled at him. "Are you throwing me to that imbecile Wang because you won't have me?"

"That wasn't my intention."

"They say that honor is everything to Shen Leung," she challenged.

"They say many things." He rubbed a hand over

his eyes. He would have preferred to not have such a reputation, but no one could control the way stories spread. People expected the impossible from him. Even the imperial court believed he could convince errant warlords to swear loyalty and bring traitors to justice. No man could live up to such expectations.

"If I could correct this, I would," he said. "But how can I marry you? I have nothing but these empty hands. No property, no money—"

"I don't care about those things."

Her voice grew quiet. She was looking at him with dark and vulnerable eyes. It was impossible to try to speak reasonably when his body was demanding that he take what she offered. All that softness, all that warmth.

It wasn't only his body reacting. He longed for much, much more from Mei Lin than a brief night in the dark, but it was impossible. Heroic poems aside, he was of mixed blood with nothing to offer.

"Mei Lin." Heaven, even saying her name aroused him. "You need to go."

Her expression hardened and she shoved the quilt away with her foot. "Fine, I'll go." She glanced around until she spied the hilt of her sword buried beneath a wooden plank. "But there is something you should know about our swordfight."

"What is that?"

She started toward the weapon, but paused to stare at the scattered pile of his belongings. The letter protruded from the knapsack.

The letter with the imperial seal.

"Mei Lin." He lunged for her at the same moment her fingers closed around the paper. "Give me that."

His body stretched over hers and she twisted until they were once again face-to-face. The paper crumpled as she tightened her grip. Her eyes narrowed defiantly.

So beautiful, and she didn't even realize it.

This time their struggle was brief. He lowered his mouth to hers and kissed her.

The first touch of his lips streaked hot through her. She had experienced Shen Leung's strength in their duel, but now his magnificent body anchored her to the ground. His hand twisted into her hair, angling her to him. He urged her lips apart and her body curved into his without thinking.

He kissed as well as he fought.

Vaguely she felt his fingers work over hers, loosening the letter from her grasp.

"You're not a gentleman at all," she murmured against his mouth.

He laughed. By now he had retrieved his precious letter, but she didn't care. He captured her mouth again. His tongue caressed hers wickedly, making her dizzy with pleasure. He tasted like rice wine. She let her arms circle his shoulders, gliding her hands over sleek, smooth muscle.

What had she come to do? Seduce him? Kill him? She didn't remember anymore. She only knew she wanted more of him.

"We shouldn't," he protested, but his hand slipped into the opening of her tunic.

His hand closed over her breast and he stroked her nipple with his thumb. She arched into him, her eyes squeezed shut to savor the feelings he was showing her. The first time anyone had shown her.

"Shen Leung."

"I like that." He worked the sash at her waist. "Say my name again."

His mouth found her throat, seeking out a spot that was especially sensitive. She lifted her chin to give him access, to give him anything he wanted. He kissed her neck before biting gently and she jumped at the shock of the touch.

"I imagined this." His fingertips trailed down over her stomach. The exploring touch sent ripples down her spine. "While you stood across from me in the town square. I could barely concentrate."

"I…I felt the same."

She didn't know what to say to him that wouldn't sound inept. How could she tell him that she'd never felt so close to anyone? That she'd felt this way the moment they stood across from each other, swords drawn. What would he think if he knew the extent of her surrender?

Her breath caught as his hand traced a line to her other breast and circled lazily, stoking a slow fire in her. He watched her so intently, breathing harder with each caress. Her body grew damp down below, responding to him in hidden ways she'd never known.

His voice was low and sensual. "I wish I could promise you anything you wanted."

She reached for him, her hand curling around the back of his neck to pull him back down. He yielded and kissed her with a raw edge of hunger that thrilled her.

He was so strong and wonderfully…male. She couldn't think of any other words. His hard member pressed against her hip. She had only vague notions of what this all meant—the secrets between men and women. The mystery of it excited her even more.

He forced himself apart, still fighting her. "I won't let this happen."

He should have known better than to challenge her like that. She raised her hips to him and Shen Leung groaned. His hands fisted in her hair and his eyes closed, the look on his face caught between pleasure and agony.

"I can't stay," he said through gritted teeth.

She held on to him. The feel of him hard against her was too wonderful to relinquish. She wanted his hands on her again, his mouth on her, touching her everywhere. Boldly she reached for the edge of his trousers. Her fingertips skimmed the hard muscle of his stomach.

"No."

He snatched her hand away, once again pinning it over her head. But this time his fingers threaded through hers. The savage tenderness of it rendered her heart in two.

Every muscle in his body strained above her and his breathing came in ragged bursts. "I have to go. There are… There are duties I've sworn to fulfill. If we gave in and made love tonight, what would happen to you when I leave?"

"What if you swear to me?" she asked.

"What?"

"Tell me you'll return and I'll believe you."

She burrowed her face against his neck to hide

from the reckless need coursing through her. She'd never begged anyone for anything. The shame of it.

"Mei Lin, you're worth more than this."

His words only made her burn for him. She choked back tears of frustration.

"Must you be so *honorable*?"

Slowly he eased her away so that he could see her face. "I can't promise you anything when I don't know what the next day will bring for me. I don't know if I'll be near or far or if I'll be fortunate enough to be breathing."

She touched a tentative hand to his cheek. "Are you saying there's a chance you can be killed?"

His eyes had grown dark and serious. He hesitated before answering. "Nothing is certain."

"It's dangerous work you do for the empire, isn't it?"

From the way his jaw tightened, she knew she was right and that he would say nothing more. Her desire faded only to be replaced by an even greater longing: the need to remain close to Shen Leung and know that he was safe.

"You should go home now," he said.

"Let me stay just a little longer," she pleaded.

"No."

He planted a kiss on her lips and then another on her forehead. Then he rested his brow against hers and for a few precious moments, she listened to the sound of his breathing and wished that the moment wouldn't end. Finally he got up and moved away.

So she went. With every step, she wondered about the stories they told about him: acts of nobility, protecting the weak and righting small injustices. There was so much more to him she wanted to know. She thought of the hunger in his eyes and hoped that if she walked slowly enough, he would call her back. But he didn't.

Chapter Three

She awoke earlier than usual to open the noodle shop. Actually she hadn't slept at all. By daybreak, she was already standing between the empty tables, staring at the stretch of road leading through town. What if Shen Leung rose before dawn and left without a single farewell?

She'd stayed up, thinking over every moment she had spent with him. The memories that had started out so bright and clear had become twisted while she lay curled up in bed. He was worldly, so much more experienced than her in every way. Her overtures must have seemed laughable to him.

But he had kissed her. Again and again, like he wanted her and needed her. He'd called her beautiful. He did want her, but not enough—

"Mei Lin!" Uncle's sharp tone cut through her meandering thoughts. "You've been wiping that same bowl for an hour."

She stared at the dishrag in her hands and the porcelain with its faded blue pattern. Uncle started grumbling his usual rant about how she ate all the rice and was nothing but a worthless girl. Her temper suddenly got the better of her.

"This bowl?" She held it high and then dashed it to the ground. An angry sound pierced the morning as it shattered to pieces. "Now I don't need to wash it anymore."

"Disrespectful! You'll pay for that." He shook his finger at her and grumbled his way down the lane to share morning tea with old Chang.

As soon as he disappeared, she regretted her rashness. Breaking things and causing a storm so early in the morning simply because she was lonely. It was the first time she'd admitted it. She was lonely here.

She bent to pick up the porcelain shards and found herself face-to-face with Shen Leung. He'd somehow come to kneel beside her. Her hands fumbled over the broken pieces while he tried to help. His fingers were long and graceful and she was so clumsy. They stood at the same time and she was at a loss as she looked up at him.

"I'm not always like this," she said in a near whisper.

His flawless manners had returned. "I can pay for that."

"Nonsense. This wasn't your fault."

But it was because of him. The sharp edges of the porcelain dug into her palms. He had filled her head and taken over her thoughts. She wanted to cry just looking at him and she didn't know why. It was unbearable to want someone so much, so quickly.

He pressed a copper into her hand. His thumb traced the edge of her palm needlessly. He slung his travel pack over one shoulder and the sight of it caused an immeasurable sadness within her.

"Won't you stay and have something to eat?" Her attempt to sound bright failed.

"No, I should go."

He was standing close enough for her to feel the heat of his body and search every expression that flickered across his face. She was still holding on to the broken bowl awkwardly and there was nothing clever she could conjure up to keep him there a few moments longer.

Her voice grew faint. "Please be careful."

"It is beyond my right to demand this, but don't accept any more of those challenges. That is no proper way for a maiden to find a husband."

It wasn't as if she wanted these ridiculous fights.

Or that she had any choice when Zhou was intent on harassing her. Still, his request was kindly meant.

"You can make any demand you wish." She looked down demurely. "You did win our duel."

He fidgeted with the strap of his pack. "Perhaps my travels will take me back this way one day."

It wasn't quite a promise, but her heart leaped. If they weren't in the middle of town, would he have kissed her? She was already spinning dreams in her head.

"Lady Wu," he said with a slight bow. And then added, "Mei Lin." He lingered over her name like a slow caress.

"Master Shen."

And with that, he was gone.

Mei Lin hefted the basket in her arms and hurried through the woods surrounding town. Auntie Yin had protested that the wash didn't yet need to be done, but Mei Lin had grabbed several clean articles of clothing before rushing out. There was a view of the road from a bend in the river. If she hurried, she might catch just one more glimpse of her swordsman.

"Eh, Mei Lin!"

The hated Chen Wang. What was he doing out

here without his cronies anyway? She skirted around him.

"Wait, where are you going so quickly?"

"I'm busy."

"It seems even the great Shen Leung can't bear your temper."

She ignored the heat rising up the back of her neck and walked faster.

He clung to her like a shadow. "Maybe toothless Lo needs a wife."

"How's the eye, Wang?" she countered.

There was a notable break in the determined rhythm of his footsteps behind her. "I was drunk!"

All of her skirmishes with Wang and his brood seemed inconsequential now, like incidents from another life. Shen Leung had brought a new awareness that her corner of the world was so small. Beyond these woods were greater towns and cities, glittering palaces and dangerous missions.

She spun around to chase Wang and his mosquito buzzing away, but a hulking figure among the trees caught her eye.

"Wu Mei Lin."

Another stranger with her name on his lips. This time a cold shudder ran down her spine as the intruder's black eyes skimmed over her from head to toe.

Wang shoved himself between them. "Who are you?"

"Let's just say an acquaintance of Lord Zhou. He sends his regards."

Zhou again. But this one didn't look like the other fools who had strutted into town. He didn't move like them. His eyes never left hers while he stalked toward them, taking up all the space in the clearing. There was a knife at his belt. Her hands tightened over the basket.

Her swords were tucked away beneath her mattress. Their little town had always been a quiet place. A safe place.

The stranger grinned. His teeth gleamed against the darkness of his beard. "You're as pretty as Zhou said."

"Wang, get out of here."

But Wang stood fast. "Run, Mei Lin."

Blood pumped through her, sick with fear. She threw the laundry basket at the stranger's head. At the same time, Wang leaped forward and threw his arm over the man's neck. The skinny merchant's son wrestling an ox by the horns.

"Run!" Wang shouted.

"Yes, Mei Lin," the stranger mocked. "Run."

There was a snap followed by a howl of pain. She looked back to see Wang on the ground. His face was twisted in agony. He had one hand clutched over his arm.

But Zhou's minion had no interest in Wang. He came after her, his long stride closing the distance between them. Her heart was hammering so hard it took over her senses. Her head pounded. Her hands shook.

She aimed a kick for his groin, but he was ready for it. Her foot landed against his thigh and he laughed at her. In desperation, she struck at his throat. The heel of her palm connected and he staggered back, wheezing. Behind him, Wang had pulled himself onto his knees.

"Get help," she called out.

She was running again, dodging toward the trees and praying she was fast enough. Suddenly the forest looked foreign to her. Nothing made sense. Her legs felt sluggish in her panic. A rough hand clamped on to her arm and jerked her backward.

Something struck her across the face. The pain blinded her and she staggered, but the stranger held her up. His fingers dug into her shoulder and she tried to claw at him. The powerlessness over-whelmed her. He struck her again and then tossed her to the ground.

She tasted blood, blood and the salt of her own tears. The pain wouldn't go away.

The stranger stood over her like a conquering lord. The faint rustle of cloth sent a new stab of fear through her.

"Zhou said to come begging at his doorstep and he might be generous. That is, if you can still walk when I'm done with you."

He stepped closer. She clutched a hand to her cheek. She forced herself to look up, otherwise the fear would choke her and she'd drown. Her master had defied warlords and defied men far more powerful than this vagrant. Mei Lin tried to summon that fighting spirit into herself, but all she could find was a ghost of her master's strength.

"When I see that coward Zhou—" Her swollen lips trembled. "I'll cut his throat."

She hated that tears stung in her eyes. Hated that he laughed at her, this man who was there to violate and possibly kill her. All because she had dared to say no to an appointed official.

A coldness took over and her body no longer felt like her own. She bit down hard against her lip as the stranger loomed overhead. He loosened his belt and his tunic hung open. She screamed at herself to flee, to fight, to do anything.

Suddenly he was dragged away. Another figure appeared before her, lean and tall and strong. One she would know anywhere.

Chapter Four

Shen Leung grabbed the man and planted a fist into his nose. His knuckles jarred against bone and flesh. He caught sight of Mei Lin crumpled on the ground and hit the man again.

"Get up."

There was no skill involved. Only brute strength and anger. He flexed his fingers and ignored the dull throb in them as he advanced on the coward. The man was larger than he was, yet he dared to hit a woman. Not any woman. His Mei Lin.

His.

A film clouded his eyes and a dark wrath filled him. The surge of power was nearly frightening. The fiend stumbled back against a tree with blood pouring from his broken nose. The man made the mistake of reaching for his knife.

The sight of a weapon sparked some instinct within Shen Leung. His hand closed over the hilt and the knife became part of him. In a single smooth motion, he stabbed the blade through the man's palm, pinning it against the tree.

The scream tore through the woods.

The sound woke him from his bloodlust and he was able to break through the anger and look at this animal impassively. Violence was sometimes unavoidable. Men like this only responded to swift, decisive action.

He leaned in close while the man cursed him. "Run far," he commanded quietly.

Shen Leung didn't watch to see how the man detached himself or where he fled to afterward. His anger refused to cool as he listened to the fading footsteps.

Mei Lin stood with her arms hugged around herself. She spoke his name as he circled an arm around her shoulders.

"Are you hurt?"

"No."

But he could see where she'd been struck. He touched her mouth gingerly. "Zhou?" he asked through clenched teeth.

She could only nod. Mei Lin had tried to be strong. He should have expected that when she insisted that the old tyrant was harmless. She pressed against his side and fitted herself against him, trembling. He led her to the river and sat her down on a flattened stone on the bank. Without a word, he bent to soak his handkerchief in the water. She sat with her hands folded, watching him. Her lip bled and he could see the darkening signs of a bruise over her cheekbone.

He pressed the damp cloth against the swelling. The grateful look she gave him pierced straight to his heart.

"I didn't know Shen Leung could lose his temper like that," she said.

He stiffened. "I don't like to."

"Why didn't you draw your sword?"

"If I had, I would have killed that man."

These weren't the barbarian pastures. There were laws to be upheld.

"I wouldn't have felt any regret." She fought to keep her voice steady as he dabbed at the corner of her mouth. The sight of her beautiful face marred like this sent a fresh wave of anger through him.

"Me neither," he said.

He should have trusted his instincts from the beginning. He should have never walked away from Mei Lin. Tenderly he ran his fingers through her hair. She closed her eyes to absorb his touch. The tension in his body transformed immediately to desire, but he fought it. This wasn't the time—yet her fingers tangled into the front of his tunic, willing him closer.

"You're only frightened," he protested.

She shook her head. He knew what she was asking. It was torture to keep denying her when he'd wanted her since his first glimpse of her standing in the sunlight. When some bastard had nearly taken her from him.

"Let me take you home."

"I thought I would die when I saw you walk away," she whispered.

"We can talk later."

"Stop fighting me."

There was trust and longing in her eyes. He wanted to wrap his arms around her and keep her safe forever. She had stopped trembling. He brushed his thumb over her jaw and her lips parted with a sigh. He kissed her, gently at first, then deeper with each moment. His hand slid down to the small of her back and she pressed feverishly against him.

Mei Lin's arms circled his neck as she explored his mouth. He grew hard in an instant. She didn't want a protector, she wanted reassurance and comfort. She wanted *him*. In a moment of decision, he braced his knee against the rock and dragged her into his arms.

Her hands stole beneath his tunic while he carried her to the riverbank and laid her down in a patch of wild grass. The touch of her hands over his bare skin drove him mad. She roamed over his chest and stroked lower over his stomach. He grew tight with anticipation, his cock heavy.

"When I saw you, I knew," he said.

He ran his hands through her hair. She was looking up at him with her eyes lidded and sensual, her flawless skin framed by the tall grass around them. She was too beautiful for words. He kissed her because he had to. He needed to absorb her, take her and make her his.

"I knew this was how it would be with us, but I denied myself. I didn't want to dream."

"You talk too much," she chided.

Her clever fingers pulled the ties of his trousers loose and suddenly he was throbbing with her hands around him, so soft. He thrust mindlessly into her grasp, reaching toward heaven.

Mei Lin's heartbeat quickened. This was so reckless of her. Anyone could come and find them and at that moment, she didn't care. Her world had narrowed until there was only the man above her, his face blocking out the sky. From all the stories the old wives told, she should be frightened. Her virtue was in peril. She would be scandalized. But Shen Leung didn't frighten her.

His flesh swelled against her palms, the skin fine and smooth like silk and hot to the touch. His eyes were closed and his expression bordered on pain, every muscle in his face taut. He had one hand fisted in the grass beside her ear and his breathing was labored.

She had no experience in these things, but she had good instincts. She ran her hand over the thick length of him.

"Mei Lin."

He gasped out her name as his fingers tangled into her hair. His kiss was almost forceful. His warm tongue took her mouth and her breath became his breath. She grew dizzy. Before she knew what was happening he had opened her top to caress her breasts.

Her fingers slipped listlessly from him as pleasure arched through her in waves. His touch was so knowing, so experienced. For a second, she wished that she could be wearing perfume and silk and be enchanting.

She parted his tunic as well, following his lead. He was as beautiful and strong as she remembered. She ran her hands over solid muscle. The image of his bare chest had plagued her through the night.

He brushed her hands aside and for a moment she was confused. But only for a moment. His mouth descended to close over her breast and suddenly her body was no longer her own. It arched into him, a wild, wanton creature. A strangled cry escaped her lips. She wanted more.

He gave her more. His tongue slid over her nipple and she writhed in his arms. He did it again, rougher this time, his teeth scraping lightly over the sensitive bud. No longer careful, almost cruel. She sobbed and held on to him while he parted her legs. There was no time to even remove all of their clothing. The wickedness of it took her breath away.

He entered her, flesh to flesh easing deep and invoking a confusing tumble of emotion. Surrender and possession. There was an exquisite pain as he filled her, a focusing of all sensation at the point where their bodies joined. And she was surprised to discover she loved all of it—the sensation of being stretched beyond bearing, even the slight hitch of pain. She cried out as he entered her completely. Her legs wrapped around him and she buried her face against his throat. His pulse thrummed against her lips, calling to her.

He groaned her name and she bit his neck. She'd learned that from him. She learned a lot of other things, too. When she lifted her hips he held her tighter. His fingers pressed into the small of her back and his movements became more jagged and uncontrolled.

The pleasure-pain reached a crest and her entire body tightened. Her vision blurred. Everything vanished. Even Shen Leung, except for the unrelenting swell of him within her and the solid muscle of his shoulders where she clung to him.

When she opened her eyes again he was watching her. He cradled her, lifting her away from the ground while he rocked into her, watching her face with each thrust.

It didn't take long. His body tightened and he crushed his mouth over hers. It wasn't a kiss anymore. The caress was raw and desperate. He ground against her lips as he pushed himself deep. Then he held her tight while he shuddered over her, groaning with his release as the skies opened.

The stillness afterward went on for a long time.

A long time.

Honor was everything to Shen Leung according to the tales they told. Would he marry her now? Was it even possible between a wandering swordsman working for the imperial court and a nameless girl in a nothing town? She blinked up at him, waiting.

He stroked her hair, letting the strands fall through his fingers. "You're so beautiful," he said finally, and she held her breath. He would tell her now. He had to.

"That dog Zhou and I are going to have a conversation," he said instead. "Today."

Chapter Five

Shen Leung took her back to the edge of town. His hand remained cradled around her the entire time, but then he left her.

"Zhou will never harm you again," he vowed.

But that wasn't the vow she was waiting for. He had to realize that. She wanted to know what it was between them, whether he thought of her with each breath, the way she did with him.

She halted when she reached the noodle stand. The tables had been upended, the bowls and dishes smashed. Uncle shuffled among the ruins and Auntie dragged her broom silently through the fragments.

"This was all because of you." Uncle's voice shook. "So disobedient! And ungrateful! Zhou made a good offer, better than you will ever have."

Uncle went on and all she could do was stand

with her eyes cast downward as he berated her. Auntie went on sweeping and said nothing.

"Now you've angered him. See all this?"

"Yes, Uncle."

It would have been disrespectful not to answer. Uncle and Auntie had fed and provided for her since her parents had died. They weren't kind, but they were far from cruel.

"What are we going to do now?" he ranted.

"I'll take care of this, Uncle."

"You'll do nothing!"

The broken benches reminded her more than ever that she had never belonged. She had brought this turmoil upon their peaceful town. She was more an outsider than even Shen Leung. The only time the world made sense was when they were together. But why had he left so quickly after the things he'd said to her? After the things they'd done?

"Worthless." Uncle left her to grumble at Auntie Yin.

Wang hovered outside the stand. His left arm hung in a sling and he winced when he saw the bruise on her cheek.

"There were two of them," he reported. "I wasn't here to stop them, but next time…"

His cronies circled the avenue restlessly, prowling for a fight. For once, she felt an itch of pride in their dogged obedience.

Wang lowered his voice, sounding genuinely anguished. "I should have never left you alone, Mei Lin."

"It would have been worse if you hadn't found Shen Leung."

"Shen Leung?" He blinked at her. "But I never called him."

She had assumed Wang had sent Shen Leung to her rescue. If Shen had returned to her on his own...

She took a deep breath. "Take care of Uncle and Auntie."

Wang nodded solemnly and, just like that, their old grudge swept away on the breeze.

She hurried to the house. They lived not twenty paces from the noodle shop, in a two room hovel that was cramped even before she had arrived. She went to the mat in the corner of the front room. The butterfly swords were there beneath it, her only possessions. She thought of Shen Leung as she lifted them.

He had returned for her.

His lips had brushed against her hair after they made love. She had nestled against him, afraid to ask what would happen next. She didn't even know the words for it. There was more than honor and the need to set things right. She had to believe that.

Once outside, she bowed to Uncle. "Thank you for your generosity all these years."

Uncle snorted and turned his back on her as she started down the road. Auntie hurried over and tried to press several coins into her hand, but she wouldn't take them.

Her fate was decided in so many little movements. No matter what happened that day, she couldn't come back. She was nothing but a burden to her aunt and uncle.

She was halfway down the lane when the patter of footsteps sounded behind her. The familiar stride brought tears to her eyes.

"Mei Lin, Mei Lin!" Little Cho grabbed on to her hand. "I'm going with you."

"What are you going to do in the wide world out there?"

What was she going to do? She pushed the thought away.

"I'm going to learn how to fight with swords," the boy insisted.

"But then who will take care of your mother and father?"

His hand tightened willfully over hers. She could have shaken free and sent him back, but instead she straightened. Like her, Little Cho only became more stubborn when someone told him no.

"All right, then. Do you need to say farewell?"

He shook his head and wiped his sleeve over his nose. She started toward the edge of town. With each step, his feet dragged more and more. By the last row of buildings, he grew stiff and his small legs locked in place, refusing to go farther. He stared wide-eyed into the trees beyond and then looked up at her, blinking furiously.

"We'll see each other again someday," she said gently.

His hand slipped from hers and he turned around, running as he always did. With a deep breath, Mei Lin faced the woods. From the moment she'd refused Zhou's demand, she'd taken her fate into her own hands. Shen Leung was out there. He expected her to stay behind while he faced her enemy, but she didn't need his heroism. She needed him.

Unlike Little Cho, her feet carried her forward without pause.

She found Shen Leung at the main juncture, standing perfectly still as he watched the road like a hawk. He was magnificent like that. Confident and impenetrable.

He cast her a long look when she took his side and then returned to his vigil. He seemed almost meditative, while she could barely stay still. All she could think of was how their bodies had joined only hours earlier and that it was torture to be so close to him and not touch him.

And it was so damn hot standing here.

"You're certain Zhou is coming this way?"

"He'll be here." The muscle along his jaw tightened. "And then I'll make sure he never threatens you again."

She knew he had some clandestine mission he'd been sent to do. Whatever it was, his work for the empire had to be more important than a quarrel between a spurned magistrate and a small town. It had to be more important than some silly, lovestruck girl.

"I don't regret what happened between us," she said.

There was a pause. "I feel the same."

She didn't tell him about what had happened back home. He probably assumed she could still return and wait for him until his travels brought him back.

"When we fought yesterday, I knew you were unlike anyone I would ever meet again," she said.

"I'm honored, Mei Lin. I truly am."

She gripped the hilt of her sword to keep from slapping him. Did he always have to maintain such discipline? She longed to have him pressed over her again, all control gone as he lost himself inside her. These feelings couldn't be hers alone. Yet he revealed nothing. Was this enduring silence a sign of strength among men?

She considered telling him that she had thrown that fight all along. He might have something to say then.

A covered palanquin appeared in the distance, hefted by four carriers and a small escort of two guardsmen. A curtain over the front shielded the occupant from view.

"Are you sure you want to be involved in this?" he asked.

"Don't insult me. I'm already involved."

She caught the very corner of his mouth lifting. The litter continued its steady approach. Her heart welled with emotion as she watched Shen Leung in profile. So proud, righteous and humble.

"So Shen Leung gets caught in local skirmishes and is praised as a hero through no fault of his own," she teased. "Is that how it always happens?"

His gaze lingered on her. "Nothing has ever happened like this."

Heat rose to her cheeks and she wanted nothing

more than to remain by his side, even if she had to challenge him to another swordfight for the right. Even if she had to seduce her way into his heart. She was new to the mysteries of men and women, but she was a quick learner.

The carriers halted before them with the palanquin balanced over their shoulders.

"Who are you to block the road?" the guardsman called out.

Shen Leung started to answer, but Mei Lin was there before him.

"Come out, Zhou, and face your *little wife*," she challenged.

The term was used to refer to a man's mistress, his kept woman. She advanced on the guardsmen before they could draw their weapons. She kicked the lead man in the groin and he fell back against the carriers. One end of the sedan toppled to the ground. The men stumbled as the wooden box shifted over their shoulders and the entire contraption crashed a moment later. The carriers shrank back when she started toward them.

"Mei Lin, they're unarmed," Shen Leung admonished.

The curtain swung open and Zhou's eyes narrowed on her. "Demon girl," he spat.

"Dog spawn," she retorted.

She raised her sword and Zhou darted back inside. The curtain fluttered over the opening.

Shen Leung came forward. "I have no quarrel with you," he said to the servants. "You may flee with your lives."

Always so honorable. They listened to him and fled. The remaining guardsmen fell back when Shen unsheathed his sword.

"It is your misfortune that you serve a dishonest master," he said.

These country louts had little in the way of formal training. In two strikes, he disarmed them and sent both of them running. Only Zhou remained, cowering inside the wooden sedan.

Shen Leung turned to her and held out his sword. "Hold this for me."

"What makes you think I won't kill Zhou myself?"

He shot her a warning look and she lowered her weapons. The moment Shen Leung's sword passed from his hand into hers, another bond formed between them.

With a sweep of his arm, he tore aside the curtain and grabbed the shrinking official by the front of his robe.

"Lord Zhou," he greeted.

"Unwashed barbarian. You'll hang for this."

Zhou tried to claw himself free. She had never noticed how much he looked like a vulture before. A vulture squabbling for its life.

"I will kill you with my bare hands if you ever threaten Lady Wu or her family again."

"That fox demon is no lady!"

Shen dragged him close, until they were eye to eye. "Look at my face and remember it. I will kill you myself if you threaten her or her family," he repeated. "My name is Shen Leung and I honor my promises. Now, I think you have a long way to walk home."

He released the man and Zhou shot her a glare before fleeing. His blue robe disappeared in the distance.

She smiled as she returned the sword. "You can be impressive when you lose your temper."

"Like a common bully."

"Nothing of the sort."

He slid the weapon back into its sheath and held out his hand. Her heart beat faster, her mind full of questions as his fingers closed around hers. But he only meant to help her into the palanquin. The gesture was pleasantly chivalrous, but so much less than what she hoped he would offer.

"Where are we going to go without any carriers?" she asked.

He climbed in beside her and, for a moment, she enjoyed the feel of being close to him, reclining in the shade upon silk pillows.

She ran a hand over the polished wood of the interior, stalling for more time. "I've never been inside a palanquin."

"If only I could offer you wealth and privilege. Your feet would never have to touch the ground."

"I don't mind walking…beside you." This was so hard. How could she confess everything she felt for him when he still hadn't said anything? She took a deep breath and held it. She might be holding her breath forever given how taciturn he could be.

"I didn't expect any of this," he began, finally. "I want you more than anything. When I'm around you, I can barely think."

"I want you, too."

"I have nothing to offer you."

He was so hardheaded! "Don't you dare apologize," she warned. "I'll kill you if you do. And then I'll shave my head and join a convent and never think of you again."

Shen Leung was just sitting there. Not holding her, not kissing her, not whispering heatedly to her and declaring his devotion. All he could think of was objections when her heart was so full she thought it would burst.

"Shave all that beautiful hair?" he asked finally.

When she dared to look at him, he was grinning. She scowled at him.

"That's a pretty face." He was laughing now.

"You waited long enough to say something."

"You don't already know?" He leaned close so that his mouth grazed her earlobe. "Every time I touch you, it's a promise." His mouth explored a sensitive spot on her neck, sending a shiver through her that curled her toes. "And I always keep my promises."

He twined his fingers around hers and she had never felt so safe, so secure. She was beginning to see who Shen Leung was: a man who was endlessly loyal. He made his decisions with the same quiet strength that he projected, and he held on to them. She would never have to doubt him.

"Wherever you're going, I'm going with you," she insisted. "I won't stay behind and wait for you while you risk your life for the empire."

"You can protect me with your butterfly swords."

He kissed her gently, turning her to draw her into his arms. Her skin warmed to him. This was where she belonged. He tugged at the curtain so they were hidden inside the palanquin.

"But we're on the road," she protested.

"I told you, you make me forget myself." He

smiled wickedly and pulled her onto his lap. "Stop fighting me, Mei Lin."

She settled onto him, all protest gone. His thighs were hard beneath her. Another part of him grew even harder as she circled her hips. It was wonderful being able to watch him like this, close enough to see every muscle along his jaw clench with desire.

His mouth found hers. His hands slipped inside her tunic and pushed the cloth aside.

"I must get you to a proper bed." His skilled touch smoothed over her shoulders and the soft skin of her breasts. "Someday," he amended, breathing hard.

He wrapped his arms tight around her to pull her nipple to his mouth. His tongue licked over her, slightly rough on her skin. She gasped and her body grew damp. He switched to the other one and soon she was writhing and clinging to him, no longer caring where they were. Only that they were together.

He lifted her momentarily and his clever hands worked between them, pushing their clothes aside. She undid his shirt and ran her hands greedily over the packed muscle of his chest. One day she would get to see him, every powerful inch of him. She couldn't wait.

"This morning, you came back on your own, didn't you?"

"Of course. I bested you in that swordfight."

"There's something I should tell you about that."

"Hmm?" Shen Leung took hold of her hips and eased her down onto him in a single smooth, powerful glide. He thrust upward and her vision blurred.

"I'll—" Her body tightened around him as he moved inside her. "I'll tell you later."

"Those were the terms, were they not?" He was watching her with such intensity, possessing her with each loving stroke. For the first time, he looked smug. "You belong to me, Mei Lin."

His voice sounded far away as the pleasure built between them.

"Yes," she sighed happily. "Completely yours."

She arched her neck back and hid her smile.

* * * * *

THE LADY'S
SCANDALOUS NIGHT

To the Tuesday critique group: Dawn Blankenship,
Amanda Berry, Kristi Lea and Shawntelle Madison.
Thank you so much for the kibitzing, the prodding,
the encouragement and the laughter.
All things big and small it takes to keep me going.

Most importantly, a heartfelt thanks to my editor
Anna Boatman for always respecting the story
and helping me untangle the many threads of this tale
to turn it into something beautiful.

Author Note

The Lady's Scandalous Night stemmed from all those late
nights at my grandmother's house, watching Hong Kong
and Japanese melodramas on television with 'the cousins'.
My idealistic young mind was always tortured because
these young, beautiful couples had to sacrifice themselves
and their love for the sake of honour and duty.

This story is linked to *The Dragon and the Pearl* and takes
place alongside the larger story. The two tales can be read
in any order, and it's my hope that reading one will enhance
the other. I was fascinated by the idea of two sword brothers
pitted against each other. These warriors swore an oath
to serve their master, yet one of them has broken it. I was
also inspired by the idea of arranged marriage. Though a
prospective husband and wife often met for the first time on
their wedding day, an arranged marriage was an agreement
between two families, often with much history and context
behind it.

What if all these vows of honour came into conflict with
one another all at once?

A few historical notes: the late Tang Dynasty is known
for the rise of the *jiedushi*, warlords who were often
promoted from the field out of necessity. Governor Li Tao
is protected by a fictional elite group of fighters known as a
Rising Guard, which is an homage to the historical LongWu
or Dragon Martial guard that formed within the Imperial
Army.

Chapter One

Tang Dynasty China, 759 AD

The shop was exactly as Chen had imagined it. The cabinets were fashioned from dark, polished cherrywood. The counter kept meticulously clean. He stepped up to it and a shadow moved in the back room. A shape through the beaded curtain.

The Yao family sold paper. They had a mill and purchased logs transported down the Great River from forests west of there. All these things Chen knew from so many stories, told over so many days. More details than he remembered of his very own family, which he'd left behind to serve in Governor Li's army when he was little more than a boy. Chen was no longer a common soldier, of rank too insignificant to mention. He was a trained swordsman and a trusted bodyguard who would die to protect his master.

As Yao Ru Shan had been. Once.

The curtain at the back of the shop parted. A middle-aged man appeared and greeted Chen with proper deference, but it was the figure still beyond the curtain that held Chen's attention. The young woman sat at her desk with a brush in hand. He only had one glance before the strands fell back in place. The wooden beads tapped together in muted harmony.

He had already memorized the curve of her neck and the perfect angle of her wrist as she bent over her writing. From across the room, filtered through the beaded barrier, there was nothing more to see but form and shape. But the shape of her was enough to capture his thoughts.

The clerk bowed behind the counter. "Honored sir, what can we do for you?"

"I am looking for Master Yao Hui-Rong."

At that, the woman stood. Chen watched her shadow approach from the corner of his eye. Before the clerk could answer, the curtain parted once again.

"Yao Hui-Rong is my father."

And now she became more than an elegant silhouette. More than a name he had repeated to himself in the dark.

"Lady Yao."

Chen greeted her, palm to fist, head bowed. In the moment before he lowered his eyes, he'd already taken in more than was polite. She resembled her brother and she didn't. Her features were strong, but tempered. Her hair was coiled tight and fixed with ebony pins. Her mouth was small and curved, the only part of her that could be considered soft. Ru Shan called her River.

When Chen straightened, River wasn't looking at him. Instead her gaze had fixed onto the sword at his side.

"I apologize. My father is ill." Her voice sounded strained. She must have noted it, because when she spoke again it was forcibly clearer. "If you have any news…"

This was harder than he thought it would be. "It is of the utmost importance I speak to him directly."

She looked to the clerk and then back to him. Her robe was blue, nearly black, like the fading twilight. The collar of it closed high around her throat. It was unnecessarily austere, he found himself thinking.

"Then I can take you to him. If you can watch the shop, Liao?" She turned uncertainly to the clerk, who nodded.

River came around the counter to stand deliberately apart from him. "My manners are nowhere to be found. Your name?"

"Wei Chen. I served with your brother in the military governor's first battalion."

"I'm Yao Ru Jiang," she murmured.

Jiang. River. He'd always thought it sounded pretty. "An honor," he replied.

He waited for her to recognize his name, but she averted her eyes as she started past. Perhaps it was too much to hope. Too needful. The clerk, Liao, bowed once, as an afterthought, and then followed them with his eyes as Chen followed River out into the street.

"Our house is outside of town," she explained.

He knew that, as well. Ru Shan had told him of this town, the mill, and of his younger sister. Chen had devoured every word and used the images to fill in empty moments and empty spaces within. He'd never thought that he would have to use this knowledge to hunt down his comrade, the brother of his heart.

"My horse is at the stable," he offered.

"Our home is not far." Her eyes grew wide before she turned away, blushing. "I'd...I'd prefer to walk."

Was it the prospect of riding with him that made her so nervous? Etiquette demanded that he do something quickly to ease her mind and set their interaction back on steady ground. He wanted to do this properly, or as properly as could be expected.

"The lady is right, it would be a shame to waste this sunshine."

He took her side at a respectable distance. River snatched a brief sideways glance at him before casting her eyes downward. He found his palms sweating.

They continued wordlessly to the edge of town. From there, a dirt path led toward the river.

"I haven't been completely honest with you," he said, breaking the silence.

She paused for a moment, her lips pressed tight, then continued down the path.

"I knew your brother well. I consider Ru Shan—" He faltered. "I consider him a friend."

"It is always good to meet friends."

Her words were brittle. She knew. Even this far within the province, they would have heard reports of the unrest, as well as rumors of who was instigating the rebellion. When he'd first learned of Ru Shan's treachery, he hadn't believed it. Doubt was quickly replaced by confusion, then anger. Now he didn't know what to feel as he hunted for Ru Shan.

"He spoke often of you," Chen continued. "Ru

Shan and Ru Jiang. Mountain and river." He fumbled for more. It was difficult to walk beside her. It was difficult to be pleasant while he held back what he'd come to tell her. "It seems very poetic."

"Our family only makes the paper. We know nothing about the poetry written on it."

"I'm no poet either," he admitted.

"No, you're a swordsman. A trained killer."

Her directness took him aback, but she was right. He deserved this coldness from her.

He was trained. An expert. A clean death was a mercy, in a way. The final mercy and the only one he could give.

She had to get the swordsman away from town. There were too many people who could have seen her brother come and go. One seemingly harmless comment could mean his death.

River knew the men of the first battalion were fiercely loyal. They had honed their skills with the sword, the knife and the bow. They would follow an oath of honor through all the layers of hell.

Now one of those men walked beside her: sleek, silent and predatory. Ru Shan had spoken of this man like a brother, not this hard-edged warrior beside her. They had suspected someone would come, but she hadn't expected it to be Wei Chen.

Her heart pounded and she grew faint as the blood rushed through her. She'd been wrong about him, so wrong.

"You're tall," Chen said.

She frowned, struggling to find a suitable response.

"You're taller than I imagined," he amended.

Why would he care to fill the silence with this and that?

"My brother is tall," she replied.

Her hands were shaking. She tucked them into her sleeves to hide them, and remained focused on the path ahead as they left the town behind them. His eyes were on her. She was certain he could see her guilt and sense the heat burning beneath her skin. Some careless remark could send this hunter after her brother.

The courtyard house stood on the river across the bend from the mill. They came to a halt outside the front. River paused with her hand on the wooden gate and forced herself to look directly at him.

"You don't have to be afraid of me," he said, almost gently.

"I don't believe you."

Of all things, her lack of trust seemed to wound

him. This hardened, steel-eyed soldier who faced death and dealt it in the same breath.

"You don't know me, but I served with your brother among Governor Li Tao's trusted body-guards," he explained. "Recently Ru Shan was released from the governor's service. The circumstances were—not ideal."

Her brother had been marched into the forest for execution. At the last moment, Governor Li had relented. Ru Shan should have just come home and then none of this would be happening. Her heart ached to think of it.

"My brother did speak of you," she admitted.

Ru Shan had spoken Chen's name many times to her father and to her. Chen was accomplished, highly skilled, disciplined. Had the warlord known to send the one man her brother would refuse to fight?

"My brother told me that you saved his life when he first went to battle." She watched his face, searching for signs of the friend her brother so admired. "Our family owes you a great debt."

Chen's eyes grew cold. "That was a long time ago. Any debt that exists is only between your brother and me."

"He hasn't come here."

She'd spoken too hastily. The swordsman pinned

her with his gaze and she struggled not to look away while heat rose up the back of her neck.

"I know," he said after a pause.

Chen had searched through the town, as she suspected, though it seemed he hadn't interrogated the inhabitants yet. Otherwise he might have discovered that Ru Shan had been there. Her brother was still too close, only three days' ride away.

"Why do you wish to speak to my father?" she asked.

"Ru Shan and I are brothers, in spirit if not in blood. I came to pay my respects to your family, as I should have done long ago." His tone was calm. So calm. "And then I must apologize."

"Apologize?"

A flicker of emotion crossed his face, too fleeting for her to catch. A chill traveled down her spine. Her next breath wouldn't come.

"His shame is my shame." Chen squared his shoulders before her. He was taller than Ru Shan. Stronger. Colder. "I must apologize for the sorrow I will inevitably bring you when I'm forced to kill him."

Chapter Two

Chen didn't threaten so much as promise. It would do no good to beg or plead. His decision had been made. River could see it in the set of his jaw and the way his tone never wavered.

She knew of the stories of the military governor's ruthlessness. Li Tao showed no mercy. His men were the same, except for Ru Shan. Her brother had never belonged among those mercenaries. She'd thought Chen would be different as well, but her first impression was obviously correct: duty came first with him.

"That is unfortunate." Her voice came out strained. She swallowed to try to regain it. "But expected."

"I am truly sorry."

Chen bowed and she wanted to shout at him. What use were such manners after what he'd just told her? But she had to remain calm.

"If I can speak to Master Yao, I will leave and no longer burden you with my presence."

Leave to hunt down Ru Shan. What did etiquette demand she say after a man she'd never met announced he would kill her brother?

"You must stay for dinner."

Chen frowned. Let him be confused. That was her one task now: to keep the swordsman distracted for as long as she could.

"The Yao family is not entirely without honor." She regarded him pointedly. "And we have nothing to hide."

She pushed the gate open and stepped into the enclosed courtyard. After a pause, Chen's footsteps sounded behind her and she breathed with relief. The servants came to greet them, expressing surprise that she was home so early. The head attendant shot her a meaningful glance. Liao had made it home before her, then. He'd warned the others.

"Our honored guest will be staying for dinner," she said. "Prepare tea for him."

"Please don't trouble yourself," Chen protested.

"But you must be tired from your journey."

Another objection lingered on his lips. She insisted again, and he finally relented. Such a simple, familiar pattern of etiquette. It was almost a comfort to be distracted in this way.

"Lady Yao." He must have read something in her gaze. His expression softened. "If the situation had been different—"

She caught a hint of sadness in his deep-set eyes. Their meeting was supposed to be a happy occasion. Ru Shan should have been there to introduce them, as he'd always promised he would.

River wanted to believe Chen was too courteous to be a hardened killer. He had a good face. One that looked sincere. She'd had so many silly, girlish dreams woven around this man and each one opened now and bled.

Chen was supposedly trustworthy and righteous, but his righteousness made him dangerous. He would always adhere to the strict code of fighting men and Ru Shan had broken that code. For sword brothers, one man's honor was equally shared. One man's shame, also equally shared. Even she understood that much.

"I'll go speak to my father," she said and Chen nodded solemnly.

She assigned one of the servants to take him to the parlor. The moment they disappeared from the courtyard, she hurried to Father's study. Liao was waiting there, pacing in a small circle behind the desk.

"Master Yao has been told," the clerk reported.

"Keep my father hidden," she instructed. "You must get him away tonight."

"But how? With the governor's man here…"

She'd invited Chen to dinner with a purpose. Within the walls of their house, she could control what he heard and saw. "I'll distract the swordsman while you take Father and the others to safety. Stay with him in the south or…or go as you will. You've done your duty."

There wasn't enough time to change their original plan. Liao would gather horses and wagons. The household would be smuggled away in the night.

"But what about you?" Liao asked.

"I have to stay."

The loyal clerk shook his head. "My lady, we can delay the swordsman for you."

She held up her hand to silence him. Wei Chen was a master with the broadsword. Deadly accurate, Ru Shan had boasted. Liao and the servants would be cut to pieces. And even if they did succeed in subduing Chen, they would only bring Governor Li Tao's wrath on all of them for daring to strike at one of his warriors. She needed to keep him here, where he could be controlled.

"He trusts me."

"This servant won't run while the lady stays!"

"You will," she said so forcefully that Liao fell silent. "Wei Chen won't hurt me." She didn't know that for certain. "I'll come and find you when it's safe." And now she was lying.

The ruthless warlord had sent only one man after her brother. If Chen failed, more men would come, but as long as Chen was alone her family had a chance to escape.

Ru Shan had made his life-or-death choice and dragged them all down with him. This was her own life or death choice. She'd never known she could lie so steadily. Her hands no longer trembled.

"It has to be me," she said quietly.

Wei Chen had looked at her. The sorrow within him had captured her for a fleeting moment and the unspoken promise hung between them. They were supposed to meet and, if all the stars aligned, perhaps even marry. It was a future that was now forsaken, but it still connected them. She would use that bond to gain his trust. It was the only way to save her brother and her father.

Liao remained hidden in the study while she left to prepare. She spoke to each servant personally to make sure they understood their tasks. Then she retreated to her room.

Her belongings had been packed. They had intended to leave that night. They would escape under the cover of darkness and become fugitives in the shadows. Everything that their family had built over generations was fading away. The mill stood empty. The paper shop would close. She was empty, all hope for a normal life gone.

One robe remained in the cabinet. It was the color of peach blossoms and threaded with gold embroidery. She ran her fingers over the smooth cloth. The delicate garment had no place where they were going and she had meant to leave it behind, but then Wei Chen had appeared to grind all their plans to dust.

She could hold him there. Not forever, but long enough.

She pulled the ebony pins from her hair and let it fall about her shoulders. She knew she wasn't beautiful in the way of springtime and flowers, but perhaps it wasn't necessary. Wei Chen had looked at her in the courtyard as if he couldn't turn away. No man had ever looked at her like that. Maybe it was only anger or regret, but she would use them both if she had to.

Her brother was preparing the rebels for battle in the mountains. She prepared now for battle with jeweled hairpins and perfume. With silk.

She would have to dress without the aid of servants. The entire household was either busy preparing the evening meal or readying for their escape. The embroidered cloth draped sensually over her shoulders. She wrapped the sash about her waist and dabbed a drop of perfume at her throat and wrists. This was how she'd prepare herself for a lover if her life was not yet destroyed.

Her hair took longer. She had to pin it and repin it, with nothing but her own shaking fingers to twist it into place. On a whim, she painted her lips. One look into the brass mirror and she wiped the tint away, horrified.

That sensual, daring creature wasn't her. Mouth like a scarlet butterfly's wings. But it was who she needed to be, wasn't it? Tentatively, she'd stroked more color onto her lips, tracing the edges with the tip of the cosmetic brush. Red as firecrackers and festival lanterns. Her eyes were drawn inevitably to her own reflection. As Chen's would be. He would look once at her, his gaze piercing and intense, and then he would look away out of propriety. Her pulse quickened at the thought.

River scrubbed her face clean again.

It was an hour before she emerged. The dining room was near the front of the house. She stood just inside and waited for Chen to be brought from the tea parlor. Her palms were damp. Her throat dry. If only she'd been brave enough to keep a touch of rouge. Maddeningly, her lips remained swollen and sensitive from the undue attention. When Chen entered, heat rushed to her cheeks.

He looked at her dress, to the table, then to the door behind him. "Will it be only the two of us?"

The servants drifted in to light the lanterns and set plates upon the table. Father had dismissed most of the servants a week ago, leaving only a few to tend to them before they went into hiding. River spoke when the two of them were once again alone.

"My father is ill with grief. My brother's shame is our shame, as well." It was easier to speak if she didn't look directly at him. Her nervousness worked well here. "He's taken to bed early tonight with a medicinal tea to help him sleep. I must beg of you not to trouble him until tomorrow."

"I don't wish to cause your family any more distress—than necessary," he added regretfully.

He was telling her in so few words that he would still find and punish Ru Shan. Why then did he insist on being so civil? By Chen's code, he could only restore his honor if he took her brother's life. Honor was not clean or civil. Neither was loyalty, nor love. They all battled one another, tearing mortal wounds, showing no mercy.

She extended her hand in what she hoped was a graceful gesture. "Please sit."

They sat opposite each other in silence while the servants poured the rice wine. What followed was a feast only seen at weddings and the lunar festival. Pickled vegetables and brined eggs. Four-ingredient soup and five-spice quail.

The kitchen was overreaching. She had only asked them to extend the meal as long as possible.

"Is everything to your liking?" she asked.

"Yes…yes, of course." Chen shifted uncomfortably as he stared at the feast, but said nothing more. Perhaps he thought her mad, dining so lavishly with her brother's would-be executioner.

"How long was your journey?"

"Two weeks from Chengdu."

"You must be tired."

"Not at all." Chen folded his hands, watching her intently.

She sipped her wine, already at a loss for conversation. His gaze strayed unmistakably to her mouth, sending a flutter to her stomach. So it wasn't necessary for her lips to be painted after all.

"I used to imagine what you must look like," she ventured.

He stiffened. "Oh?"

"I thought you must be tall enough to scrape the

ceiling. Arms like tree trunks, the way Ru Shan described you. Frightening."

Chen managed a small smile. "Your brother certainly could tell a story."

It became a little easier to breathe. "You'd be covered in scars and missing teeth after all the battles you've waged," she teased.

His laugh resonated through her. Things could have been different, that laughter told her.

"You were wrong about the teeth," he said. "Unfortunately I can't do anything for the scars." Chen ran a hand over the back of his knuckles. A map of lines ran across them as a testament to the battles he'd seen in the warlord's training grounds and beyond.

She had thought about Wei Chen in the past. In more innocent times, she'd hoped he was handsome. At the very least, she'd hoped they would speak like this and find their temperaments compatible.

It might have been easier if his appearance was as fierce and cruel as she feared. Chen had a high forehead, a strong chin. Proud features. She wished she hadn't noticed how his eyes lit up when he smiled.

Such fantasies meant nothing now. Soldiers like Chen believed in honor and duty before all else, but she couldn't put country before family. Ru Shan was her brother. He was the mountain and she was the river. She had to do everything in her power to save him. She searched deep within herself for the strength to carry out this deception.

Another dish was brought out. Chen reached for his wine cup. Boldly, she leaned across the table to pour more, only to spill it when their movements collided.

She fumbled with the flask. "Forgive me."

Chen steadied her hand with his own. "Forgive me," he echoed.

Their eyes met and she knew he wasn't speaking about the wine. Her skin grew hot where he touched her. She twisted free and retreated back to her seat, the clumsiest seductress in the world. Despite the awkwardness of her attempt, she saw how Chen's eyes grew clouded.

The more she saw of Wei Chen, the more he confused her. He didn't strike her as a cold-blooded executioner. He was more than the master swordsman her brother described.

"I remember when the governor's soldiers first came to recruit Ru Shan," she said. "He was fifteen. He had never even held a sword, let alone knew how to wield one."

"That was the Spring Rebellion," Chen said. "It

was the first year after Governor Li took this position. Many men were recruited to his service."

She was supposed to distract Chen from her brother, not remind him, but suddenly she wanted Chen to explain to her how a man could hunt down someone he considered his own blood.

"My brother spoke often about you, but he was always vague about how you met."

"You don't want to hear the story. It's about warfare and battle."

"I do," she insisted.

The rebellion was led by the former military governor of the district who had fallen out of favor with the Emperor for one reason or another. Her brother hadn't protested when he was selected to serve, but none of them had been given much choice.

After a pause, Chen drained his cup. "We marched against the insurgents and cornered the last regiment in the valley of the Sichuan basin. The rebels made one last desperate push and we were cut off from reinforcements. The foot soldiers panicked, but not Ru Shan."

"But he would have died if not for you."

The muscles of Chen's jaw tensed, but he said nothing.

"My brother told us you were one of the governor's trained warriors of the *Xining*. The Rising Guard rode into the center of the fighting and held the rebels back. You saved him."

"It was only duty," he said, his voice rough. He reached for his cup, only to realize that it was empty. She poured for him without error this time. She hoped he wouldn't notice that there were no more servants attending to the meal.

"After the battle, I recommended that Ru Shan be accepted into the Rising Guard," Chen went on.

"Because he had been ready to die so bravely?"

"Because he had been ready to die," he concurred somberly.

Now Ru Shan was the rebel and both men were ready to die. The *Xining* had changed her brother. He'd trained as a warrior. He'd become hard and fearless, but in his soul River had known he wasn't one of them.

"So after all that has happened, you came for him yourself," she said quietly.

Chen's eyes glittered, black and cold. "I asked Governor Li to allow me the chance to bring justice to Ru Shan with my own hand. He's my burden. *My* responsibility."

River could almost understand Chen's anger. Her brother had betrayed more than just the warlord. She and Father were being forced to go into

hiding. Their home was lost and their future upended. Perhaps Chen was right. The last face Ru
Shan looked upon should be one he knew and re-
spected. Not the cold, blank stares of assassins or
the shame of a public hanging.

The path of her thoughts shocked her. She would
never side with her brother's executioner, but she
saw how Chen faced a decision as hard as her own.

"You don't want to do this," she said.

"But I must."

Chen set his cup aside. The rest of the food had
gone cold. It seemed neither of them had an ap-
petite.

"Thank you for your hospitality," he said formally. "It was good to finally meet you, Yao Ru
Jiang, despite the circumstances."

He spoke her name with care, savoring it. He
sounded so sincere that her heart ached.

"It was good to meet you as well, Wei Chen,"
she replied.

"With your permission, I'll come by tomorrow
to speak with your father."

He was leaving.

"Wait." This was the moment. She had to keep
him distracted. If he left the house, there was too
much risk that he'd discover the escape. Her throat

went dry as she tried to speak. "Where are you staying tonight?"

"There must be some place in town."

"But it's late and the way back to town is dark and unsafe." Her heart pounded so loud it would give her away. "You must stay here. In spite of everything, you and Ru Shan were once brothers."

Chen looked troubled. "I can't accept—"

"I insist." She placed her hand at the crook of his arm in what she hoped was a meaningful and enticing gesture—except she was shaking.

He swallowed with some effort. Her face burned hotter with each moment he regarded her. The awkward, awful invitation dangled between them.

"I'm very grateful," he replied, holding her gaze until she was the first to look away.

Chapter Three

He had to refuse her.

Chen lay in the soft darkness of the chamber, facing the ceiling and looking into nothingness. The bed was heated by coals laid beneath the mattress boards. River had put him in one of the innermost rooms at the far end of the courtyard—the most private and luxurious. Like their dinner together, it was more than he deserved.

It wasn't possible that she had worn that dress for him. Perhaps the delicate perfume wasn't meant to lure him, nor the coincidences which had the two of them dining alone. Chen could have been mistaken about her intentions, but if he wasn't, then he had to refuse her.

There could only be one reason she would come to him tonight, and he didn't want her that way.

Ru Shan had spoken often to him about growing up in this house with his sister and his father. Chen had asked Ru Shan to tell him about the smallest details. Usually when they were drinking, and Chen could hide his longing behind the wine and the lateness of the hour.

River hadn't turned him away despite his confession. The family was too humble and too honorable for that. Public before private, the proverb said. Country before family. The family understood that Ru Shan had condemned himself. They must be mourning for Ru Shan the same way Chen mourned. He lay in the quiet house with reminders of his old friend all around him, while regret choked the life from him.

"Defeat me today and I'll give you my sister in marriage," Ru Shan had teased once, twirling his sword so it caught the sunlight.

It hadn't been so long ago, had it?

Between the boasting and the insults, Chen had known what Ru Shan truly wanted. He was proposing that they become brothers in name as well as spirit. He was offering family. Ru Shan owed Chen his life. It was a debt that could never be repaid.

"If she looks like you, it would be a punishment!" Chen had retorted.

Then he had defeated Ru Shan soundly.

That night, Chen had lain awake imagining shining black hair and pale, smooth skin. He'd spoken her name aloud. *River.* The name itself sounded like a dream. *River.*

He no longer had to imagine. He knew her face and how she held herself. He knew how utterly beautiful she was in sadness and he knew he'd never be able to see her happy.

Chen's eyelids grew heavy a moment before the door creaked open. Languidly, perfunctorily, he stretched toward his sword, but there was no danger there. At least not the kind that a sword could defeat.

A tentative hand covered his. Cool, delicate fingers.

"River," he said.

She sat on the edge of the bed and freed the pin from her hair in one perfect motion. He lay back and watched it fall, afraid to move. His breath came and went in uneven pants. She was here, in his bed as he hoped and feared. He had to refuse her, but he didn't want to.

"This—" He swallowed past the dryness in his throat. "This won't change anything."

"That's not why I came."

She was dressed in her sleeping garment, a pale tunic over loose trousers, as if she'd already retired to bed before rising to come here. A band of moonlight slanted across the lower part of her face, leaving the rest of her in shadow. He followed every line and curve of her in the dark.

"I can't spare your brother."

"I don't want to talk about him anymore," she whispered. She came closer. "I don't want to talk about anything."

They did share one thing. They both loved Ru Shan as a brother and shared the pain of his betrayal. Did she need to close her eyes and forget as much as he did?

Maybe there was no answer to that. River touched her fingers to his wrist and he went hard beyond reason. He raised himself up and her jasmine perfume surrounded him. By the time he curved his hand over the back of her neck, he was blind with desire.

A small gasp escaped her lips before he crushed his mouth to hers. She was soft. She was soft and warm, and he was being too rough, but she tasted so right.

He pulled away, but couldn't let her go. The pulse in her throat fluttered beneath his fingers. She regarded him with wide, startled eyes, and in them he saw decision. Resolution.

She reached for his tunic. He reached for hers. He tugged at the linen until her arms were free, her breasts bared. He removed the rest of her clothing, but all he could think of was the soft sloping curve of her breasts. The entire time he reminded himself, be gentle. Be gentle. Be gentle.

He stopped her hand when she reached for his trousers. Instead he laid her back against the bed and stretched himself over her, shoulder to hip, legs intertwined. He needed to press himself against as much of her as he could, breasts, thighs. His *yang* member strained against the final cloth barrier between them. His mouth scraped hungrily at the base of her throat. There was nothing gentle about it.

River was panting. Her chest rose and fell beneath him. When her arms found their way hesitantly around his neck, his heart opened and bled. Heavens, she was innocent.

He raised his head to look at her. "You've never done this."

It wasn't a question. He could tell from the way she trembled when he kissed her.

She trailed her hand down his back. "Show me," she murmured.

He couldn't refuse her, or himself. Not when his blood was pumping hot through him, and she was looking as if she could only see him before her and nothing else. Not when he hadn't felt like this, hadn't felt anything for too long.

He bent and took her nipple between his lips. River stiffened, her entire body arching up. He should have started slower, as untried as she was. Kissed her mouth, her throat. Whispered how beautiful she was. And River was beautiful. He'd tell her a hundred times.

After.

River sobbed with tortured pleasure as Chen's tongue stroked over her breasts. He circled his arms beneath her to drag her tight to him. She was grateful for his strength. She needed to be held fast or she would come apart.

From the first moment she touched him, she couldn't hide any longer. She told herself she was deceiving Chen, but she had been deceiving herself, as well. Part of her didn't want to flee and disappear into the far reaches of the empire. Her spirit demanded that she stay and fight her battle here, in this very chamber. She was as rebellious as her brother after all.

Chen's hair was untied. It fell over his face as he bent over her. She wound nerveless fingers through the black strands. He was licking and, dear heavens, biting. His teeth nibbled fleetingly over a sensitive spot below her nipple, on the curved underside of her breast. Who would ever think of such a thing?

She let her head fall back, eyes closed to let the sensations flow over her. This was duty, she had told herself on the cold walk from her chamber. She needed to distract Chen to save her brother and her father.

But this surge of desire was certainly *not* duty. Not when her body was damp and restless with yearning.

When he pulled away, she tried to kiss him again. Her knowledge was so poor. She wanted to entice him, but what did she know beyond a few kisses, an awkward embrace or so? Chen was a rich expanse of hard muscle and heated skin. She wanted to run her curious hands over all of him, but she was afraid. So she tried to press her lips to his, even though she knew it was clumsy.

He accepted her offering. A low rumble rose from the back of his throat as he took command and showed her how to really kiss. It was an exploration, she learned. A dance. Lips parting, caressing. Different angles. Feeling for pressure and give. And taste. His tongue found hers. He tasted of spice. Cloves and the sweetness of plum wine.

Emboldened, she slid her hand down the sculpted

plane of his stomach. But Chen stopped her just as her fingers dipped below the waist of his trousers.

"I don't understand." Her voice sounded thick like sugar syrup.

He trapped her wrist and pinned it over her head. She would have protested, but her body wanted him to do to it whatever he willed. And he was kissing her again. An all-consuming kiss.

His next touch was light, against her knee. Her heart pounded. He was still kissing her, but she could no longer concentrate on his mouth. The next touch after that was not as light. On the inside of her knee, parting her legs. She couldn't breathe. Her skin was flushed and alive.

She whimpered as he found her center, drawing her open with two fingers. One moment a cool rush of air and then heat. He was touching her down *there*. Stroking her first, and then circling. Indescribable pleasure with each small movement. Hard fingers slipping over soft flesh. More pleasure, growing. She bit down hard on her bottom lip.

She had expected to be taken quickly. Perhaps a bit rough—not with any cruelty. Cruelty wasn't in him, she was certain of that from the first moment they met. Chen's touch was rough in an unexpected way. He was direct and unrelenting, drawing out the sensations within her without mercy, while she writhed beneath him.

"Later, I'm going to put my mouth there," he promised.

A shiver ran down her spine. Could she even bear such an act?

His voice was harsh, but his touch went featherlight. Just the tip of his finger now. Quick and subtle. She'd never been so aware of her own body. She wanted to scream and cry.

Her muscles clenched suddenly. She struggled against the hand that pinned her wrist and against the weight of him draped over her. But it wasn't a struggle for escape. Her pleasure sharpened to a single point.

She did scream. She suffered a moment of bliss and anguish, and there was nothing to do but cry out.

"Shhh..."

She became conscious of the frantic beating of her heart. Still fast, gradually slowing. She was breathing in gasps. Chen was breathing hard, too, though they had barely moved for the last of it. His face was above her. His eyes glowed.

There was a hint of low laughter in his voice as he hushed her. "The servants will hear you."

Her first coherent thought in a long time was that he didn't need to worry. No one would hear them.

His smile faded until only the glint in his eyes remained. Rising up, he removed his trousers and stood naked beside the bed. She tried to take in every detail at once. Bronze skin, broad shoulders, narrow hips. And between his hips... She wasn't too sated to blush.

He climbed over her, his muscles flexing as he positioned himself. Once again he parted her thighs. She opened willingly, knees lifting to accept him.

Her breath caught as the smooth tip of him rested against her. He paused at the sound of her gasp. A tiny barrier of doubt returned. They had become suddenly familiar with each other's bodies, but they were still strangers. She explored him in the darkness, her hands running over his shoulders and down the muscles of his back.

This was what had remained unspoken between them throughout the night. She would have never dared to sacrifice herself, even for the sake of her brother, if it hadn't been Wei Chen who had arrived at their shop.

Chen must have seen the question in her eyes, because he kissed her again, giving her precious moments for her body to relax, before taking hold of her hips and easing his hard length slowly into her.

Heat. Slick, encompassing heat and nothing else.

Gradually he became aware of River clutching his shoulders and the rhythmic pant of her breath as he thrust steadily into her. He groaned her name, watched her eyes close and her lips part.

His release was going to come too soon, but he wanted this to last.

The pleasure rose and took him over until he could think of nothing but thrusting deeper into River's welcoming body. He tangled a hand into her hair. Her legs curved and locked about his hips. They became nothing but shapes and sensation in the darkness.

River. His River. The reason why he'd come all this way. One final, fierce thrust and he spent himself into her.

Afterward, they lay together unmoving, skin flushed and damp with sweat.

"I dreamed of this," he murmured, letting his head sink onto the curve of her shoulder. "I dreamed of you."

Chapter Four

River was asleep on her side with her back turned to him. Her long hair draped over her shoulder and neck like a curtain, the darkest black against ivory pale skin. It wasn't long before he went hard again.

He woke her gently, his lips brushing over the back of her neck. She shivered, before turning to fit herself into his arms.

"Why?" he asked.

But she shook her head and wouldn't speak of it. If they spoke, the delicate bond between them might break apart. Instead of words, he made love to her the way he should have the first time. Carefully. Patiently. Then they slept. Or rather, she slept while he stayed awake a little longer to hold her.

Once he and Ru Shan had run up a mountain trail, pushing themselves farther and harder until their legs ached and their lungs nearly burst. They had expended every last shred of energy. Then, with their minds clear of everything, they began their sword training.

This is what he had done. He had run a hundred *li* as fast as he could, but not with his body. His spirit was purged and his soul bared. At that moment, he'd conjured a single thought.

This was why he'd come. He'd sworn loyalty to Governor Li's army, but he'd made another promise in spirit to this woman, long before he'd ever met her. When he'd seen River, that bond pulled tight within him. She felt it, too, he was certain of it now.

He touched River's cheek. She'd captivated him with her courage as much as her beauty. They had both trusted Ru Shan. They both suffered now that he had turned traitor.

There was no escaping his duty. He was going to find Ru Shan and give him an honorable death. But Chen also needed to do something to put the scales in balance. He could become River's protector. He'd do everything within his power to honor her and her family.

Eventually, he drifted. When he awoke, it was morning and River had left, but he remembered what he had resolved to do. Chen would bow before the ailing Master Yao that morning and ask to marry his daughter. He hoped their grief would heal in time.

His own family probably still lived on in the hamlet where he was born, but he had been fostered out as a child, handed over as a servant to the nobleman who served another nobleman who served Governor Li Tao. He was meant to be in the infantry, a foot soldier like Ru Shan, but Li Tao's commanders were always looking for skill. He'd been chosen and trained. The Rising Guard had become his new family, until Ru Shan had offered brotherhood and friendship.

River's perfume lingered in the blankets. Breathing deep, Chen closed his eyes and thought of her long legs clasped about his hips. She'd disappeared before morning broke. She'd accepted him into her body for one night, but would she accept him as a husband, knowing exactly what he needed to do?

Chen splashed water from the washbasin onto his face and took extra care retying his hair. He ran his hands over his outer robe, trying to smooth out the wrinkles. His pulse beat relentlessly as if an army of hundreds awaited him with broadswords and axes.

He should have come prepared to make a proper proposal, but his thoughts had been far from marriage when he came here. Ru Shan's father wouldn't be happy to receive him. River had asked him not to upset the man further because he was ill with grief. The meeting this morning would be tougher than any battle. Chen's stomach churned, just as it did before combat.

He was thinking of River as he left the room. Already anticipating the next time he'd see her. He could make her happy. He knew he could.

The courtyard outside was empty. Odd.

The sun appeared high enough to indicate they were well into the Snake Hour. He'd stayed in bed unusually late with thoughts of River keeping him warm.

Hadn't Ru Shan told stories of being awoken before dawn to work in the mill? The servants would all be up, sweeping, cooking. The smell of rice would float from the kitchen. Yet the courtyard was empty. No morning sounds from the kitchen or from any of the rooms surrounding it.

Chen went to the first door and opened it. It was another bedchamber, larger than his, but the furnishings were gone. All personal belongings had been removed. He closed the door and went on to the next room, his muscles tensing. Black bile rose in his throat.

All the rooms were empty. Abandoned.

* * *

River sat in the study at her father's desk. The walls had been stripped bare of all scrolls and paintings. She'd instructed the servants to take anything of value with them. Those items could be sold or used for bribery if it came to that. If nothing else, the objects of their household would have some sentimental value to Father. Something to remind him of the home his family had built.

She balanced a calligraphy brush over a sheet of paper. Her characters formed a tidy column from top to bottom, right to left. A door slammed nearby and she startled, ruining the character she'd been so carefully writing.

The letter to her father was already finished. This one was to Ru Shan. She hoped it would find its way into his hands somehow.

Another door slammed, followed by the heavy stomp of boots. Her pulse jumped and her palms grew damp. Valiantly, she tried to continue, but her brushstrokes wavered and the characters came out uneven. Ru Shan would see how broken her thoughts were if he were ever to read this.

The door to the study flew open and Chen stood before her. His expression twisted into rage.

"A trick," he accused through gritted teeth.

Her grip tightened on the brush. The ink pooled

below the tip to soak through the paper. She set the implement down with a shaking hand. She'd made a dangerous wager by remaining here.

"They're all gone," she replied. "The servants, Father, Ru Shan—"

He marched across the study until only the desk separated them. "Ru Shan was *here*?"

She closed her eyes. She hadn't expected the sight of him to make her stomach flutter or his closeness to render her body weak. It wasn't fear that made her tremble. She had given herself to this man. He had shown her passion and tenderness, but he would hate her now. She'd betrayed him.

When she opened her eyes he was still glaring at her, his eyes black and endless. She would have done anything to be back in his arms. In the scarce hours between dusk and dawn, she had pretended that the lies didn't exist between them.

"This won't save your family, River. This only implicates your father, as well as you, in Ru Shan's treachery."

"We were already implicated," she said sadly. "Such is the burden of family."

"Why?" Chen demanded.

The last time he'd asked that of her, they'd been skin to skin. He had looked at her as if he would never let her go. Now he looked as if he couldn't stand the sight of her.

Her chest clenched painfully and her throat went dry. "Just a trick," she whispered.

"I told you, seducing me would not change my mind."

"I know that."

She could no longer tell herself she had gone to his room out of duty and sacrifice. Loneliness and desolation had crawled through the empty rooms like vermin after the last of the household departed. She could have tried to escape with them and risked Chen discovering the deception. Instead she'd stayed. She had gone to Chen searching for something. Anything.

He gripped the edge of the desk and leaned ominously over her. "If I fail, Li Tao will send his personal guard after your brother. They won't be as merciful as me."

She needed to calm herself. Her heart was beating too fast. "You won't find him."

Like her brother, River was now marked for death. Chen's sword was strapped to his side. The only time she had seen him without it was in bed. Perhaps she was wrong about him. She'd dishonored and humiliated him. Maybe he would kill her now like he'd vowed to kill her brother. He would call it mercy.

His frown deepened as if he could read her thoughts. He turned and stormed from the room, striking the door frame in anger as he passed. After a moment to steady herself, she followed him out into the courtyard.

She found Chen tugging at the doors of the front gate, both hands gripped around the brass rings. The wood creaked and rattled, but the doors held. They'd been chained from the outside.

"I knew that you couldn't be swayed. Not a man with your code of honor," she said to his back. "But all we needed was time. How long until Li Tao assumes you've failed? My brother has until then to find a safe place."

He swung around. "I'll be out of here before then."

"The Yao family still owes you a debt," she continued, hiding behind formality. It was hard to look at Wei Chen in the daylight, after giving a part of herself to him. After knowing how tender he could be in the night. "If you hadn't convinced the governor to let you go after Ru Shan yourself, we wouldn't have this chance."

She prayed her brother wouldn't learn about Chen and try to return. That was probably what the two of them wanted: honorable battle, face to face. The fools.

"Don't say that name to me." Chen paced toward her. The hardened warrior was finally showing. "He told me you were right-minded and honest."

"Well, now you know I'm none of those things."

"Two faces," he spat. Chen glared at her with a mixture of anger and disgust and her soul withered. "Exactly like your brother."

River disappeared into the recesses of the house while Chen circled the courtyard like a caged wolf. That was the only way to describe how he felt. Feral and prowling. It was good that she'd left him. He was ready to lash out at anything to rid himself of this rage.

Her every sigh had been a betrayal.

He wasn't going to think of her or her nameless dog of a brother. Instead Chen stared at the walls. The brick had been piled unusually high, as if the elder Yao had feared thieves this far outside of town.

A search of the storage areas and servants' quarters yielded nothing. Of course River wouldn't leave anything as useful as a ladder. If he stacked furniture beside the wall, he might be able to climb over.

He scavenged through the rooms of the abandoned house. The desk in the study appeared heavy, but he could probably drag it outside. He wasn't certain the dining table would fit through the doors. The rest of the tables and chairs were low, but he could stack them.

Chen rolled up his sleeves. In the later part of the hour, he managed to heave and shove the pine wood desk from the study into the courtyard. It was solidly built and he was sweating in the midday sun. He needed the hard labor to burn the memory of River from his skin. She was still there, all around him, inside him.

River was likely laughing at him. Her less than nefarious plan, his less than glorious escape.

He dug his heels into the dirt and pushed against the desk with all his strength. The smell of smoke drifted into the courtyard. Something was burning.

He abandoned the cursed desk and traced the acrid odor to the kitchen at the eastern wing of the residence. River was standing fearfully over an iron pot on the stove. The lid bobbled from the heat trapped beneath. She reached for the handle, then jumped back, yelping in pain.

"What are you doing?" Chen grabbed a rag from the chopping block and moved the pot away from the stove.

"I was hungry," she snapped.

He lifted the lid and turned away from the rise of steam. The smoke made him cough. The rice was both burnt and uncooked on top. A feat indeed.

"There's not nearly enough water and you need to stir it." He was no cook, but he had boiled enough rice by a campfire to know.

Her chin jutted out defiantly. "I'll try again, then." She stuck her scalded finger into her mouth to soothe it, suddenly looking very young and vulnerable.

She'd looked just as lost when she'd propositioned him. When he'd taken her into his arms, she'd trembled and clung to him. She might have tried to deceive him for the sake of her brother, but if he'd been lured into a trap, it was because he'd wanted to be.

He knew then that he was already in love with her.

Chen said nothing as the realization took awful root in his chest. River hadn't seduced him. He'd been in love with her before he ever saw her. He had come here with his soul open, waiting for the sight and shape of her to lock into its rightful place in his heart.

He fought hard not to let his emotions show as he led River to the basin and guided her hand under the water. A small welt had formed over her fingers and the skin was red, but it wasn't all that bad. Still, he held on to her wrist beneath the cool water.

"It—it's better now," she said.

Her voice curled around his heart and stole his breath. He released her, going both hot and cold at once. The inevitable confrontation with Ru Shan would tear out Chen's soul and leave him gutted. It would be like falling on his own blade—but nothing so clean and quick.

"Your plan would have worked better if you had put a knife in me while I was sleeping," he muttered.

River made a show of scraping at the pot, her back turned to him. "My kitchen skills are quite lacking. I know less about knives than I do about cooking."

The conversation dwindled away, but Chen found it hard to leave the kitchen. Other than the pain twisting like a blade in his gut, nothing had changed. He still needed to bring Ru Shan to justice. Yet he had another duty to protect River. Not only because they had been promised to each other in an arranged marriage by her brother. River belonged to him. She'd given herself to him and he'd accepted. Which meant he belonged to her, as well.

If she ever realized that, then he would truly be lost.

He retrieved more wood for the stove while River started another batch of rice. Together they scrounged the kitchen for odds and ends: cold dumplings, some yams that were easy to boil, salted duck eggs. This time the rice was mushy, but at least edible. They piled everything onto a tray and went to sit at the same table where River had presented him with a feast the night before. A feast neither of them had been able to enjoy.

Chen positioned himself with the tray between them. River selected a dumpling with her chopsticks and bit carefully into it. He watched her eat, his heart growing heavier with each passing moment. She was wearing the somber robe he'd first seen her in with the collar closed high over her neck. There was no need to tempt him any longer.

"Why would you give yourself to the man who was going to kill your brother?" he asked.

There wasn't as much force behind his question as he'd wanted. He was drained from more than just pushing Yao's desk through the yard.

She stared at the center of his chest. "Isn't it plain enough? Even an impenetrable warrior can be distracted in the bedroom."

The dear girl couldn't lie.

"Your virtue isn't worth the sacrifice," he said evenly.

"As if my virtue is worth anything." She met his eyes then. "Look around us. Our home is gone. Our name, gone."

He bit savagely into an egg. The saltiness lodged in his throat. He didn't know if he was angrier at her or for her. "It didn't have to be this way. Li Tao would have left you alone."

"If we had denied Ru Shan and turned him in," she countered bitterly. "What would warriors like you think of that sort of disloyalty?"

"You didn't answer my question. Why did you give yourself to me? I know you weren't pretending."

She blushed. "You had wine. You could be mistaken."

"I remember every moment, River."

River was no skilled seductress and he wasn't blind. She had clung to him, cried out his name. But desire and intention were not the same. The room fell silent except for the methodic click of her chopsticks as River became enthralled by their sparse meal. She swallowed slowly, staring into her bowl. He let her have the pause.

"You were never going to kill Ru Shan," she said finally.

"Because of your plan?" he challenged.

"Because I know you."

Her words struck like a blow to his gut. "You don't know me."

She set the chopsticks down. "I know you, Wei Chen," she repeated, with more hope than certainty. She searched his face with her eyes. "You came here looking for something besides Ru Shan. You were hoping to be dissuaded."

"That's not true."

"In your soul, you don't want to do this."

Her voice trembled, but then she stopped cold, embarrassed by her outburst. Chen sat rigid beside her. He could see how much she wanted to believe it—so much that he even doubted himself for a threadbare moment. He was searching frantically, reaching for something he couldn't name. Was it direction? Was it forgiveness?

Then River stood to go, leaving emptiness in her wake. Eventually he stood and returned to the courtyard, where he stared at the abandoned furniture. River had disappeared into the depths of the inner chambers. He could no longer see her, but he could sense her there.

He resumed his efforts, shoving the desk against the wall and then going to scavenge more furniture. He'd never turned his back on duty. Soon he'd climb free and continue his hunt. Ru Shan was days away, a week at most.

He'd leave what happened here out of his report to Governor Li. Outside of these walls, he'd insist that he'd never seen River or spoken to her. Or touched her. She'd remain safe as long as she stayed away from Ru Shan and away from him. That was all he could give.

The afternoon sun had begun its gradual descent. Chen threw himself into his work. He tried to focus on this one task and nothing more, but the loneliness devoured him from within. There was no peace.

Chapter Five

For the rest of the afternoon, Chen dragged furniture out into the courtyard. He attempted to stack the tables beside the lowest point of the wall near the gate. River hovered at the edges of the courtyard to watch him labor away. She never doubted he would find a way out. Their house wasn't a fortress or a prison. Not like the one she'd be thrown in when Li Tao's men caught her. Or would Chen turn her in himself?

For a dim moment, she saw the point of his desolate warrior logic—better to meet your end at the hands of someone who knew you. Who, at one time, cared for you.

Night came swiftly. She retired to her own chamber and her own bed only to find she couldn't sleep. The lanterns burned away and the movement of the shadows over the walls kept her company. Maybe she had chosen to lock herself in with Chen out of protest. Deep in her heart, she resented having to abandon their home and their life.

A silhouette appeared outside the window and her pulse skipped. Chen hesitated there. Holding her breath, she watched his shape through the paper windowpane. If he moved away, she didn't know if she was brave enough to call after him. Her heart was already torn into jagged pieces.

After too long a pause, Chen entered without knocking. His sleeves were rolled up over his forearms and his skin glistened from physical exertion. The lantern light washed over him in a warm glow. Her mouth went dry. He was handsome, she realized with dismay.

It was just too much for her to find him handsome now on top of everything else she felt about him.

"It's cold in here." He came to the bed as she had done in his room the night before.

She shrank a little beneath the quilt. "I was afraid if I tried to light the coals, I might set the bed on fire."

He didn't smile. "By tomorrow morning, I'll be gone."

"Then we have nothing more to say." The chill around her came from inside and out. It was inescapable.

"There's something I need to know before I go."

He lowered himself to sit on the edge of the bed. The gesture should have been only a small intimacy after he'd taken her virtue and brought her to the highest tide of pleasure. Yet her breathing grew shallow at his nearness. She tracked every shift of his weight beside her.

"You didn't come to me as part of some devious plan," he said calmly. "Tell me why you did it."

She couldn't. Already her skin warmed and her muscles loosened. The sound of her voice alone would give away how much she wanted him.

He placed a hand over her ankle. His grip was firm through the layers of the quilt and she savored the heat of his touch. Chen had come to claim her. From the moment he'd set foot in their shop, he'd claimed her.

River squeezed her eyes shut. "I don't have an answer for you."

He made a move as if to rise, and she sat up in a panic. If he left, she'd die of heartache.

"We were going into hiding. Ru Shan was talking of rebellion," she explained. "I wanted to know what it was like between a man and a woman before I died." Her next pause went on for a lifetime. "And I wanted to know…with you."

His eyes sparked. "Nothing is going to happen to you."

The blanket became an unwanted barrier. River stared at the determined set of his lips. Shamefully, she remembered Chen's promise to use his mouth on her. He hadn't yet fulfilled that promise.

"I did want to trick you," she continued faintly. "I wanted to seduce you, but I wasn't any good at it."

Chen's gaze grew deeper, darker. He watched her expression while he shifted his hand higher onto her calf. Her sex flooded. She was so much more aware of her body now, so much more aware of his.

River peeled back the blanket to reach for him. His hair was disheveled from his labors in the courtyard. She pulled the tie loose so that it fell about his face.

"This is impossible," he told her gently.

But he was here, when he could have gone.

She threaded her fingers through the dark strands. "I know."

Then she kissed him. She was better at it tonight. Chen's eyes closed, but she kept her eyes open. She wanted to be able to conjure his image long after he was gone. River had done everything to convince him, but Chen remained headstrong and unyielding. She'd tried to convince her brother, as well. These men lived by a code she would never understand.

This was why they called the midnight chamber the woman's domain. This was all she could claim and all she could have. Private and hidden moments. She cradled his face in her hands, feeling the structure of his cheekbones beneath her fingertips. Chen circled his hands around her waist to bring her closer.

She removed his outer robe first, then his tunic. Her hands explored him, brushing over sculpted shoulders, and a torso lean with muscle. Chen permitted her touch, eyes closed, breathing deeply. Not the dominating and impassioned lover she'd known last night.

Her own heart was pounding. She was dizzy from the rush of her pulse, and his reticence confused her.

"Wei Chen?" She was begging and demanding at the same time.

A look of pain crossed his face and finally he opened his eyes. Her breath caught. She saw too much in them. Longing and fear and a desperate hunger.

"There is no one here but us," she said.

She wasn't going to let him fight this. She locked her arms around his shoulders, willing him to take her in his arms. Together, they lowered themselves onto the bed. He pulled her clothes away along with the last of his. Then he feasted.

Chen parted her legs and tasted her, as he'd promised. His tongue slicked over her once, lingering indulgently. Then again, soft and unerringly gentle. Her body went limp and she cried out her surrender, all shame gone, until he gave her more of what she needed. Soft and then hard, his hands digging into her hips to hold her captive while she panted and writhed and climaxed. He continued to torment her until the last of her tremors eased.

Later she did the same. First caressing his sex with her lips, discovering smooth, silken skin over the hardness beneath. He exhaled sharply when she finally dared to take him into her mouth. She circled the broad tip with her tongue and his hand tightened in her hair.

"River." His voice strained to the breaking point. "Stop. Please stop."

Chen pulled away and stretched her flat on her back. He entered her in one swift thrust that stole her breath. River arched her back to accept him into her. Tonight the ache inside was familiar and welcome. There was no other pain or pleasure like it.

When her eyes opened again, he was watching

her. His fingers twined with hers and held on as he withdrew in a slow glide before pushing deep again. Each movement resonated within her. Each shift sent exquisite sensation through every pulse point and meridian in her body, transforming into joy and elation and hope.

"Stay," she sobbed.

Chen stilled above her. It was cruel of her to demand it now, but how could she not? Her eyes flooded with tears.

He kissed her tenderly, but wouldn't answer. His body resumed its rhythm after a pause. Slower now, with purpose. His mouth closed around her breast. He wanted her release, willed it. She cleared her mind of everything but the feel of him, and soon she was shuddering in his arms. He followed closely behind. They found each other in climax.

They stayed awake in each other's arms, refusing sleep, fighting the coming of morning. But it came nonetheless.

"You need to go quickly, River. Don't tell me where."

They stood on the path along the bank. The same one they had walked down together only two days ago. The residence was abandoned behind them.

Chen had scaled the stone wall and broken the chain over the gate. At first he was afraid River wouldn't leave, but she went to him as the doors opened. A single travel pack was slung over her shoulder. Her look was sullen, with a storm cloud around her that wouldn't lift. He wanted to draw her into his arms and hold on.

He needed to make sure River was protected before he left. She was in more trouble than her brother now. He cursed Ru Shan for putting his sister in so much danger. There was no way to shield her against a charge of conspiracy and treason. Li Tao did not tolerate disloyalty on any level.

"Is there someone you can go to?" he asked.

She nodded and started to speak a name before stopping herself. "There's a friend in town that will help me."

He smiled ruefully. "Your brother always knew how to gain allies."

Ru Shan was out there, building up the rebellion. The situation had become dangerous for all of them: Ru Shan, River and himself, as well.

"Chen, I apologize for asking that of you…last night." She hesitated, but went on. "I don't want you to face my brother."

There was nothing left in her, but raw and naked honesty. He loved her for it. He would always love her.

"Nothing is certain," he replied. "Ru Shan might end up killing me should we meet."

"I don't want that either." Her resolve broke. She pressed a hand to her mouth as if she could hold back the tears.

Chen crushed her to him so she could bury her face against his chest. He couldn't go with her, and it destroyed him. He wanted to defy country and honor to stay by her side, but if he didn't report back, Li Tao would send the others. Two or four or forty of their brethren from the Rising Guard, all of them fervently dedicated to bringing Ru Shan's death.

"It won't come to that if I can stop it," he said, his lips brushing her hair. He didn't know if she believed him, but it was all he could promise.

He and River were meant to walk different paths. The only way to keep her safe was to continue to serve Li Tao. The warlord had to believe he was hunting for Ru Shan.

River broke away and pulled out a paper hidden in her sash. "Don't open this until I'm far away. Swear you won't."

Before he could answer, she raised onto her toes to kiss him. She slipped the letter into the fold of his robe. Her fingers brushed the spot over his heart. This was farewell.

"I swear," he said as she stepped back.

She turned and hurried down the path, never looking back. He watched her long after she disappeared around the river bend.

He never should have made that promise. It was a damn, stupid oath. She'd looked so vulnerable, face tilted to him, his lips warm as they held on to the memory of her touch. He was certain that the message contained something irrevocable. It would destroy her father and her brother. It might destroy him, as well. When he read it, he'd have no choice but to act.

So he waited a day with the folded paper tucked inside his robe. Burning against his breast. First thing the next morning, in a cold bed at the inn, he'd opened it.

The brushstrokes bled on the page and he finally had the answer she wouldn't give him.

I also dreamed of you.

Chapter Six

River knew who was upon the horse the moment he came over the rise. Chen had sought her out. For the last three months, she and Father had lived far away from the main roads and cities of the province. It was safer that way. She didn't know where Ru Shan was either. That was also safer.

If Chen had found and challenged Ru Shan, she didn't know what she would do. There was no such thing as a good death in her eyes. It was all loss and pain. Her father would never recover and she… she had already decided to bury her heart. Yet against her wishes, it came to life at the first sight of the swordsman.

She walked to the edge of the path and held her breath. She couldn't go to him until she knew. His gaze fixed onto her as he neared. Her heart caught in her throat as Chen dismounted and even when he stood before her, it was as if a veil still clouded her eyes, separating them. His presence was both beautiful and terrifying.

"Is he dead?" she whispered.

Chen paused, taking her in from head to toe as she had done him. "Ru Shan is not dead. At least not that I know of."

She could breathe again, but she kept her hands clenched at her sides to keep from reaching for him. There were still too many questions. "What is that?"

Chen had pulled out an official-looking pamphlet from his saddle pack, but he lowered it to his side as if it were unimportant.

"Do you still dream of me, River?"

She blinked furiously. It was the sunlight, she told herself. It was too bright. "Why did you come here? Are you still hunting Ru Shan?"

"I searched for him," he admitted. "I followed news of him into the mountains. There was a skirmish somewhere in the south, but your brother escaped."

He came closer and she allowed it. She was too caught between hope and fear to move. Chen held up the pamphlet again.

"A pardon. Governor Li has declared that the debt between the two of them is settled."

She took the decree from him and read through it. "Can this be a trick?"

"Li Tao can be harsh and brutal, but he doesn't believe in deceit."

"The governor would rather kill his enemies as public examples," she said contemptuously.

"Sometimes these matters can only be handled warrior to warrior. Only Li Tao and Ru Shan can understand what has happened."

"Then Ru Shan is safe? We don't have to hide any longer?"

He nodded and she nearly collapsed with relief.

"I wouldn't have taken Ru Shan's life," he told her. "I knew I couldn't do it the moment we parted. I wanted to see you again, even if it was only in another life, and I knew the forces of heaven wouldn't allow it if I went against what I knew was right."

The weight of a hundred stones lifted from her. She'd known he wasn't a coldhearted killer. "I was so afraid. I thought of you every day, wondering."

Chen was finally there beside her. The barriers lifted away and the sight of him filled her, pure and uncorrupted.

He looked beyond her to the window of the cabin. Father had pulled back the curtain to stare out at them. "Is that the elder Master Yao? I've always wanted to meet him and pay my respects."

"Father will be very happy to hear that Ru Shan has been pardoned," she replied.

They started toward the door, side by side. She was no longer the sheltered girl by the river, but being close to Chen brought back those days of hope and longing. She could dream again.

"I didn't just come to talk about Ru Shan," he admitted. "There is something else I've been meaning to ask your father."

"Oh? What can that be?" She looked away, coy and uncommonly pleased.

He reached out to take her hand and all the pieces of heaven and earth came together. Chen smiled at her for the first time since he'd returned, a true smile full of promise and happiness.

"It's about his daughter."

* * * * *

AN ILLICIT TEMPTATION

Sometimes a story just flows from your mind onto the page. This is *not* that story.

I must dedicate this story to my husband, who was busy setting up a nursery and buying a minivan while I was hospitalised and attempting to type up this new story. I owe a huge debt of gratitude to Shawntelle Madison and Amanda Berry for offering emotional and writing support during a very trying time. I wouldn't have been able to finish if you hadn't been with me every step of the way. Thank you to Bria Quinlan and Stephanie Draven for lending your tough love and critical skills to the final product. Special thanks goes out to Alvania Scarborough and Sandy Raven for their input on horses and horsemanship. I've only ridden a horse once and he didn't particularly like me.

Author Note

An Illicit Temptation continues from where *My Fair Concubine* ended and shows a journey into Khitan in Inner Mongolia, a land that at the time was considered by the Tang Dynasty to be savage and primitive. It's easy to see parallels to the American West and interactions with Native American tribes. For this reason I think of Dao's journey as a 'Tang Dynasty Western' akin to the stories of frontier romance in historical westerns.

The research for this short story nearly equalled the amount I collected for *My Fair Concubine*. This time was on the cusp of change for Khitan culture. The Khitans largely had an oral tradition until during the later part of the Tang Dynasty, when they united under an emperor and formed their own autonomous empire under the Liao Dynasty. Unlike many other peoples who were consumed by the Chinese, the Khitan were dedicated to preserving their culture even as they adopted many Han customs.

I tried to recreate Khitan culture from a blend of information from later Khitan writings and brief references in Tang records, and I used Mongolian culture to fill in the gaps. I hope the steppe emerges as a wild and untamed land with its own sense of power and beauty. A perfect place to discover love!

Chapter One

Tang Dynasty China, 824 AD

Pretending to be a princess wasn't any hardship. Dao hadn't grown up in a palace, dressed in silk and jewels. She didn't miss her cot in the Chang family's servants' quarters. Now there were no more clothes to mend, floors to sweep, chamber pots to empty. The only thing required of her was that she recline inside a gilded palanquin while the wedding procession made its way through the steppe toward the Khitan central capital. She even had an army of her own attendants to wait on her. No hardship at all…another day of it and she would go mad.

Dao stabbed her needle through the eye of the crane she was embroidering. The afternoon was lazy and warm as the palanquin rolled over the wild grass of the northern plains, lulling her to sleep with the rhythm. It seemed that was all she did on this journey: embroider or nap.

With a snap of her wrist, she pulled the curtain aside. A square of sunlight opened up revealing the endless green of the steppe and cloudless sky beyond. Khitan tribesmen on horseback surrounded the procession to serve as her escort. She was in an exotic land and she was squandering the experience in meager glances through this tiny window.

She searched among the riders. "Kwan-Li!"

Kwan-Li was tasked with bringing her to Khitan to be married to the khagan, the chieftain over all chieftains of this land of nomadic tribes. The khagan was without a wife so the two empires had negotiated for a peace marriage.

Kwan-Li was astride a horse at the head of the procession and absorbed in conversation with one of the tribesmen. Despite his responsibilities, she didn't have to repeat herself before he broke away to ride up alongside the window. Princesses gave commands and others obeyed. Dao still felt a foolish little thrill whenever it happened.

Kwan-Li was tall and looked more like an imperial soldier than a statesman. He wore the traditional *deel*, the heavy folded tunic favored by the nomads, except his was fashioned from a vibrant blue brocade. A broad yellow sash wrapped around his waist, highlighting a lean, masculine frame. His features were strong, almost harsh, with a distinctiveness that she couldn't quite place.

"Princess An-Ming," he acknowledged, his expression stern.

The court had also seen fit to bestow an imperial name upon her. It meant Bright Peace and she quite liked it. The name sounded very princess-like to her ears unlike her own name, which simply meant Peach. She was so very tired of being plain.

"I want to ride," she said.

He blinked once. "Now?"

His eyes had the sharpness of an eagle's with gold flecks within them that caught the sun.

"Yes, now," she said simply, pleasantly.

The procession continued to move along. He kept pace with her as he took in the caravan of wagons transporting gifts from the imperial court as well as an army of attendants to take care of her every need.

"It's nearly time for us to stop and rest, isn't it?" she asked.

She could see from the uncompromising line of his jaw that it wasn't.

"The princess might find it more suitable to practice at the end of the day when the sun is low,"

Kwan-Li suggested coolly. This was what a refusal sounded like from the very proper diplomat.

"I'm not afraid of a little sunlight. Have a horse ready for me when we next stop for rest."

Dao let the curtain fall back in place, ending the discussion. When she stepped out of the palanquin an hour later, the Khitans were tending to the horses while her attendants erected canopies set on bamboo poles to shield the party from the sun while they had their tea and refreshments.

A tent was erected for her privacy. Moon, her personal attendant, helped Dao change out of the light silk *hanfu* into the sturdier *deel*. The tunic was long, reaching almost to her ankles, and was lined with fox fur at the collar. Dao tried not to fidget as she watched Moon secure the clasps. Not two months ago, Dao had been in the girl's place, dressing and tending to her own mistress.

Pearl had been more than her mistress. They shared the same father, though the two of them had never acknowledged that they were related by blood. Pearl's mother was First Wife while Dao's mother was a household servant who was never even a concubine. Pearl had been chosen by the imperial court to go to Khitan, but when she ran away with her lover, Dao had taken her place.

Marriage to a chieftain was a better future than

she had ever hoped for. It didn't matter that her husband was much older than her or that she had to leave her home behind. These were small sacrifices. She was very fortunate, she had to remember that.

When Dao emerged from the tent, the caravan was in the process of repacking. Kwan-Li oversaw everything with quiet efficiency. He had the respect of the nomads and spoke their language with impressive fluency. She could see why he objected to the small delay she had caused. There was nothing simple about managing all the wagons and trunks and people.

Ruan, the eldest of the Khitans, was waiting with her horse, saddled and ready as she had commanded.

"Old Wolf," she greeted him.

"Dragoness," he returned cheerfully.

Ruan had been given the nickname due to a wolf attack that had left ragged scars across the right side of his face. He was old, grizzled and surprisingly good-natured, making frequent use of what remained of his smile. As one of the few tribesmen who spoke Han, he'd quickly become her favorite.

It was Kwan-Li, however, who came to help her onto the saddle. She braced her foot into his hands and had to grab on to his shoulders as she wobbled.

The sudden press of his body against hers startled her. He was made of hard, unyielding muscle. As he lifted her, their eyes met briefly and her face flushed with heat. Princesses shouldn't get embarrassed so easily, should they? His expression was serious, his movements brusque. After a few moments of struggle and indignity, she was able to seat herself. Kwan-Li lifted himself onto his horse with a natural grace that she envied.

"Stay beside me," he instructed.

Dao held her back straight and tried to relax into position, determined to show him she wasn't entirely incompetent. It was said the children of Khitan could sit on horseback before they could walk. If she was to live among them, she had to be able to do something even the youngest among them found to be second nature.

Kwan-Li guided her toward the center of the line and rode beside her as the caravan started moving once again in its endless trek across the planes. Dao had grown up in the city where distance was measured by wards and divided by gates. Out here there were no walls, no streets, and the grassland seemed to go on forever. An expanse of blue sky hovered over them and a cool breeze swirled around her. There was something meditative about the rhythm of the horse beneath her and the feeling of being suspended between heaven and earth. No boundaries existed.

"You're displeased," she said when Kwan-Li remained silent and brooding. Yes, brooding was what it was, the way he stared into the distance and purposefully avoided even looking at her, though they rode side by side.

"Of course not, Princess," he said.

"What's the loss of one hour in a month-long journey?"

"Indeed." A terse pause followed. "Princess."

She wouldn't go so far as to call him rude. He was the court's appointed official and treated her with deference, yet he had always been distant toward her. Almost cold in nature. Perhaps he hadn't wanted this appointment. It was common knowledge in the imperial city that Khitan was a wild, uncivilized land.

"I can demand you explain yourself," she said lightly, only teasing in part. He was one of the few people who would speak openly to her on the journey. He seemed to be in a particularly bad mood when all she wanted to do was enjoy the touch of the breeze on her face.

Kwan-Li met her gaze. A flicker of defiance lit in his eyes. It lent something daring and exciting to him and her heartbeat quickened. She looked away, searching for something to lighten the air between them.

"Such barbarian customs they have here," she murmured, watching one of the nomads place his fur cap over his head.

"Barbarian?" Kwan-Li echoed stiffly.

"It seems odd to shave the top of your head like a monk, but then leave the sides so long," she mused.

"It is to open themselves to the grace of the sun," he explained.

Alarm crept into her voice. "Will I have to do the same?"

"The princess has nothing to worry about. The women do not follow the same practice."

He nudged his horse forward and she did the same, keeping stride beside him as he had instructed. As a ranking official from the imperial court, Kwan-Li was the only one who felt he could speak to her without averting his eyes and agreeing to her every word. She found herself missing the comfort of conversation.

"You seem to have studied their customs very thoroughly," she said.

He regarded her with an odd expression. "I am from Khitan."

Her eyes widened. "But you don't look—"

"Like an unwashed barbarian?" He allowed a slow smile to reveal itself.

"I didn't say unwashed," she protested.

In the capital, they spoke of the barbarians of the northern steppe to be a roughened, warlike people. The Khitans that rode along with them certainly had the hard-eyed look of survival amidst the unforgiving elements. Yet Kwan-Li's bearing had the mark of education and culture.

"But you speak our language so fluently," she said fascinated. "You even look Han."

"You are mistaken, Princess."

She traced over the shape and line of his face with unabashed curiosity. Kwan-Li grew his hair long and had it pulled back into a topknot as they did in the empire. His skin also lacked the dark, sun-drenched quality of the nomads. Perhaps there was a slight difference in the shape of his eyes, a broadness of his nose and chin that she had overlooked before.

"How unexpected! I would have never known."

He was taken aback by her reaction. "I assumed the princess would have been told—" He stopped himself, his eyes narrowing as he considered her.

Dao's pulse jumped. "I have no knowledge of the day-to-day dealings of the outer court," she said quickly. "We princesses are kept so sheltered away in the palace."

She attempted a smile. He frowned, but seemed to accept her answer. Or rather he rode on in silence. Dao realized she was gripping the reins too tight when her horse tossed his head, flicking his ears in agitation. She relaxed her hold and concentrated on the trail in front of her.

She had to be careful what she said around Kwan-Li. He was intelligent and likely well-versed in court etiquette and politics while she knew none of the things a princess should know. It was fine for him to think of her as a vacant and innocent as long as he was convinced she was a princess.

When she dared to glance at him again, he was looking over the caravan, ever watchful. She had assumed that he was a diplomat, appointed by the court to accompany her. This new information made her even more curious about him.

"Your name sounds Han," she remarked.

He turned and regarded her as if surprised she was speaking again. "Kwan-Li is the name I was given by the imperial court. A courtesy name."

She refused to be intimidated by his cold demeanor. She was the princess here, after all. "How long were you in Changan?"

"Twelve years."

"You came to the capital to study?"

"I came to be educated." There was a pause. "And for diplomatic reasons."

All sorts of foreigners lived within the walls of Changan. The public markets were full of stalls set up by merchants from neighboring lands, but this was the first she'd known of a barbarian—of a foreigner—who was taken into the imperial court.

"I remained in the capital to ensure peace between our two lands," he said in response to her questioning look.

"Much like an alliance bride, then," she suggested.

He paused to think. "Perhaps a very similar arrangement…"

She grinned. "But in your case, you weren't bound into marriage."

He blinked at her, taken aback, looking flustered. "No…I was not."

In that confusion, his expression lost its sternness, his eyes their coldness, and his speech relinquished that distinctive formality that she now knew was due in part to his having come from a foreign land. Without that wall in place, his entire demeanor changed.

"No woman would have you, barbarian that you are," she teased.

His mouth curved upward slightly, with a crookedness to the smile, which sent a small flutter to her belly. He suddenly appeared approachable. More than approachable. For all its hardness, his face wasn't an unpleasant one to look at. A slow rise of heat invaded her cheeks and she had to look away.

Dao prided herself on being practical. She had lived a life of servitude and constant toil. Cunning was more important than charm. She fought to keep her observations impassive as she gazed at Kwan-Li in profile: the hard shape of his jaw, the arch of his cheekbones, the curve of his mouth that took on an unexpected sensuality when he smiled.

Wayward dreams of romance would lead only to ruin. She had known that truth since birth. So Dao had no such romantic thoughts now as she rode beside Kwan-Li. Instead she tried very hard to forget that in a few weeks she would be wed to a stranger.

They stopped to rest again several hours later, after which Princess An-Ming insisted on getting back onto the saddle.

"The princess will be sore tomorrow," Kwan-Li advised.

"She won't be." She positioned herself beside the horse and prepared to mount, ignoring him.

"She will."

"She *won't*."

An-Ming braced a foot on his knee while one hand grasped his shoulder, fully expecting compliance. He hefted her up with a bit more force than necessary and she tottered as she clambered into the saddle.

Her eyes flashed fire down at him. He kept his expression blank as he mounted. Her touch on him, however brief and impersonal, lingered, as did the scent of her perfume.

Perfume. Out here among the dust and needle grass of the steppe.

It had been easier when he had only been subjected to brief glimpses. A tantalizing flutter of yellow silk as she went from the sleeping tent to her sedan. He had expected the princess to maintain her distance and a proper sense of formality throughout the journey. Instead she insisted on riding in the open, on redirecting the entire caravan if there was some sight she wanted to see. She was as restless and vibrant as a summer wind across the grassland.

At least Princess An-Ming had donned more modest clothing for riding. Those elaborate robes she wore only gave the illusion she was hidden under layer upon layer of silk. Every movement hinted at the rounded curve of her hips, the enticing indent of her waist, and in a swirl of color that could not be ignored against the starkness of the plains.

"Why do you always have that scowl on your face?" she asked.

He'd been gazing at the horizon, taking in the long-awaited sight of the land of his birth and preventing himself from looking too long at her.

"I am thinking." He tried again to turn his attention away, but she wouldn't allow it.

"What about?"

It always surprised him how easily she fell into informal speech with him. The intimacy was out of place. It was the same way with the sly, sideways glance she wielded so masterfully.

She was watching him now, eyes bright, mouth pink and pressed just so. Her face was sensually rounded and he could lose a day just watching the expressions that danced across it. He turned to her, resigned. That intriguing dimple on her left cheek was showing itself.

Why this woman? Why her, when he'd been indifferent to all manner of beautiful women in the capital? She was a princess and the Emperor's niece. Most importantly, her arranged marriage was meant to ensure peaceful relations between their lands.

"Our progress is not as I had hoped," he said.

"You're still upset that I wanted to ride today." She smiled at him, amused. He *amused* her.

"I have no objection to you. This, however—" He gestured toward the impossibly long trail of wagons in the caravan.

She frowned, affronted. "I didn't ask for all this. I don't need people to dress and feed me."

He eyed her skeptically.

"But I should have such luxuries…being a princess," she amended, lifting her chin haughtily.

There was something very, very strange about Princess An-Ming.

"The princess must know how important it is to travel swiftly," he explained. "The Uyghur delegation has sent their own alliance bride to petition for marriage. They may already be at the khagan's central camp."

An-Ming paled. "Another princess? But I'm supposed to be the khagan's bride! He wouldn't dare go back on his word." She paused and looked at him imploringly. "Would he?"

Had she truly been locked away in some dark corner of the palace? It was told that the princesses of the Tang Empire were formidable women. An-Ming certainly upheld that reputation when it came to her audaciousness, but she seemed to know nothing of the politics of the imperial court.

"This was why the journey was moved ahead several months," he explained, a bit impatiently.

"But the Khitans asked for this alliance to our empire."

"The alliance is important to many of the southern tribes such as mine, but Khitan is a confederation of many tribes. We have been caught between the Uyghur and the Tang empires for hundreds of years."

Her usual airy tone vanished. "So there are other tribes that support this other marriage." She frowned and her expression took on a serious, calculating look that he'd never seen on her before. "I thought everything was already decided."

His mood darkened. "So did I."

At that moment, her horse faltered a step and the princess fell slightly behind. She was inadvertently pulling back on the reins, signaling her horse to slow. He started to remind her to relax her hold, but the section of the caravan before them had come to a stop.

One of the horses had become agitated. The rider worked to steady the animal while the other Khitan horsemen soothed their mounts. Kwan-Li scanned the area and saw the remains of a fresh animal carcass. Signs of a wolf attack with the smell of blood still in the air. It should have been nothing more than a routine distraction, but the princess was still fighting to regain control. Her horse snorted, his hooves stamping the ground in agitation.

Kwan-Li sensed disaster before it struck. The horse shook his head defiantly and suddenly reared up. His front legs lifted from the ground and the princess shrieked. The scream set the horse off and he bolted off toward the open plain in a storm of dust.

He cursed and set off after her. The beast was head down in a full run. An-Ming was reduced to a small huddled figure clinging to the saddle. As he came nearer, he could see her clutching on to the horse's mane. She cried out for help, but her distress only made matters worse.

He hoped she could hear him above the pounding hooves. "Princess!"

Kwan-Li directed his mount alongside hers, edging gradually into the path of the runaway horse. He crouched low and used his heels to push forward. Faster. The earth rushed by beneath him.

He had to try to slow the runaway down. The horses turned in a wide circle, gradually matching speeds. An-Ming lifted her head to seek him out. Her knuckles were bone-white as she held on.

"Take the reins," he shouted.

The leather strap whipped against her knuckles as she grasped blindly for them. She made another desperate lunge. The motion unseated her and she was thrown over the horse's shoulder, landing hard with a sickening thud. Kwan-Li's heart stopped. The runaway horse continued heedless through the grassland while the princess lay in the dust.

Kwan-Li dismounted and ran to her. The princess was curled onto her side.

"Princess!"

He called out her name when she didn't respond. With great care, he rolled her onto her back and she opened her eyes slowly. The headdress had fallen away and her face was streaked with dust. Her chest lifted and lowered shallowly as she struggled for breath. Only a thin wheeze escaped her lips.

"Are you hurt? Is anything broken?"

She was able to focus on him, which was a small relief, but she appeared confused.

Kwan-Li realized he'd reverted to his native tongue in his panic and had to repeat himself in Han. Wincing, she pressed a hand to her midsection.

There was no time for fear. He ran his hands along the sides of her rib cage, trying to feel through the tunic. He unclasped the front of her *deel*, ignoring the flimsy silk garment beneath. Pressing his fingertips lightly to her abdomen, he checked for swelling, for pain. She didn't wince at his touch, but continued to struggle for breath. He ran his hands over her arms, her legs, searched gingerly along her scalp. Nothing seemed broken. She'd simply had the wind knocked out of her.

"Breathe slowly," he instructed, his voice low and calming.

After what seemed like ages, she was able to draw a shallow breath followed by a deeper one. His own breath returned as she let out a sigh and the color returned to her cheeks.

Relief flooded through him. Their eyes met as he helped her sit up and something unspoken passed between them. He had a hand on the curve of her waist and another braced behind her shoulder. She was watching him, her eyes deep and dark, lips parted. Her hair was in wild disarray. He reached up to brush at a smudge of dirt on her cheek and suddenly it was more than relief that warmed his veins.

He'd avoided this for so long. Avoided even the thought of it, but she was so close and his hands were on her, touching skin. Hungrily, helplessly, he bent and pressed his mouth to hers.

Chapter Two

Dao's eyes shot open. Kwan-Li was kissing her, his breath becoming her breath. His fingers sank into her hair to hold her to him as he tasted her. She went still like an animal hunted. The roughness of it sent her heart racing, harder and faster than it had during the wild chase across the plain. But the kiss had barely begun before he tore away.

She was left staring up at a blank sky. It was several moments before she could gather her wits. It was much longer before she could catch her breath. His back was still to her and his breathing was low, harsh.

"I didn't even think you liked me," she said, her throat dry.

He turned to her, an incredulous look on his face as if *she* were the one who had lost her mind. "We must return to the caravan," was all he said.

Her hands shook as she fumbled with the clasps on front of the *deel*. In the distance, she could hear the sound of horses and in a matter of minutes, several of the nomads from the caravan appeared on the horizon.

When Kwan-Li helped her to her feet, his expression was wooden, but his eyes continued to burn. He kept his hands fisted by his sides, refusing to reach out to her even when she stumbled. Her horse had finally stopped and wandered back toward them, bending his head to graze tranquilly upon the wild grass. The beast.

Kwan-Li retrieved both of the horses as the escort came closer. "You'll ride with me," he said as he mounted.

"But that would be highly improper." She was still dizzy from the harrowing ride, from the fall, from his nearness. From…everything. "For a princess," she added. "Wouldn't it be?"

He gave her a hard look and held out his hand, stopping all argument. She climbed onto the horse behind him. She considered trying not to touch him, but the danger of falling again had her holding on tight. The muscles in his back tensed as her arms circled his waist and he flinched when she sank her cheek momentarily against his shoulder.

What had just happened? What would happen now?

"Kwan-Li?" she began tentatively.

"Not now," came the muttered reply.

He kicked in his heels to set the horse in motion, guiding the second one by a rope. Her chest was pressed to his back and she could feel the rhythm of the ride through him.

Before today, Kwan-Li had never said anything to her outside of what was absolutely necessary. He remained just as quiet now, as if willing the silence to scour away that one unforgettable moment. It had come and gone too quickly for her to react, but her mind and body reacted now.

Kwan-Li. Looking at her with unmistakable desire in his eyes. Kissing her. It was as if heaven and earth had changed places—she had never considered such a thing.

"The princess is unharmed," he reported tersely as they rejoined the other riders.

They rode without a word back to the caravan, where he returned her to the sedan, enclosing her safely away. Even when she was alone, her heartbeat refused to settle down.

This was not good. She was adrift in a wild and

foreign land. Another princess was trying to take her place and Kwan-Li was her one tie to the imperial court as well as to the khagan. She needed his guidance. She didn't need…whatever this was that had her skin flushing and her stomach all nervous and swimming.

Dao had assumed an alliance bride would be assured a position of respect. As a household servant, she'd had no chance of marrying well. Her mother had been seduced and then cast aside by the master of the house. At least her mother had been allowed to remain in the household and not forced to raise Dao on the streets. It might have been different if Dao had been a son. Instead she was born into the same humble servitude, growing up alongside a brother and a sister she could never recognize as her own. Being married to a chieftain was a brighter future than she could have ever hoped for.

Suddenly that bright future had become clouded. She had not come to this strange land to be cast away as a second wife, a concubine. Little better than a servant. She had come here to become someone new. As a princess, even a false one, Dao could finally determine her own fate. She had that power now—or did she?

Thoughts of another caravan and a rival princess, a *real* princess, haunted her.

Kwan-Li had said she would be sore the next
day. Dao was already sore within a few hours. She
was bone-weary and every part of her ached. She
slept inside the palanquin and continued sleeping
as they reached a Khitan settlement.

When the palanquin stopped, she lifted a heavy
head to peer out the window, searching first for
Kwan-Li, but not finding him.

The settlement resembled a village. About thirty
yurts, large circular huts wrapped in felt, were arranged around a cistern at the center. Plumes of
smoke vented from the huts and pale-colored sheep
flocked in pens around the camp.

Dao stared in fascination at the women and
children milling about the dwellings. She wanted
to explore, but was ushered discreetly from the
palanquin into one of the yurts. Princesses weren't
meant to be seen.

The yurt was luxurious compared to the sparse
tents they had slept in during the journey. A sturdy
lattice-work frame and a fan of wooden beams,
much like the spines of an umbrella, provided the
structure. While the outside had been wrapped
with a plain canvas, the inside was furnished with

a low bed and sitting area. Woven rugs in rainbow colors covered the floor and the yurt was heated with a central stove. A precious basin of water was brought to her. Not enough for a bath, but Dao was able to wash away the layer of dust from her skin.

Several attendants came in bearing trays laden with bowls and pots trailing steam. Dao took a sip of a pale, thick drink that they explained was mare's milk. She managed to keep her face still until the attendants left before washing the sour taste away with a dose of strong tea.

There was no rice with the meal, but there were plates of golden pastries and thick stews and generous portions of roasted lamb. As delicious as the food looked and smelled, Dao was only able to finish a few bites before exhaustion claimed her again and she fell into a deep, restless sleep. When she awoke, the yurt was dark and she was alone.

Curse that skittish horse and her insistence on riding it! She'd meant to summon Kwan-Li after dinner, but the day had taken everything out of her. From outside she could still hear the drone of conversation along with the muted wail of strings singing an unfamiliar song. Perhaps it wasn't too late.

She crawled out of bed and felt her way through the darkness until she reached the flap that covered the entrance. Dao opened it to let herself out into the night. A scatter of torches lit the settlement and a blanket of stars greeted her overhead. More stars than all the people in the empire.

She stared up at the dots of light, feeling dizzy beneath their watch. It was said that the stars told of celestial designs, the will of the heavens. Had they always known she would be here, on a journey to be presented to the ruler of Khitan? She, who was born to a mother who was the lowest of servants and a father who never recognized her as daughter.

The sound of a male voice startled her. Dao recognized the young man as one of her guardsmen.

"Where is Kwan-Li?" she asked.

He responded with a string of sounds that meant nothing to her. Dao hadn't learned enough of the Khitan language to make her purpose known so all she could do was shake her head in frustration and move toward the sound of voices. The guardsman could do nothing but trail after her. She wove around the dwellings. The settlement was still very much awake and the voices grew louder. Soon she arrived at a gathering around a fire pit. She stopped at the edge of the light, not wanting to intrude.

An elderly man pulled a bow across a stringed

instrument with a long, thin neck. The wailing sound she'd heard earlier now took on an effusive, resonating quality, filling the entire circle with a racing song, like the stomp of hooves across the plains. The music was as indecipherable and mysterious to her as the language and customs of this land.

She scanned the crowd and her skin flushed as she caught sight of Kwan-Li. Dao wasn't one to be taken by romantic notions. She had agreed to pose as princess to elevate herself from a life of servitude. Still—to be kissed without restraint, without warning. Kissed almost savagely by a man who was always so impeccably well-mannered. Any woman, whether she be a lowly maidservant or a princess would weaken a little.

He had traded the blue *deel* for one of tanned felt, similar to what the other nomads wore. A fur cap hid his topknot. He could have easily blended in as Khitan, yet he stood at the edge of the circle. An outsider.

Dao had been set apart throughout the entire journey. When night came, her attendants would see to her needs and then disappear. She was left isolated in her sleeping tent while the entire caravan gathered around a fire to trade stories. She could have called them back to provide her company, but she used to enjoy that small peace at the end of the day when she was a servant. When there were no more demands on her and her time was her own. Besides, what did attendants have to say to a princess? She could sense their discomfort whenever she tried to converse with them. It always left her feeling so lonely, but she understood the boundaries of status. This was the price of her deception.

Kwan-Li spoke more directly with her than the others, but even he treated her with a sense of detachment. Until today.

He turned then, as if sensing her presence, and found her among the shadows. His eyes glowed in the firelight as he moved toward her. Her palms began to sweat.

"Kwan-Li," she began.

"Princess."

His voice was low and quiet. She was at a loss at what to say now that he stood before her. There was a wariness to his expression. These next moments would dictate how they moved on from all that had happened that afternoon.

She stared at the curve of his mouth. How long had the kiss lasted? No longer than a heartbeat or two. Not even as long as this strained silence between them, yet it had changed everything forever.

"How fast can we ride to the central capital?" she asked. "If we didn't have to carry all those trunks and so many people, how long would it take?"

He appeared relieved. "With a small group on horseback we can be there in perhaps two weeks, but it would be a tough journey. Staying in the saddle all day is not easy."

She narrowed her eyes at him. "I can ride a horse."

The corner of his mouth twitched. "I said *stay* in the saddle."

Humor now? From Kwan-Li? She didn't know whether to scowl or laugh.

"It was your clan that negotiated the peace marriage. This alliance is as important to you as it is to the empire."

He sobered at that. "It is very important to us," he agreed.

"Then we'll ride out tomorrow morning. No barbarian princess is going to take my place."

His expression, as usual, was unreadable. "As the princess commands."

With nothing else to say, the memory of the kiss once again loomed between them. Her stomach twisted into a thousand knots. Dao considered retreating to the safety of her bed, but her gaze drifted to the fire pit surrounded by song. The yurt was a dark and lonely place by comparison.

The musician began another song. There was an accompanying melody in a low drone that sounded like some sort of pipe or winded instrument. It took her a moment to realize that the man was somehow creating the sound in his throat. The sound of it was eerie, ethereal in quality. A sense of freedom filled her. She was no longer hidden away in seclusion. After the long journey through the plains, she had only now arrived.

"I never thought I would ever leave the walls of Changan," she said, lost in the warmth and laughter of the gathering.

"I never thought I would stand before the Son of Heaven in Daming Palace," Kwan-Li replied. "Then after several years in your capital, I thought I would never return here."

She stood very still beside him as they let the music encompass them, very much aware of how his shoulder was just a touch away from hers. The chill of the night air vanished.

Kwan-Li knew what it was like to leave his homeland behind. He had lived in a foreign land and adopted a different language and way of life.

"How old were you when you were sent to the empire?" she asked.

"Fifteen."

She was only a handful of years older than that. "What did you study while you were there?"

"I learned the ways of the Tang Empire—its laws and methods of governing. For the betterment of our land. There are many in Khitan who would be content to become subjects to the empire. To accept its protection and adopt its culture."

She had indeed seen Khitan nomads living among her own people in the settlements they had passed through the borderlands.

"Did you long for Khitan, being away for so long?"

His shoulder lifted in a gesture that wasn't a yes or a no. "I never forgot where I came from," was all he admitted.

He was a tough Khitan tribesman. Of course he wouldn't admit to being homesick. The realization that she would never return to Changan finally settled into her heart. This was her new home: the open frontier, a place without walls, without roads. But she had chosen this life. She would learn what she needed to know to become a part of it just as Kwan-Li had done in the empire.

She had already learned a lot that day. They spoke of the Khitan as fierce warriors, savages even, but Dao could feel the spirit of openness and generosity around her. Life on the steppe was harsh, yet they found ways to celebrate.

She studied Kwan-Li more carefully now. There were so many things she hadn't known about him. Kwan-Li was educated, cultured, well-mannered. He was an expert horseman who rode off to rescue princesses. And the way he kissed...

It was a good thing she wasn't a swooning romantic.

"I should go now," she said in a rush. "We have a long journey tomorrow."

He moved to accompany her without being asked. Would he be so attentive if she weren't a princess? If it wasn't his duty to watch over her?

As they neared the yurt, she realized he was no longer beside her. He held himself back, out of arm's reach.

The darkness highlighted the hollows of his face and the distinguished shape of his cheekbones. He was striking with a rugged handsomeness that she had somehow overlooked. He was impossible to overlook now.

"I should be punished for what happened today," he said grimly.

It took a moment to find her voice. "It was my fault. I didn't know what to do when the horse started running."

"I wasn't speaking of that."

"Oh. That…"

A wind picked up and rustled through the grass, punctuating their conversation.

"That was an accident," she said faintly. "Wasn't it?"

He straightened. "It will never happen again, Princess."

She could see his chest rising and falling while the rest of his body remained still, tense. Some part of him didn't want to leave and some part of her didn't want him to either.

She should have kissed him back. They had been alone out on the plains and no soul but the earth and sky would know what happened. They were alone now beneath the light of the stars.

Her pulse quickened and she took a step toward him. No. Heaven and earth, no! She immediately took a step back with two additional ones for good measure.

She wasn't nearly brave enough for that.

Kwan-Li didn't move from his position. Not a hair. He was watching her curiously.

"Sleep well," she said, her tongue struggling with those two simple words.

He nodded.

Dao retreated into the yurt and lay down, staring

up into the darkness for a long time. Finally she closed her eyes and tried to recapture that perfect storm of heat and pressure and touch. Kwan-Li was probably too honorable to ever attempt another kiss, even if she happened to once again be caught on a runaway horse. And that itself was highly unlikely. A shame.

Chapter Three

Kwan-Li enjoyed the freedom of riding from sunrise to sunset unburdened for the next week. This was the land he remembered from his youth. Princess An-Ming rode beside him while the sun cast its final rays of the day. The golden light washed over her and she glanced over at him with a soft and fleeting look. A look drunk with warmth and the pleasure of the open air. He wanted to touch her so much he ached with it.

The single touch of her lips he'd stolen continued to torment him. He buried that feeling most days, but there were moments, like this one, when something burned hotter inside him than desire. The spirit of the steppe was seeping back into his blood and An-Ming was there for every rediscovery. He could see in her face how the sight of the earth and sky affected her. He was coming home while she was a stranger to the steppe. Yet here they were…fellow wanderers between worlds.

They were flanked by Ruan and three of his fellow tribesmen. Each of them led two additional horses by a tether, providing a small fleet for their use. The horses were rotated throughout the day to distribute the burden of carrying a rider. This allowed them to cover a greater distance with shorter rest periods in between.

"Old Wolf!" the princess called out to Ruan who had taken the lead.

"Young Dragoness!"

"How does anyone find their way in this land with no roads?"

Ruan laughed. "The sun, the rivers and the distant hills tell us where we are." He went on to describe how to use the shadow of the sun to determine direction.

The hidden language of the steppe had once been second nature to Kwan-Li. He, too, knew how to read the clouds and sky. The rhythm of the wind across the plains was in his blood. But for the last twelve years, he had lived in the imperial city of Changan, confined within walls surrounded by more walls. He had studied a new sort of knowledge that came from scrolls and books. The same books had proclaimed that his people were barbarians. That they had no language of their own. That they worshipped the sun like savages.

At times he had almost believed that his people were ancient and primitive. The Tang Empire had swallowed his spirit whole and he had come back changed.

Before sundown, Ruan navigated them down into a ravine and they set up camp beside the river. Belu and Ruan took care of setting up the sleeping tents while Kwan-Li brought the horses to water and refilled their gourds and waterskins in preparation for the next day's journey.

An-Ming came and knelt at the edge of the stream, dipping a cloth into the water. He watched, transfixed, as she washed the dust from her face. Her skin had taken on a warm golden tint from the sun, with a faint scattering of freckles appearing on her cheekbones. The Han women he'd known in the empire had valued pale skin as a sign of beauty. They used powders to appear like porcelain dolls and hid behind parasols and curtains at the faintest ray of light.

When he had first seen An-Ming in the palace, her face was similarly powdered. Her lips were painted red, her cheeks unnaturally pink. Her hair was pinned and laced with ornaments and she was encased in silk and gold. He had only caught a glimpse before she was shut away.

The princess had been impossible at the beginning of the journey, insisting on delicacies at every meal, baths at inconvenient times because she was hot, entertainment because she was bored. Such behavior was expected of a spoiled princess, but An-Ming seemed to grow weary of it. On the steppe, where the journey became most difficult, she was no longer willful and demanding. She'd become curious to learn their ways.

Her hair had fallen loose as she sat by the river. The ends of it trailed over her shoulder to tease at her breast. He watched in fascination as she gathered it up and twisted it into a knot, exposing a slip of pale skin at her neck. His chest tightened, as well as other, more insistent parts of him.

"You're staring at me."

She had stopped what she was doing to meet his gaze. The washcloth was still pressed to her cheek. He was caught.

"There is not much else to look at out here."

Her lips curved into a mischievous smile that once again revealed her dimple. "Where I come from, there's a penalty for that."

"What would that be?"

"Twenty lashes."

It would be worth the risk. His heart was beating fast from nothing more than this careless banter. He willed himself to show nothing.

An-Ming filled a basin with water and disappeared into the sleeping tent while he forced his attention elsewhere. He turned to find old Ruan grinning at him. There was no escape.

"You need a wife, Tailuo." Ruan used his name. His true name.

He scowled at the elder tribesman.

"A woman, then," Ruan amended.

He'd had lovers during his time in the empire. Courtesans who knew how to smile and speak and sway in ways that made a man burn. This was a different sort of woman. This heat within him, a different kind of fever.

Kwan-Li regarded the elder tribesman with a grave look. "This agreement with the Tang Emperor. Will the khagan honor it?"

Ruan's grin faded. "We have served as vassals of the Uyghur Empire for nearly a hundred years."

"But their hold is weakening. We can be free of them."

"By paying tribute to the Tang Emperor instead? Many of the chieftains of the eight tribes don't see the difference."

The Uyghurs were another tribal confederation.

They wanted Khitan land and horses and men to fight in their wars. With the Tang Empire, there was at least chance for diplomacy. For peace. That was why his father had sent him there to learn from them.

"You must be discussing serious matters."

An-Ming returned from the tent and settled in beside them at the fire without a moment's hesitation. Her hair was damp and pinned up in a loose knot with a few strands pulling free. Beads of moisture remained on her, pooling at the hollow of her throat.

"Princess." Kwan-Li bowed his head in deference. What he really wanted to do was put his mouth on her and run his tongue over her neck. He swallowed forcibly.

"It's only because you can't have her." Ruan spoke in Khitan. His grin was back, but there was a dark wisdom in his eyes.

"I'm no fool. I just need to get her to the khagan," Kwan-Li retorted.

An-Ming looked expectantly between them, not understanding. She pouted when neither of them offered any explanation. "You have to teach me your language once we reach the central capital," she said to Kwan-Li.

That stopped him short. "I am not staying, Princess."

Confusion crossed her face, then alarm. "But I thought—"

Ruan conveniently backed away to help the others with the provisions.

An-Ming looked so lost that he was reminded of his own journey long ago into a foreign land. He'd been left adrift there, practically a hostage trapped in the imperial city.

He and An-Ming had embarked on this journey together. He had never considered she would expect him to stay with her. He had never considered she would ever want him to.

His throat clenched. What she was asking for was impossible. He was the one who had negotiated the peace marriage from his position within the imperial court. The responsibility lay in his hands, but duty and honor weren't enough to keep him away from her. His control had already slipped once and if Ruan wasn't hovering nearby now…

"There are others within the khagan's court who speak your language. They can teach you." He shouldn't have to explain, but he did anyway. "I have my own tribe to return to. My own kinsmen."

For the first time, he saw a break in her resolve and the loneliness underneath. He wanted to protect her. If this fire inside him were nothing but desire, An-Ming wouldn't have such power over him. He was angry at himself for this weakness.

"I don't suppose I can command you to stay," she said softly.

He responded with an iron look. "I am not your servant to command, Princess."

Kwan-Li took the lead that day. Ruan had explained the route. They would follow the river north to where the ravine opened into a valley. From there they would be only days away from the khagan's camp.

An-Ming chose not to speak with him, favoring Ruan's company instead. She was pointedly asking the Old Wolf to teach her Khitan.

The day was otherwise uneventful, until around midday as they navigated along the inclines of the ravine. Kwan-Li noticed movement in the pass ahead. A dark shape moved out of the shadows followed by another.

"Riders," he called out.

Ruan came up beside him. "A hunting party?"

A low sound punctuated the air. Kwan-Li knew it at once and his heart seized. One of their companions doubled over in the saddle, the shaft of an arrow protruding from his chest.

"Stay back!" Kwan-Li commanded.

There was a startled cry from behind him. The princess.

Confusion spread as the additional horses became untethered. Ruan moved to the front, bow in hand to return fire, while Kwan-Li positioned himself between An-Ming and the intruders in the distance. Her face was pale, her eyes wide with shock.

"Head for the other side of the river. Go!" He leaned over to strike her horse's backside.

An-Ming held on as the horse took off while he followed behind her at a gallop. There was little cover in the ravine. She needed to get out of range of the archers.

He led An-Ming behind a growth of brush by the bank. Her horse pranced in agitation, his hooves splashing in the shallow of the river. She was fighting to keep her hands from shaking, but she managed to steady the animal.

"Uyghurs?" she asked.

"Khitan," he replied without emotion.

They were outnumbered and he needed to decide now. Fight or flee. Tension rippled through his body as he detached his bow from the saddle pack.

"If I fall, you ride north." Kwan-Li indicated the direction with his hand. "Ride hard."

"Wait—"

There was no time to see if she understood. He hooked the bow over his shoulder and gave her one final look before kicking his heels in to ride back into danger.

His kinsmen had regrouped to face the oncoming riders. The attackers outnumbered them two to one, by his quick assessment. A few of them had broken through the pass and were charging forward.

Kwan-Li urged his knee against the horse's side, using the pressure to direct the animal, while he reached for an arrow and nocked it. The rhythm of the earth thrummed through him. The cadence of his breathing joined it. The pace of the enemy horsemen rushing toward them became a dissonant harmony. He took it all in.

Kwan-Li sank his weight onto the iron stirrups and rose, standing upright in the saddle. His horse continued its charge. This technique of shooting from the saddle allowed the Khitans to dominate the steppe, but it had been years since he had done this. A lifetime. He drew the arrow back and let it fly.

The body remembered. The heart remembered.

Kwan-Li aimed and fired again, his arrow once again finding its mark.

"Go!" Ruan shouted. "They only want the princess."

Kwan-Li hesitated. His tribesmen had pushed the attackers back to the pass and were holding their ground.

Ruan exchanged his bow for a halberd. "Go." His face creased into a grin. "This Old Wolf won't be dying today."

With a bellow, Ruan rode into battle.

Chapter Four

No matter how far they fled, Dao could still feel danger chasing them. She had grown up as a household servant in a wealthy section of the city. She'd polished furniture and haggled for good prices on chickens at the market. The only place she'd seen a bow drawn was at the archery park.

They rode for hours before stopping when the sky faded to red and gold. The land had once again flattened out into wide expanses of wild grass. Kwan-Li did one final scan of the horizon in every direction before setting up camp. He started a fire and broke off a chunk of a tea brick into a pot of water.

"They won't harm you," he said when she looked over her shoulder warily.

"How do you know that?"

"You are the Emperor's niece and an imperial princess."

"Not out here. Bandits don't care who we are," she argued.

He fell silent, a frown creasing his brow as the tea brewed. After a few minutes, he handed her a cup filled with steaming liquid.

"Those were not bandits," he said. "They were from another tribe and they wanted to keep us from reaching the capital."

He sounded calm now. Deadly calm.

"What about your tribesmen? What about Ruan?"

"Ruan has survived much worse. Now drink, Princess." Kwan-Li had to close his hands around hers to get her to grip the cup. "You will feel better."

"Does it have mare's milk in it?" she asked after a pause.

He laughed. It was brief, but it was a laugh. The touch of his hands was also brief, but they were warm and strong and did more to reassure her than anything else.

"You said the men were Khitan," she began.

"I couldn't tell which clan they were from, but none of the tribes would dare raise a hand against you. The wrath of the Tang imperial army would be too great."

His jaw clenched and he radiated a low, simmering anger. The warrior in him had come out in battle and it remained. Dao could sense the change in every part of him. She had been so naive. This wasn't a grand adventure to an exotic land. Being a princess meant more than wearing silk and having servants attend to her every need. It meant being caught in politics and power struggles. Things she knew nothing about.

She sipped at the tea. It was bitter, yet fortifying. "Is there always such fighting among the tribes?"

"There have always been disagreements."

She thought for a long time. "Khitan is a dangerous place."

His eyes darkened at the statement. "No more treacherous than your imperial court."

At that moment, Dao felt like she didn't know anything about anything. Neither the dangers of Khitan, nor the imperial court. In her innocence, she believed that it was an honor to be selected to be an alliance bride. Her half sister had had the good sense to flee.

Kwan-Li was watching her carefully. "You regret coming here."

It was too late for that now. "I won't be writing any laments about being married to the other side of heaven, if that's what you're wondering."

Again, the half smile. "I did not think you would."

The poetry of the frontier was always filled with homesickness and sorrow, but Dao hadn't come all this way to wallow in misery. She was a princess now.

"What do I need to know about the Khitan court?" she asked.

"There is conflict in any court," he said roughly. "But the princess will be protected at all times."

Was he trying to protect her by keeping her in ignorance? Her half brother had been the same way. When the family had been on the brink of ruin, he'd tried to take all the troubles onto his own shoulders, thinking to shield them from worry. But the entire household had always known. She couldn't remain ignorant if she wanted to survive.

"Tell me," she insisted. "I'm to become the khagan's wife, after all. And you'll no longer be with me."

Kwan-Li gave her a hard look. She stared back with a harder look. She won.

"The tribes of the south have lived among the Han, learned your language, in many instances adopting your ways. Other clans have similarly aligned themselves with the Uyghurs," he continued. "For generations, the Khitan have balanced themselves between these two enemies, trying to appease both sides. The Tang court withdrew support when we became vassals of the Uyghurs, but within the last few years our clan has once again paid tribute to the Emperor to reestablish relations."

She thought of Kwan-Li, who had been sent to the capital to be educated. "Your clan would rather be allied with the Tang Emperor."

"I would rather we were our own masters."

There was so much pride and conviction behind that statement.

"You risked your life for the sake of this alliance today," she said.

"No." His gaze burned into her. "I did what I did for you."

It would have been the same had he known she wasn't royalty. She was certain. He called her princess and almost always did what she asked, but she never thought of him as a servant.

"I'm very grateful," she said, feeling the words were inadequate. "For all that you've done for me."

His only answer was a brief nod before he went to tend to the pot that simmered over the fire. It wasn't the first time she regretted how the difference in their positions kept him at a distance.

The rest of the brew was used to cook up a thick gruel of tea leaves and millet. They ate the simple meal in silence while she was aware of his every movement beside her. Kwan-Li was a constant puzzle: scholar and warrior. He was at ease with the silence as they watched the sun melt into the horizon. This land suited him with its harsh beauty.

"The princess should rest," he suggested finally. "I will remain on guard."

She started toward the tent, but paused as Kwan-Li scattered dirt over the fire.

"It is unlikely we would be found out here, but the fire would make us visible from afar in the darkness," he explained.

They were down to a single sleeping tent as well as a limited number of supplies. All he had for warmth was a wool blanket and the steppe could become frigid once the sun was down.

"There's enough room in the tent," she offered.

He stared at her for a moment then looked away, shaking his head. The corners of his mouth lifted wryly. "You are…very beautiful, Princess."

Their gazes locked. Blood rushed to her face and her heart was suddenly beating too fast. She wasn't so very beautiful. She doubted Kwan-Li would have ever noticed her if he didn't think she was a princess, but the way that he said it was more than a compliment.

"I should go," she said.

"Yes."

Only in the shelter of the tent did she allow herself to consider what was happening between them.

His words sounded like a warning...and like a promise. As if he wouldn't be able to resist her if tempted. Her heart pounded.

It was impossible not to have these thoughts. Kwan-Li was young, strong and handsome and she was stranded on the endless steppe with him. They were being pursued. Her future was clouded and she was a little frightened. The khagan was old and...and nothing. She knew nothing else about her husband-to-be.

Darkness descended and a lone wolf howled in the distance, but no mate answered its call. Dao lay down on the rug and closed her eyes. Her thoughts floated outside to where Kwan-Li remained in order to preserve her honor. She realized that she did want very much to tempt him.

The sky was hanging on to the last orange threads of daylight as the warmth from the fire ebbed away. Kwan-Li seated himself beside the tent and prepared for a long night. Everything had changed. Nothing had changed. It was still his duty to guide the princess safely to the khagan. The security and future of his clan rested upon it.

He could hear the rustle of movement from inside the tent. There wasn't a moment of the day where his body wasn't acutely aware of her. The princess wasn't yet asleep. After a long moment, there was silence and Kwan-Li stared at the empty horizon beyond. Anything to keep from looking at the tent and thinking of what awaited inside. Loneliness overtook him, a loneliness that came not from the starkness of the land, but from hovering between two worlds.

Out here, there was an intimacy that could never be found within the city. Two strangers meeting quickly became friends. A man and a woman alone quickly became…

He had kissed her only once. That was all he'd ever have, yet the soft press of her lips lingered with him. The open plain provided nothing to distract him.

The princess was moving again. His heart lodged in his throat even before the tent flap lifted. Her shadow slipped over him and her hands settled lightly on his shoulders. She was a fox-spirit in the moonlight.

"Princess," he acknowledged her.

He spoke with quiet forcefulness. She faltered when he made no move toward her. Holding her breath, she closed her eyes and leaned forward, her lips touching his almost fearfully. He let her go on and waited for her to lose her resolve. It was almost cruel, except she was killing him, as well.

Her mouth pulled away, but only to descend once again, searching in a caress that was too sweet for what he truly wanted.

"Princess," he said again, his voice husky.

He already knew he wouldn't fight her. In a dark corner of his heart, he'd known this moment was inevitable. There was no avoiding one another when they were the only two souls around.

He gathered up her hair as she had done by the river and pressed his mouth to her neck. He inhaled the scent of her skin as her pulse throbbed beneath his touch. He wanted to use his tongue on her. His teeth on her. There wasn't a part of him that didn't want her.

An-Ming lifted a hand to his jaw. Her eyelashes fluttered delicately against his cheek. "I didn't want my first lover to be a stranger," she whispered.

She pressed against him and kissed him again, bolder this time. He'd heard all sorts of stories in the palace about princesses who flaunted authority, who took lovers without shame. He'd never thought it of this princess, but it didn't matter now.

They moved together, clinging to one another. He shoved the canvas flap aside and the darkness of the tent closed over them. He untied his sash and pulled his tunic open before reaching for An-Ming. He felt her touch momentarily against his chest, pressing softly just above his heart.

More pulling and loosening of cloth. The moment's delay stretched on for too long before his hands were on bare skin, running up the curve of a knee, the softness of her inner thigh. He parted her, stroking deep with just his fingertips in that most sensitive place where heaven lay waiting.

She gasped, her breath hitching on a sibilant cry that went straight to his groin. Her legs curved naturally around his hips while her mouth sought his. Every part of her body was urging him on. Commanding him. He positioned himself, his organ hard against soft flesh, his mind a storm. He thought fleetingly that she was a princess, that she was inexperienced...that he had a duty. Then he was inside her.

She closed around him, hot and tight. He abandoned all other thought in the wake of the dark pleasure. He began to move in slow, gradual thrusts. An-Ming consumed him and he gave himself over to her. For the first time in years, he no longer questioned where he belonged.

Chapter Five

Dao closed her eyes to concentrate on the feel of Kwan-Li inside her. He was holding her, kissing her. His weight anchored her to the rug. This first time taking another person into her body was… confusing. The heat, the pressure. The feeling of being stretched and invaded. The longing. The pain. The strange pleasure beneath it.

She was being taken. Undeniably so. His every movement radiated through her. The coupling was rough and hungry and unapologetic. Yet when his tongue touched hers, desire curled through her, making her want the things he was doing to her even more.

Soon the pleasure outweighed the pain. Soon there was no more telling what was what in the darkness. There was nothing but the harsh rhythm of their breathing, his weight above her, and a feeling of being anchored and held to the earth while the heavens spun around her.

She pressed her lips to his throat, feeling the pulse that pounded there.

Dao was never one to be taken with romantic notions, but she wanted this. She wanted this. Her body strained against him, becoming single-minded with need.

His thrusts became more forceful. Kwan-Li was flying headlong toward completion. The women gossiped in the servants' quarters saying that this was the usual way of the bedchamber. Fast. Urgent. Satisfactory for the man, perhaps sometimes for the woman.

Kwan-Li took hold of her hips and shifted them. She was angled up and against him. His hold on her was confident as he slid deeper, his movement within her changing to assail her with a new rush of sensation. He was pushing her to a peak, willing her climax. She ran her hands along the sweat-slicked planes of his back, digging in to urge him on. Her back arched in a plea for more. In that moment, she surrendered herself completely to him, yet her body, this pleasure, was selfishly her own. She cried out into the darkness as every muscle in her tightened and a flood of pleasure gripped her.

He continued thrusting into her as she convulsed

around him. Kwan-Li buried his face against her neck, his breath harsh with exertion. His muscles clenched tight as he finally allowed himself his own release.

In the stillness afterward, he remained on top of her, heavy and indolent. Their pulses combined in a mismatched rhythm. Dao ran her hand over the contours of his back, appreciating the musculature beneath the warm skin. The dusky light played delightfully over him. He was lean in build, brimming with wiry strength. The years of living in the empire hadn't softened him.

He indulged her for only a little while longer before planting a kiss against her shoulder and rising. She was left cold at his sudden departure. The evening was upon them and the tent was dark, casting him in shadow and hiding his face from her. The shuffle of cloth punctuated the silence.

He was getting dressed.

Dao gathered her robe against her breasts and sat up, inhaling sharply at the soreness between her legs. Was it only moments ago she was clinging to Kwan-Li, crying out with his body hard inside her? Her face grew hot at the memory. Now his movements were brusque.

Kwan-Li came back to her. His fingers brushed

through her hair. "I need to keep watch outside, Princess."

The ambush. Not to mention the threat of wolves. All of that had seemed far away while she was in his arms. She felt embarrassed for thinking the worst of Kwan-Li when he had been nothing but loyal. Her doubts were not about him, but about herself.

She was the one who had chosen this. Chosen him. She wasn't beguiled or seduced.

He held his hand at her nape as he kissed her, his touch possessive, his mouth demanding. "Get some rest, but do get dressed. We may need to leave quickly."

By the time he left, she was warm and dizzy with all that had just happened. Her forbidden lover was leaving her bed in the darkness of the night. Her toes curled with the decadence of it.

She remained undressed, pulling the blanket over her to keep the heat of their joining close for just a little longer. Outside, Kwan-Li was watching over her, protecting her against whatever danger lurked out there on the steppe, but soon he would be gone. And soon she would be married, exactly as she had planned.

Despite her best efforts, the air grew cold around

her. She sat up and struggled back into her clothing, fumbling with the clasps in the darkness. Quickly she lay back down and cocooned herself in the blanket, trying hard to recapture the warmth. This was her stolen moment. She needed to hold on to every detail.

In the years to come, she would come back to this small tent in the middle of the wild grassland. She would remember the smell of Kwan-Li's skin and his weight above her. Even if the memory had faded, it would still belong to her.

Dao was aware of a stream of sunlight and then a presence moving beside her.

"Princess." Kwan-Li's voice tingled against her spine.

She opened one eye to the sight of him leaning over her. "Don't call me that," she murmured.

"What should I call you, then?" His gaze was warm as he tucked back a strand of her hair. "Beautiful? Beloved?"

His fingertips following the curve of her ear in a caress that made heat pool in her belly and her limbs go weak. She felt an alarming twinge deep in her chest. It was easy to see why people did tragic and foolish things for this. Nothing felt as warm and safe and perfect.

"Aren't we still in danger?" she asked as he began undoing the clasps along her side.

He smiled at her. "Only you, Princess."

His knuckles brushed the underside of her breast as he opened the front of the *deel*. He parted the garment down the length of her, his eyes following the path of exposed skin. She swallowed as the cool morning air washed over her legs. She was already breathing hard, her pulse frantic, when he positioned himself between her knees. His mouth parted and his eyes met hers a moment before his warm breath bathed her sex. She had to close her eyes.

Her embarrassment lasted only half a heartbeat before ecstasy consumed her. His lips were on her. Then his tongue, licking a slow, intimate path. He parted her with long, deft fingers. His mouth was unerring, teasing lightly, finding secret places on her she never knew existed. He was making her sob, making her scream. Making her love him.

He entered her in the aftermath, with her body shaken and too sensitive to take all of him without a whimper. He was mindful of her as he took his own pleasure, moving with such tender care that it broke her heart.

She opened her eyes. He held her gaze the entire time as his movements became rough and his breath shallow. He climaxed like that, still watching her.

This time, she was the first to turn away. She had to. She was starting to wonder and she was starting to dream.

Kwan-Li slipped abruptly out of her as she sat up. Dao fumbled with the clasps on her garment, staring down at her hands rather than at him. Her heart was beating too fast and there was no way to escape. In his eyes, she had seen both a promise and a demand and she was frightened of how he made her hope for more. Maybe princesses could dream, but she couldn't.

After a long pause, she could hear Kwan-Li getting up, as well. The silence grew oppressive.

"Princess."

She turned to see him raised onto his knees beside the rugs and blankets that served as her bed. His pupils were dark, his face a mask. He knew something was wrong.

She fought to keep her voice steady. A low throb of pleasure still vibrated through her. "You should know this changes nothing."

A muscle in his jaw ticked. "I would not presume it would."

Dao could see the anger that vibrated through him.

"I am still marrying the khagan," she said, gathering up her hair.

She suddenly wanted more than anything to set herself right: her hair, her clothing. If she could wash the scent of him from her skin, she would. He'd somehow gotten inside her, mind and body, and the memory was too hard to fight. She needed to get out of the confines of the tent and remove all other reminders of what they had done. She didn't regret it, she just needed it finished. This was how affairs were conducted, weren't they?

"Your clan negotiated this alliance. You have a duty," she reminded him. She struggled with the hairpins. "I have a duty."

"Everything that you are saying is true," he said tonelessly.

Dao didn't realize she had her hands clenched. She released them and let the blood flow back into her fingertips. "I told you. I didn't want my first lover to be a stranger."

Why was she explaining herself? Men were known to love and then turn away from one breath to the next.

He closed each clasp on his *deel* methodically, one after the other, all the while watching her with the eyes of a hawk. "The princess can rely on this humble servant to be discreet." His mouth twisted over the words.

Did he think she considered him beneath her? The horror of it made her blood run cold. The Kwan-Li she had come to know took nothing lightly. Not a kiss, not a single word. Surely not a night like the one they'd spent.

"I'm not a princess," she blurted out.

He blinked at her. His frown deepened as he rose to his full height and came to stand over her. "Not a princess?" he asked slowly.

Her heart raced. "I haven't a drop of royal blood. I was given the title by imperial decree—or rather my master's daughter was, but Pearl ran away so I came in her place. But I am still a princess by decree," she amended. "Your treaty will still be honored."

"Such lies! Send a false princess to the barbarians. How would they know the difference?"

His hair was untied and there was something powerful and frighteningly beautiful about him as he glared at her. She was no longer pretending and he was no longer restrained by civility.

"Did you really think every alliance bride was truly a princess?" she asked impatiently.

"The imperial court thinks it can play whatever trick it wants to on the ignorant Khitans."

She narrowed her gaze at him. "A trick? Like pledging loyalty to both the Uyghurs and the Tang Empire at the same time?" she snapped.

He fell silent.

"Why did you choose to speak now?" he asked finally.

Because she'd grown to respect him. Because what they had between them was changing too quickly for her to catch her breath. No man had ever taken such good care of her or shown her such loyalty.

"You risked your life to protect me. I thought you should know the truth."

It was a poor explanation, but how could she explain how she truly felt?

"I chose to come here," she told him fiercely. "No one forced me into this arranged marriage. The Emperor needed an alliance bride and this was the only way that I could help my family. Me. The lowly servant."

A lowly servant instead of a daughter. In a family that never accepted her as one of their own until this sacrifice. Dao looked down at her hands.

"Men seem to think they're the only ones who know about responsibility and honor," she said, her ire spent.

The chill in the air seeped into her skin and the

ache over her heart refused to go away. She had known everything would be different after their night together, but not like this. She'd become more attuned to his smell, his touch, his very presence. Even the sound of his voice made her stomach dance in circles.

For the first time since she'd begun this journey, she doubted her decision. She could lose everything. All because a man had taken her to bed and she had liked it. She had loved it—she might even love him, but it changed nothing. She was not a silly, romantic girl to be blinded so easily.

"I will marry the khagan," she said, keeping her voice steady. "And you'll go your own way, just as you said."

"Princess." Kwan-Li stopped on the title, no longer knowing what to call her. "You had decided this before you came to me last night."

"Yes. I even considered that there could be a child."

Out here in Khitan, Dao finally had control over her own life. At first it had felt like freedom. Now she was exhausted, drained of every emotion. He tried to reach for her, but she wouldn't let him.

"What if there is a child?" he asked softly.

She met his gaze without flinching. "So close to the wedding, no one would ever know."

"No man would ever allow that."

She was reminded of her father, who wasn't a bad man. Merely a typical one.

"You're wrong," she said, forcing her heart to harden. "Plenty of men do."

Chapter Six

Kwan-Li had only traveled once to the encampment where the khagan held court. He was little more than a boy at the time, riding alongside his father as they went to pay their yearly tribute to the ruling clan. He used the distant mountains and the sun as a guide as he'd been taught. It wasn't long before the land spoke to him once again.

As they reached the northern region, the land became green and lush. The journey brought them to a cliff overlooking a wide valley down below. Tall grass rippled in waves with a tipping of yellow that signaled the beginning of the autumn season. The glitter of water could be seen in the distance.

The first time he'd seen An-Ming, his princess who wasn't a princess, was two months ago at the start of the journey. She had been wrapped in silk and jewels as she stepped down from her palanquin. An-Ming dismounted now and ventured to the edge to peer into the valley. Her chest rose and fell with the sway of the breeze.

"Your land is really quite beautiful," she said with an air of wonder.

"It is." He had forgotten it at times himself, but he was rediscovering his homeland now with An-Ming beside him.

"How much longer?" she asked.

He knew what she was asking. "Two days."

"So soon..."

Her voice trailed off. They hadn't so much as brushed by each other for the last few days. Not since that morning. He sensed that she didn't want to be wooed or coaxed back into his arms, so he had waited for her to come to him. He stood behind her, just at her shoulder, with less than a hand's span between them. Not touching, but close enough for the hint of it.

"The alliance with your Emperor is important to us, but it is not written in blood." He wanted to try to explain to her. The different ruling tribes formed a complicated union.

She looked away from him, her chin tilted upward in a sign of stubbornness and pride. "This is not only for me."

Kwan-Li understood sacrifice. He also knew what it was to lose one's sense of self to duty. The thought of An-Ming being placed in the khagan's court suddenly pained him. He had desired her from the start—perhaps the way a man coveted beautiful things he had no chance of possessing—but he admired her now. He was in awe of her.

It wasn't that he was afraid she would lose herself, he realized. It was that he didn't want to give her up.

They returned to the horses and he untacked the animals to set them to graze. When he returned to An-Ming, he was surprised to see she had started the cooking fire without his assistance. She started to pour herself some tea, but he took over the task.

"You don't have to serve me," she protested as he handed her the cup.

Wordlessly he poured another cup for himself. For a moment, they sat facing the valley, shoulder to shoulder without touching. He drank. She drank.

"Do you think that everything—" He cast her a sidelong glance. "That our night together was me serving you?"

She almost spit out the tea.

He hid a smile as she sputtered. She deserved some punishment for tormenting him. For the long nights he slept on the cold ground while she lay hidden away, so temptingly close.

She looked around in desperation as she recovered. "So how good are you with that?"

He followed her gaze to the saddle packs and extracted his bow. "Better than any of your Han archers."

She raised a questioning eyebrow. "Teach me, then."

He laughed.

"Don't Khitan women know how to ride and shoot?" she asked.

"Some, but…"

An-Ming set her teacup aside and held out her hand for the bow. "Teach me."

"You are not strong enough to bend this one."

"Come now. I'm not as soft as you think."

Indeed she wasn't, but she was soft in all the right places. Gamely he handed the bow over. It was fashioned from wood and sheep's horn and designed to be fired from horseback.

He stood when she stood, taking a moment to position her with his hands on her shoulders.

"You're taking liberties now that I'm no longer royalty," she accused, shrugging out of his grasp.

"You asked for the lesson, my false princess."

She made a face at him that he doubted he'd ever see on a princess. As he predicted, An-Ming was unable to make any progress pulling at the draw-string. She returned the bow after a few attempts.

"Can you hit that tree over there?" she challenged.

There was a poplar tree a good distance away. This sort of game was commonplace to any boy growing up on the steppe. Suddenly he found himself in the mood for bravado. He stood laconically and aligned himself with the target.

"The first branch on the left," she identified.

Kwan-Li nocked an arrow against the drawstring and took his time sighting the target. "If I hit it, you spend the night with me."

An-Ming made a choking sound as he released. The arrow flew true, but continued past the tree to land in the grass beyond.

"You missed," she said after exactly three heart-beats, her voice faint.

"I didn't."

She gave him a doubtful look. He returned it with some arrogance. Together, they walked toward the tree with purpose. The bark on the under-side of the branch had been grazed away. An-Ming touched her fingertips lightly to the pale telltale mark before turning on him.

"I never agreed on the terms," she protested.

"Another target, then?" he suggested, enjoying

himself more than he had in years. His gaze moved up to a dark shadow in the sky. "I can hit that eagle, if you wish."

He started to take aim without any true intention behind it. An-Ming grabbed his arm with a look of exasperation. "Scoundrel."

She turned on her heel and strode away, leaving him to admire the sway of her hips. The wager remained enticingly unresolved. He looked back up to the skies, tracking the flight of the golden eagle over the valley. He was glad to spare the creature. He felt a kinship to it at that moment as it soared high above its domain.

He felt boastful around An-Ming today. He wasn't the barbarian struggling to be a gentleman in a foreign city any longer, but he wasn't a youth learning the ways of the steppe either. He had come home and An-Ming was inextricably part of that journey.

There was little conversation for the rest of the day. When evening neared, they stopped and followed the usual routine: tying down the horses, the fire, the tent, a simple meal of ground tea brick and millet.

His princess who wasn't a princess then retired into her tent without even the generosity of a single kind word for him. He grinned and let the first stars appear over the horizon before going to her.

She lay on the rug inside with a blanket draped over her. Her eyes were open. They glittered in the darkness.

Without a word, they were in each other's arms. Clothing was only a momentary distraction. They unfastened just enough for skin to find skin. An-Ming wove her fingers into his hair to pull him to her. He liked it when she was demanding. He liked her any way at all.

He laid himself down and pulled her on top of him. She made a startled sound, but the confusion didn't last. She braced her palm against his chest as she straddled his thighs. Her hair tickled against his throat. His hands circled her waist, angling her just so. With just a lowering of her hips and an upward thrust of his, he was inside her, sliding into sultry heat.

This was good. Very, very good. Soon they were both shuddering, lost in each other.

An-Ming melted onto him afterward, her curves molding perfectly to his body. She hid her face against his shoulder.

"I must still marry the khagan," she said, tormented.

"You don't have to."

She shook her head, refusing to look at him. She was determined to bear this burden and nothing could convince her otherwise. Nothing that could be said with words. He rolled her beneath him and hushed her, kissing her forehead, the tip of her nose, then her lips. The sort of kisses a long-time lover would bestow. She responded to him so sweetly. She wanted to be hushed.

"What is your name?" he asked when they broke apart to catch a breath. "Your real name."

"Dao."

"Dao." He said it to test the feel of it on his tongue.

"But I prefer An-Ming," she insisted. "It's so much grander."

"Dao suits you." His lips made a trail down to her shoulder. "Like a sweet, ripe—" he curled his palm over the lush shape of her breast "—summer peach."

He nipped at the soft underside of it and she gasped.

"Scoundrel."

"Why this new name for me suddenly?"

"Because a man changes after he has a woman," she accused.

"How would you know? You haven't had any men before me."

"How do *you* know?" she challenged.

"I know."

She had called him her first lover. First. She had already decided there would be another. He was like any man with his share of jealousy. He countered it by positioning himself between her knees and easing his length into her again. Her breath caught and she made a soft, startled sound as her body accepted him that told him all he needed to know. That she was his.

A man did change. He became ensnared, bewitched. A handful of days without her and his body had become impatient and greedy. He sank fully into her sooner than he meant to. His hips lifted and pushed forward slowly. He closed his eyes and rested his forehead against hers. Her breath grazed his cheek. Her nails dug into his shoulder as she throbbed around him.

"This is the last time we'll be together," she said once they had stilled.

Her tone was heavy, resolved. Sad. She ran her fingers lightly over his face, tracing the lines of it as if she were etching a picture of him in her mind. He tried to kiss her fingertips as they skimmed past, but the touch was too fleeting to catch.

He couldn't reassure her when he wasn't certain himself what would happen. Instead he hushed her again. His kiss was tender this time, trying to reach past her stubborn head into her heart. To the part that, for all her outward fierceness, was still abandoned and afraid.

He dreamed of more nights like this. Days, as well, until the end of time. He had dreamed about turning the horses and riding west. Or even south back to the cities of the Tang Empire. Any place where he wouldn't have to give her up. But running away would mean exile and isolation and that wasn't what he wanted. Not for Dao or for himself.

Chapter Seven

A cluster of yurts came into view in the distance. As they approached, more dwellings appeared. This settlement was four times the size of the one Dao had visited in the southern region. A patrol of armed horsemen rode out to greet them. The men dismounted and bowed to Kwan-Li. One after another, they clasped his arms in greeting as if long lost brothers while she looked on in confusion. After the exchange, the riders climbed back into the saddle to escort them. With each step, she could feel Kwan-Li slipping further away.

Her entire purpose for coming to Khitan was to become an alliance bride. There was no place on this earth where they could be together. She couldn't spend their last moments in regret.

At the border of the camp, Kwan-Li instructed her to dismount and reached out to steady her as she lowered herself to the ground. Dao took his hand, but he held on long after she had her footing. His fingers tightened over hers and he gave her a look so intense that her heart was in her throat.

"Is this proper?" she whispered. She had to be a princess again.

His only answer was a half smile before he let go.

Ruan came out to meet them. His grizzled face broke into a grin as he clasped Kwan-Li's arms in greeting. The grin faded as he looked from Kwan-Li to Dao.

"Princess," he said, with more seriousness than usual.

She looked about worriedly. "What of the others?"

She didn't see the other tribesmen who had ridden with them, but Ruan laughed. "Good. Strong. We Khitans are tough," he boasted.

Ruan switched to his native tongue to speak to Kwan-Li. The two men conferred briefly before Ruan left them.

"The Uyghur delegation is here," Kwan-Li reported to her. "They arrived a few days ago. We are going to see the khagan now."

His expression had become as guarded as it had been at the beginning of their journey when they had been strangers to each other. The sight of it sent a stab of panic through her. She wanted Kwan-Li back.

They walked toward the center of the camp. With each step, her stomach twisted. By the time she saw the large canvas tent surrounded by banners, she was so tangled up she couldn't remember the greeting she had rehearsed. The speech had sounded so stately and grandiose a few months ago.

Dao had filled her head with ideas that this would be easy. She would be covered in jade and gold and no one would ever know that she was nothing but a floor sweeper. For the first time, she lamented that her ridiculously lavish procession had been left behind.

"Do I look like a princess?" she whispered frantically.

Kwan-Li's gaze traced over her face. "Always."

She didn't feel like a princess. She was covered in dust and her hair was wind-battered and uncombed. They paused at the threshold of the yurt. The entrance flaps had been pulled wide and several grim-faced guards stood at the opening.

"Do you truly want to marry the khagan?" Kwan-Li asked softly.

"It doesn't matter what I want."

She wanted to be back in the endlessness of the steppe. With him.

As they entered the yurt, she could feel the circular wall enclosing her and trapping her. Each breath was forced and her tongue grew thick and useless. Her feet sank to the floor like lead.

The structure was large enough to encompass an assembly of thirty men, but there was only an elderly man inside flanked by two advisers. The khagan was seated upon an intricately woven rug. His headdress was decorated with several silver fox tails.

This was the man she was here to marry. His complexion was swarthy from a lifetime in the sun. There were crinkles at the corners of his eyes and creases around his mouth, but he wasn't as fearsome or as old as she had thought.

She knelt at the edge of the rug facing him. Kwan-Li lowered himself between them to translate the conversation. The khagan was honored she had come. She was honored to be there. His land was vast and plentiful. Her empire was the greatest under the sun. How fortunate that the khagan would be blessed with two brides.

"Two brides?" Dao ranted.

"The khagan has already given his word that the Uyghur princess will be his first wife," Kwan-Li explained gravely.

"Tell him he can't catch fish with both hands!"

"I cannot tell him that."

The khagan was looking at them with interest. Dao swallowed her retort. All their struggle and the khagan didn't want to marry her. She knew what happened to secondary wives. They were used, cast aside, ignored. Apparently it was the same for servant girls or princesses. A woman's fate was decided by her husband.

"The khagan assures the princess that she will be treasured. That she will be given a position of respect which is her due—"

"In his harem." Her blood boiled. "This is an insult."

Kwan-Li's eyes danced with light as he pressed his mouth tight. Was he trying not to laugh? Her future depended on this!

She wasn't an underling anymore. She had power. For all they knew, she was a princess. A princess from the most powerful empire in the world.

"Tell him—" Dao grasped at the right words. How would An-Ming react? "Tell him he's an old lecherous goat!" she raged.

The khagan's eyes shot wide. Kwan-Li made a choking noise.

"Tell him I won't have this," she told Kwan-Li. "That the Emperor will be angry. That *I* am angry."

It seemed Kwan-Li was spending his energy trying to calm her down rather than serve as interpreter. That upset her even more.

"I was shot at," she complained directly to the khagan. "With arrows."

The khagan said something to Kwan-Li in response, which she had to wait impatiently for him to relay to her.

"The khagan says he thought Han princesses were supposed to be elegant and graceful."

"You *are* laughing," she accused.

Kwan-Li's gaze was warm. He all but caressed her with his eyes, making her heart flutter. She tried very hard to ignore it.

How could Kwan-Li be so calm? His demeanor was impenetrable.

"You tell him the Emperor's niece is no lowly concubine," she demanded. "Tell him now."

Kwan-Li turned to the khagan and spoke with a sense of authority. Apparently he was well-spoken in any language. Whatever he was saying, it must have been very good because the khagan was nodding. Then a messenger came in. Whatever he had to say sent the two advisers into a whirlwind of chatter.

"What is it?" she asked beneath her breath. It was so difficult not being able to understand anything.

"The Uyghur princess is now outside demanding an audience," Kwan-Li informed her.

"Tell him that if he marries her, I will take his fastest horse and ride back home."

The khagan looked like he would rather be on his fastest horse, riding headlong into battle.

Kwan-Li presented the khagan with a stream of words that she was certain contained much more than a translation of her threat. The khagan made a weary gesture toward them at the end of the exchange. He appeared to have aged a few years.

Kwan-Li stood and ushered her to the side of the yurt. "The khagan has given me leave to explain the situation to the princess. I have proposed a compromise."

"What compromise?"

"Another peace marriage. Not to the khagan, but to the Yelu chieftain's son."

"He wants to appease me with a marriage of inferior status—" She stopped as Kwan-Li's eyes darkened. The earth shifted beneath her feet before settling again. "You're the Yelu chieftain's son."

The pieces all came together. Kwan-Li would have to be a very valuable hostage to be sent to the imperial court to ensure peace. Despite his courteousness, he'd never acted like an underling. Throughout the entire journey, he had commanded everyone around them. The Khitans had deferred to him, but Dao assumed it was his affiliation with the Tang imperial court that gave him status. She, like all others in the Tang Empire, assumed the sun rose and set on their kingdom. She was a fool.

"You are blushing, Princess."

She was more than blushing. Her face was on fire. Her mortification knew no bounds. When it came to diplomacy and politics, she was an ignorant peasant and he was practically a prince.

"But the alliance—"

Kwan-Li lowered his voice. "When you revealed you weren't truly a princess, I realized how little the Emperor must value this alliance. As you can see here, it is also obvious the khagan would rather uphold relations with the Uyghurs than the Tang Empire."

"So no one wants this marriage?" she asked skeptically.

"Apparently not, but no one can admit this. It would cause ill will."

She made a face that was certainly not princess-like. "Diplomacy is complicated."

"I did spend twelve years in the imperial court learning about it." Kwan-Li smiled and she felt herself warm all the way down to her toes. He leaned close and his voice dropped low. "So I must ask again, what do you want, Princess? Will you accept an inferior marriage?"

His frown deepened as he waited for her reply. He looked so serious.

"If I must," Dao replied. It was very, very difficult not to smile.

The khagan let out a sigh of relief when he heard the response. "Let this be done quickly," he declared in roughly accented Han.

Kwan-Li held his hand to the small of her back as they were ushered outside.

"For a moment, you looked worried in there." It was the first time she'd seen any break in his confidence, now that she thought of it.

"I spoke of politics and diplomacy, but the one thing I could not negotiate for was your heart." He regarded her with an earnestness that touched her deeply. "You have always been so adamant about what you wanted, but I could never be certain whether you wanted me."

Her throat tightened. Kwan-Li had given her the choice. Her. A lowly servant who was a lowly servant no more.

"I do," she told him. "More than all the gold in the empire. But what would you have done if I had refused?"

"How cruel to even ask such a thing." Kwan-Li

straightened and glanced down at her. He was quite handsome when affronted. "I have been your slave ever since you insisted on falling off that horse."

Her chest swelled with so much feeling that it was wonderful and painful all at once. She had loved him from the moment they stood together by the bonfire that very same night. She had been surrounded by strange music in a foreign land full of mystery, but she knew she would be safe as long as Kwan-Li was with her.

She reached out to him, lacing her fingers through his. "Once we're married, will you still call me 'Princess'?"

The corner of his mouth lifted. "Always."

* * * * *

CAPTURING THE
SILKEN THIEF

Special thanks to Stephanie Draven and Amanda Berry for lending their keen and critical eyes to this story on such short notice.

Author Note

Capturing the Silken Thief was inspired, surprisingly, by my time as a student at the University of California, Los Angeles. Everyone was filled with such hope for the future and all things were possible.

The many late nights and that restless energy of those college years fed into my vision of what the North Hamlet in Changan—the setting of *The Lotus Palace*—must have been like during the ninth century. Scholars and beautiful courtesans and song girls intermingled. The drinking and music would continue late into the night.

One of the most popular short stories of the Tang Dynasty tells of a romance between a scholar and a song girl. *Capturing the Silken Thief* revives this classic pairing, and it was a refreshing change for me to write a different sort of hero from my usual swordsmen. I hope you'll find this distant land and the characters that inhabit it not as foreign as they at first appear to be.

Chapter One

Tang Dynasty China, 823 AD

Luo Cheng turned his back on the chorus of cries and the rosy glow of the lanterns that swung over the doorway of the drinking house. The entreaties from his fellow scholars were well-meaning enough, but the pleas to stay and be sociable quickly died away, fading behind gales of laughter and carousing.

How did his fellow scholars manage to stay out drinking all night, every night, and hope to pass the imperial exams? He'd woken up with his face pressed into the pages of a book for three days now, after having fallen asleep in the middle of another treatise on statesmanship and duty. And heaven knows, there were many. The empire had an abundance of paper and these politicians were intent on writing on all of it.

At twenty-five years, Cheng was no longer the young prodigy that the local magistrate had boasted about to his exalted peers. Any man, no matter how humble his birth, could become a ranking official by proving himself in the civil exams. The hopes of his entire county had been behind him when he'd passed the provincial test three years ago. He had journeyed in triumph to the capital only to fail at the imperial level. If he failed again, Cheng would not only lose face, he'd have to lose several body parts to repay Minister Lo for sponsoring him.

He slung the sack of books over his shoulder and headed toward the southern gate of the ward. A soft, feminine voice floated from the pavilion doors at the end of the street. The words of the song rose over the plucked notes of a stringed pipa. The lute-like instrument had become one of the most popular in the drinking houses.

The light of the last lantern slipped by him as he ventured toward the edges of the pleasure district. His apartment was located in a quiet corner of the ward, through winding streets. The pavilions with their retinue of entertainers had sprouted up around the student centres of the city. The two populations fed on each other: the scholars with their cash and nights of leisure, the courtesans with their enchanting smiles and soft, scented skin.

It was only after he passed the third corner that he realized a group on the other side of the street had been following him. He glanced briefly in their direction before turning away. They didn't look like scholars, but they didn't look like street thugs either.

The footsteps quickened behind him. Cheng tightened his grip on his knapsack and turned to see five black shapes converging on him like a pack of rats. There was no getting out of it now. He swung his pack hard at the head of the gang. The weight hit the leader square across the face and the scoundrel fell back with a grunt.

Damned fools were attacking the poorest student in the district.

Cheng punched the next one in the nose. There was some advantage to being a country boy. The imperial capital had educated him in custom and civility, but he still knew how to handle himself in a brawl.

"Give us the bag." A sharp-nosed fellow hedged back as he issued the demand.

"Dog-born bastards," Cheng spat.

They lunged for him once again.

Someone threw an arm around his neck. Cheng

wheezed as the weight pressed against his wind-pipe. He was going to get knifed right there for a couple of history books and three copper coins.

With a roar, he threw the one clinging to him over his shoulder. Suddenly his left eye exploded with pain and he staggered back, cursing from the blow.

"Let's go," one of them shouted.

The footsteps scrambled away as the pain rang in his skull. Blinking furiously into the darkness, Cheng spat out a few insults involving pack animals and body parts.

By the time he could see again, the alleyway was clear. Music continued to flow from the entertainment district behind him as he searched the ground for his satchel. Gone.

The books that Master Wen had lent to him. The essay on statesmanship that he needed to submit before taking the imperial exams. The last of his luck.

Gone. Gone. Gone.

He considered having a drink. A strong one. But his three coins weren't enough to buy a flask of wine or the courtesan to pour it for him in this part of the city. Cheng pressed a hand to his eye. The area around it throbbed dully as he trudged back to his apartment.

It was five days until the imperial exams. That commentary had taken him over a week to compose the first time. He had better start writing.

Jia checked the desk, the cabinet, the little tight corners behind the bed. She'd been crawling around on her hands and knees, searching for clever hiding spots, too nervous to light even a tiny oil lamp.

The room was square and tidy, with a scant few personal belongings packed away in the wooden trunk. She flipped through a book she found at the bottom, squinting to stare at the characters. It wasn't what she was looking for. The scholar must have kept the journal with him after snatching it. She set the lid back down and turned to slip out, when the door rattled.

Death and destruction, he wasn't supposed to return yet!

Her gaze darted left and right, frantically searching for a place to hide. She'd run her hands over the entire apartment. It was as sparse as a monk's cell.

She could run. Just bolt right by him once the door opened and hope she startled him enough that he wouldn't call for the city guards.

That plan stalled the moment the door swung wide. The hapless scholar stood there, blocking the entrance with the shoulder span of an ox. Jia went very still beside the bed as he kicked the door shut. The frame rattled with the force of it.

Maybe he was drunk and she could still run.

"What—who's there?" he demanded. His massive shape tensed in the darkness.

Her throat seized. He was bigger than the gossip had indicated and he was angry.

"Honourable sir," she began, affecting the courtesan's lilt she'd heard so many times. It was meant to soothe tempers and stroke egos. She was no good at it. "Your good friend thought you needed some companionship."

"Friend?"

He sounded clear-headed enough to not be drunk, which was unfortunate for her. She didn't know how she was going to get out of this.

"What friend?"

"Li," she blurted out.

He moved closer and seemed to be busying himself with something at the desk beside the far wall. She'd have to dart past him to reach the door. Taking a deep breath, she pushed away from the bed only to find him in front of her, now with a lamp flickering in his grasp. A pale yellow glow filled the chamber, encircling both of them.

His features were broad and square, not like the

pale-faced scholars she was accustomed to. His cheek appeared swollen below his left eye. He was too big, the room was too small, and, on her grave, now he had seen her.

"Li?" he scoffed. "Li hates me."

She spoke quickly. "Then I must be mistaken. This must be a joke. Farewell."

Her attempt to slip by was again thwarted when he leaned in close to look at her. There was nothing menacing about his manner, other than he was too close for her to breathe easy.

"What is your name?" he asked.

Name. She needed a name. Some fancy courtesan name. Flowers were always popular.

"Rose. Precious Rose." She winced. That was awful.

"Rose."

His gaze traced over her, and a spark of unmistakable interest lit in his eyes, but it was immediately banished with a frown. "Yes, a joke. They are all so very clever."

His tone indicated this wasn't the first of such pranks.

"I'm sorry," he continued. "I can't…I can't pay you."

Heat shot up her neck, rising to her cheeks before she could stammer out a reply. "Oh no, you don't have to pay." She realized how her meaning could be mistaken and blushed even more furiously. "No! I mean—"

He looked away, but not before his gaze flitted briefly over her. He raised a hand to scratch the side of his neck nervously. It was too late. She'd already seen his pupils darken with a flash of interest.

Insufferable bastard.

She was furious, embarrassed, then furious again, ignoring the fact that it was her ruse that had started it. He should have at least questioned her story. She wasn't dressed in the finest silk robes of the elite courtesans, but she hardly resembled one of the lowly tea house prostitutes. And certainly not one foolish enough to sneak into a man's private chamber uninvited. These scholars and their arrogance.

"You should go." He appeared more weary than arrogant as he stepped aside.

"I should go," she echoed, not quite understanding why she hadn't gone already. She started for the door, but then turned. "I've given you my name." Well, not quite. "What's yours?"

"Luo Cheng."

She watched as he turned his back to her to set the oil lamp on the desk. This one certainly wasn't built like the pampered scholars that came and went year after year through the academic halls of the capital. Curiosity took hold of her.

"Like the famous general," she ventured.

He regarded her with an odd look over his shoulder. "Yes, like the general," he sighed.

Indeed Cheng looked more suited to the imperial army than the civil exams. A quick scan confirmed that he'd returned empty-handed. Her cronies must have succeeded in stealing the book. She would return to her quarters, pay her troupe members, and receive the spoils.

Cheng had seated himself at the desk. He pulled out half an ink stick, then paused with the black stub in his hands.

"Miss…er… Rose?"

"Yes?" She was staring.

He wasn't so frightening in the light. In fact, he seemed somewhat earnest and vulnerable. From what little she'd heard of him, she'd expected a wastrel. The North Hamlet pavilions were filled with eager students and enough wine to fill the Great River that cut through the centre of the city. They would stay until their pockets were empty of cash, not even knowing if it was night or day outside the curtains of the drinking houses. Yet Cheng had come back to his chamber early and she didn't smell any liquor or perfume on him. He seemed ready to work, except for her intrusion.

"Do you need me to escort you home?" he asked uncertainly.

The model of politeness and chivalry, too. She suddenly felt guilty she'd had him robbed, but for all his manners, he was more a thief than she was. The book hadn't belonged to him. He'd taken it from the Lotus Pavilion.

Of course, it didn't belong to her either—but it did now! She'd paid for it, or at least she'd paid to get it. Paid dearly from her meager earnings in hopes that her gamble would be rewarded.

"Take care." She affected a bow as she retreated to the door. "Master Luo."

He was watching her from the desk as she closed the door. Finally free, Jia hurried from the court- yard and escaped onto the street. She followed the glimmer of the lanterns back to the heart of the district. Drinking houses and tea parlors lined ei- ther side of the street, marked by colourful ban- ners.

As a musician, she was accustomed to the com- ings and goings of the North Hamlet. Strangers arrived, became fast friends in an hour, and didn't remember a thing the next morning. You couldn't trust anyone in the entertainment district.

Cheng didn't know what a treasure he'd had in his grasp. Most likely he'd taken it as a souvenir after one drunken night in the Lotus Pavilion—though Jia was certain she'd never seen him there, or at any of her other performances, now that she thought of it.

She returned to the musicians' hall where her troupe stayed. A string of tattered yellow lanterns marked the front gate. The troupe was out in the open courtyard, sharing a jug of wine beneath the stars.

"Goddess of Beauty and Light!"

Jia affected a tigress snarl at them and they laughed. She supposed it was better than the other names they used to tease her. Grandmother. Hag. Spinster. She was not even twenty-four, but in the floating world of courtesans, she was becoming a relic.

Perhaps if she was better at smiling pleasantly and being coy, every coin wouldn't have been such a struggle. As it was, no one wanted to watch an aging pipa player when they could watch a young, pretty one. If she didn't gain her freedom soon, she could be turned out to the streets to beg by the time she reached thirty. Like most of the entertainers in the district, she owed her troupe leader for taking her in as a child and training her. Every mouthful of rice she'd ever been fed was accounted for and with each performance, he collected two coins to her one. The cash would continue to dwindle as time went by and the debt would keep growing. She could play her fingers raw every night for the next six years and never earn enough.

"Where's the book?" she demanded.

The flute player held a bloodstained cloth to his nose. "Your lover hits hard."

"He is not—" Jia exhaled slowly. They only did this because she always rewarded them by getting angry. "He is not my lover. The book. Now."

The men nudged each other, grinning and re-marking cheerfully about women scorned. The lot of them still insisted she'd paid to have the scholar robbed as an act of revenge. Let them spin their less than imaginative tales. She was getting out of here and would never have to look at their ugly faces again.

A fellow pipa player pulled out a bag from under his feet. "Here," he said, dangling the sack before her. "And don't forget, you owe us cash."

She counted out the coins from her purse and slapped them into his outstretched hand. In the same movement, she grabbed the pack.

Before she reached her door, she was already working at the knots. She'd missed out on a night's wages by passing up the chance to entertain at a court official's banquet. Another fifty in cash she'd given to the dogs in the courtyard for waylaying Cheng, but the journal was worth a hundred times that.

She slipped into her room and closed the door before loosening the last knot. Her hands shook with excitement as she lit the oil candle. There were several bound books in the pack. She flipped through the first one, searching for the precious lines of poetry that would signal her freedom.

It was a treatise on the history of the later Han dynasty. She cast the book aside and flipped through the smaller notebook. The cover was plain, with none of the adornment she'd expected.

She scanned through the pages, her chest growing tighter with each column of neat black characters. Page after page, backward then forward, the characters didn't change. There was no poetry there. No words of wit and genius worth thousands in cash. She could feel the coins slipping through her fingers like desert sand.

This was going to be the death of her. She was already headed to the afterlife. How had this gone so wrong?

She could storm back to the courtyard and demand her money back, but that would only get her ridiculed. Somehow this was the scholar's doing. Luo Cheng had what she wanted, and she was going to get it even if she had to search heaven above and earth below.

Chapter Two

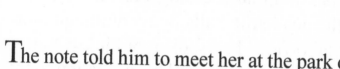

The note told him to meet her at the park on Longevity Street. It had to have been from the intriguing Rose. He could almost smell her perfume on the folded scrap of paper that had been tucked beneath his door.

The street was crowded with the midday traffic. It was the busiest lane in the ward, leading from the bustling East Market to cut through the heart of the North Hamlet. Cheng pushed past the basket-laden carts and street vendors toward the grey brick divider that bordered the park.

He had stayed up all night, grinding through an entire ink stick to try to recapture the words of that cursed essay. The examiners would accept such offerings of poetry and short writings, through a so-called "passing of scrolls," before the official exam as an informal introduction. With his uncultured upbringing, Cheng had failed to recognize such traditions during the previous examination period. He'd been completely overlooked as a no-body during the oral inquiry.

Most of the fresh-faced scholars who crowded the city wards had fathers and grandfathers of notable birth and name. They were practically assured a passing mark. Cheng was only allowed within the academic halls by recommendation. Their local official had spoken of him to Minister Lo, who'd then sponsored his excursion to the imperial capital for the exams. This was his last chance to rise above his birth and bring honour to his family and hometown. He would follow every rule and custom if that's what was required.

Yet the words wouldn't come, no matter how much he willed them to. He needed inspiration and it had sadly abandoned him. Rose had been the one bright glimmer in an otherwise dim evening. He paused to smooth a hand over the front of his tunic at the park entrance.

She was inside the gate, standing at the edge of the grass with her back to him. Unlike the previous night, she wore a long grey tunic over trousers. With those colours, she could almost disappear against the grey brick structures of the ward. It wasn't quite what he'd expected. Not that he knew what to expect, but he'd allowed himself a few whimsical fantasies.

"Rose!"

She didn't answer. Cheng had to call her name again. He was nearly upon her by the time she swung around, startled.

"You scared me," she accused.

"I was calling for you."

In the close quarters of his chamber, she'd seemed so tempting. In the sunlit park, she took on a different appeal. Her skin was pale and radiant, her lips unpainted. He'd been thinking of her face all night in between verses about civic duty. Rose was more intriguing than immediately noticeable as pretty. Her almond eyes seemed too large for her face and her chin narrowed to a point like a cat's.

Once again he was caught with his tongue stiff, his words tangled. "You sent me a message."

She glanced over her shoulder once before whipping those deep eyes back to him. "Have you been to the Lotus Pavilion?"

The pagoda stood high just beyond the line of shops. The green tiled roof made it an easily identifiable landmark of the district. At night, the eaves would be hung with a cascade of lanterns. Even in the drunkest of stupors, one could tell where he was by the pavilion's radiance.

"I can't afford to drink at the Lotus Pavilion," he said with a smirk. "Is that where you entertain?"

"Of course not," she snapped, with the same force of denial he'd affected. She waved her hand about for effect. "If I did work at the Lotus Pavilion, would I be out here? I would be sleeping off the night beneath silken covers."

The Lotus Pavilion employed the most sought-after courtesans and entertainers. Noblemen and ministers of the highest ranks hosted lavish gatherings there. Only the most fortunate of scholars were ever invited: ones with the right name or connections. Never him.

Rose shook her head, agitated. "What a mess."

"Is there trouble?"

"A mess," she muttered again, for dramatic effect. She fixed her hands on her hips, perplexed.

Cheng was quickly reminded of why he'd ventured there, despite the crumpled draft of his essay that he'd fed into the fire for warmth. He liked mysteries. He also liked her impossibly slender waist and the flare of her hips beneath it. She was much nicer to look at than a blank page.

She looked him up and down. "I don't understand. The description fit perfectly—tall, shoulders like an ox. Down to that prominent, jutting brow."

"Really?" His hand flew self-consciously to his forehead.

He was trying to discern whether the description was unflattering when Rose snatched his hand away. Her long, delicate fingers circled his wrist. They were the only thing delicate about her.

"There was a large banquet at the Lotus Pavilion a week ago," she said impatiently. "One of the attendees looked like you. Another scholar. Do you know him?"

Rose hadn't been searching for him last night at all. He couldn't help but be a bit disappointed. "What were you doing sneaking into a man's bedchamber, anyway?" he asked, leveling his gaze to hers.

She realized she was still holding on to him and let go abruptly. "He took something that belongs to me. Something valuable."

With an impatient huff, she turned away, staring at the narrow width of the park while dropping deep into her own thoughts. Something about her impetuousness fascinated him. She was bold, single-minded, and very much a riddle—like the ones hidden in lanterns for lovers to solve.

"So you're not a courtesan," he said.

She made a disgruntled sound in response that was answer enough, but he already sensed she wasn't one of the peach-blossom beauties that enchanted men to their chambers. Rose was a good name for her. She definitely had more than a few thorns to her.

Her gaze narrowed. "You're going to help me," she declared.

"What?"

"Yes." She straightened to square off against him, which still left her a head shorter. Still she had the look of a marauding barbarian. "I have your books."

"But those dogs in the alley—"

"I sent them."

"You?"

He was shocked more than outraged. His knuckles were scuffed from the fight. Her eyes flickered to his left cheek, the same spot where a bruise had formed. She flinched before glancing away. At least she felt some remorse.

"I should go to the city guards and have you arrested," he growled.

His threat brought her fire back. "I know every official in the district. And what evidence do you have? Another drunken student got himself mugged. The magistrate hears that story every day."

His retort died before it left his lips. The ward station had been less than helpful when he'd gone to them. They'd appeared bored, not even caring that his name had been marked down incorrectly in the report.

He tried to appeal to her sense of reason. "There's an essay in there that I need before the imperial exams."

"Then you have no choice but to help me."

He folded his arms over his chest. This woman was going to be the end of him. "What do you propose?"

"You find this other student and bring me what he stole from the Lotus Pavilion."

"And what is that?"

"A book."

"A book?"

"It's a very valuable book." She tucked her hands into her sleeves nervously. "A book of poetry."

Rose didn't strike him as a connoisseur of poems. There was something else there. A hint of desperation had crept into her expression. She tried to play as if she held something over him, but in truth she was the one in need.

"It's the personal journal of the courtesan Xue Lin," she continued.

"Xue Lin?"

The infamous courtesan was well known. Her poems had been presented within the imperial court to the Emperor himself.

"I have no interest in her exalted verses. Someone is offering a fortune for that book. Enough to pay my debts and be free of this place." She looked away, but he'd seen how her mouth grew tight. Her tone was thin, forced. "I could play the pipa until my hair turns grey and I wouldn't earn that much."

In profile, her fine bone structure appeared more delicate and vulnerable. It was as if he were seeing her again for the first time: the plain clothing, the slightness of her frame. She didn't have the soft, rounded curves of a well-fed courtesan or a pampered singsong girl. Rose earned her stay in the North Hamlet as a musician, coin by coin.

Perhaps her sharp, snappish nature worked on the people she consorted with. It made her formidable enough to be taken seriously, to have some measure of authority. She didn't have a courtesan's seductive ways, so she'd put on another layer of armour, warding people away with the fierceness of her scowl.

"The book doesn't really belong to you," he said.

"I have more right to it than that dog who took it from the Pavilion. I live here, grew up here. You scholars just come to drink and laugh until the cash runs out. And then you write home to rich fathers for more."

A moment of guilt washed over him. He'd considered writing to Minister Lo that morning to ask for more funds, but he couldn't bring himself to do it. He'd already failed the exams one time. If he didn't pass this time, it would be another three years before the exams would be administered again. Cheng would rather return home a no-name than ask for another chance. He'd work the fields for the rest of his life to repay the minister what he already owed.

All Rose wanted was a chance, as well. She wasn't so different from him.

"I knew you weren't a courtesan," he began. "When you were in my room you seemed so nervous."

The perfumed flowers of the evening didn't solicit men in their private apartments. Patrons came to the courtesans to worship. He had been drawn in by her awkwardness and her sincerity—though she'd been lying to him at the time.

"And also so uncultured," he added.

Her gaze narrowed menacingly. It was good to get the best of her for once.

"That's not to say you're lacking in grace—"

Rose's eyes flashed like a sleek tigress ready to lunge for his throat. He imagined her claws unsheathing beneath her manicured nails.

"Or charm." He grinned, decidedly unapologetic.

"For a scholar, you show a great talent for an improper choice of words." Her lower lip pouted fuller than her upper lip and he knew he was about to do something foolish.

"I do know the man you're looking for," he admitted.

"You do? Where is he?"

That got her interest. She was all mercenary, this Rose.

Zhang Guo was his height and build. Other than that, they were night and day. Guo was the son of a merchant who did lucrative business within the city. His father had money. His father had influence. Guo went on and on about it.

He couldn't let her try to sneak into Guo's chamber. A little musician could get her hands broken for stealing from someone with Guo's status. His words escaped before reason settled in.

"I'll have to show you."

* * *

She met Cheng in the courtyard outside his chambers that night. The moon was high and round, with that faint harvest gleam that marked it as a night for recitations of poetry. She'd come straight from her last performance with her pipa in hand. Cheng was waiting just inside the front gate which led into the courtyard. Three wings formed the walls of the enclosed space, with each wing containing a series of private apartments.

Hopeful scholars preparing for the exams stayed in courtyard houses such as these throughout the city, paying for the rooms by the month. Year after year, a new cycle of students came and went. Jia wondered what would happen to the imperial capital without the yearly crop of scholars to fill its drinking houses and tearooms.

Cheng's hands were folded behind his back as he gazed up at the sky contemplatively. What was it with scholars and the moon?

He must have heard her footsteps as he turned to her the moment she entered. With a long look, he took her in from head to toe. She was once again in full costume. Her robe was turquoise and embroidered with lilies along the seams and the silk flowed down her figure like a cascade of water.

Her hair was coiled and pinned, her lips stained with a shock of red.

"You look pretty tonight."

Men were so predictable. "You scholars with your honey-and-sugar words," she scoffed.

Cheng's crooked grin surprised her. "I haven't even begun to wield my poetry on you."

"Come on. I don't have much time," she snapped, but a small spiral of unexpected pleasure curled through her.

They had agreed to meet at the first hour, the Hour of the Rat, and though it was late into the night, it was early when it came to the nightly festivities in the district. She had been playing at a lakeside gathering for a minor official and she'd had to leave early, leaving all those precious coins behind. Maybe after tonight, it wouldn't matter.

"Where's my bag?" he asked.

"When I have Xue Lin's journal."

He shrugged and led her into the courtyard. She froze when he beckoned her behind the branches of a potted tree in the corner. What kind of mischief was he thinking of? Her grip tightened around the neck of the pipa. She'd hit him over the head with it if he even blinked at her wrong. Not that the instrument would stop a man of his size, and breaking it would add several hundred in debt onto her ledger.

"We're supposed to go get the book," she protested.

He stopped a respectable distance away. "Guo lives there." He pointed to a door across the courtyard. "You weren't too far away when you wandered into my chamber."

"Is he in there now?"

"At this time?" Cheng sneered. "Guo's evening is just beginning. He'll be gone for hours. Stay here."

"Wait." She grabbed on to his sleeve as he started toward the door. "You're going in there alone?"

"If I'm caught, I can always say I was drunk and wandered into the wrong room." His mouth twitched as his eyes met hers. "You would be more difficult to explain."

She could see the bruise over his cheek. It looked worse than it had that morning. He'd taken a decent blow to the face to earn that mark. Something didn't feel right about this. Why was Cheng so willing to help her?

"Keep watch for me," he said.

She sank back into the corner behind the shrubbery while Cheng moved across the courtyard. Within moments, he disappeared through the door. No locks in these quarters. They were so trusting.

Luo Cheng wasn't at all as she expected. There was something pure about him. His desk had been stacked with books and pamphlets. That morning, there had been dark circles beneath his eyes and his fingertips always held a faint stain of ink. While his colleagues drank the nights away, it was clear Cheng returned to his rooms each night to study.

She imagined his broad hand closing around a calligraphy brush. He wasn't born to be a scholar any more than she was born to be a musician, but she'd scrubbed floors and fetched and carried for years to be accepted into the troupe. At the same time, she'd trained on the pipa every moment in between. The only other prospect would have been on her back as a common drinking house whore. She didn't have the beauty, elegance, or breeding to be anything more.

She turned the instrument around and around in her hands nervously as she glanced from the courtyard gate to the door. It was clear Cheng had come from a place very different than these crowded streets. A place where a young man with all the prospects in the world would risk himself to help a stranger after she'd wronged him.

She'd wronged him. Her gaze stopped on the

door. No man save the Buddha himself would be so forgiving.

Jia swept through the garden, weaving around the shrubbery. How could she be so foolish? She'd made the mistake of telling Cheng how much the book was worth. She had to get to it before him.

She slipped into the room and found Cheng at the opposite end of the room with his back to her. He swung around, a scroll in hand. A single oil candle flickered from the edge of the desk.

"It will be quicker if we both search," she explained hastily.

He didn't look pleased with her decision, but he nodded toward the far wall. "Look inside that chest."

The wooden trunk stood beside a wardrobe. Whoever this Guo was, she could already tell his room was larger than Cheng's and more elaborately furnished. The candle provided a small halo of light at the opposite side of the room. Jia knelt and rummaged through the trunk, searching for anything that felt like a book. She even ran her hands along the edges and the bottom searching for secret compartments.

"Nothing," she reported.

"Nothing," Cheng echoed.

"Maybe he found out how valuable the book is.

It might be hidden inside something." She opened the wardrobe. "Bring that candle here."

Cheng held the flame up to illuminate the interior. Jia dug her hands through the layers of silk and linen inside. She became restlessly aware of his presence behind her as they both peered into the cabinet.

"He has a lot of clothes," she muttered in frustration.

"Guo's father is a textile merchant."

"He must have some status to drink at the Lotus Pavilion."

"Maybe Guo didn't take the book after all," he suggested.

There were thousands of students in the city. She couldn't investigate all of them. "It has to be him," she insisted, renewing her search.

Her pulse skipped as her arm brushed against his. Immediately her insides pulled tight. This sudden sharpening of her senses on him was entirely inconvenient.

"Is the book so important to you?" Cheng asked quietly.

"How important is it to control one's own future?" She turned her head to find him close. His arm was nearly around her as he held up the candle. He'd never understand. "There are no imperial exams for song girls," she said in a whisper.

He fell silent, scrutinizing her. A faint orb of light enclosed them like a secret embrace. Even in the darkness, she was afraid the glow would reveal too much. She dropped her gaze to the point just below his chin as her stomach fluttered.

She struggled with her next words. "Where else can we look?"

A voice rang out just beyond the door. Cheng tensed. She tensed.

"I can't believe you lost it all so early!"

"Quiet, you drunken dog."

Cheng blew out the candle and ushered her into the space between the bed and the wardrobe as the door rattled. He shut the cabinets and shoved himself into the tiny enclosure against her. Right against her.

Jia bit back a protest as she was pressed flat against the wall at one end and flush against a male torso at the other. The two men were inside, making as much noise as the lunar festival. She sucked in a breath and held it. She could feel the solid thump of Cheng's heartbeat against her cheek.

"Only a minor delay," one of the men was saying. He grunted laboriously and she thought she heard a scraping sound. His companion continued to crow about the good wine they were missing every moment they were away and the girl with the peach-shaped face that fancied him.

Heavens, she hated these types. A few drinks in them and they were higher than the Emperor himself.

She became acutely aware of Cheng once again. It was hard not to with her face pressed into the front of his robe. He smelled of sandalwood, earthen and mysterious. For a moment, the rest of the room disappeared. She shifted slightly, trying to find some position where she wasn't so over-whelmed. Finally she was able to breathe again, but somehow Cheng's hand ended up on her hip in their subtle movements.

She braced her arm against the solid mass of his chest. Cheng relented, or seemed to. His touch lifted from her hip but only to slide lazily to the curve of her waist. Tilting her head up, she caught the glint of his smile in the darkness. Demon.

"Shhh," Cheng hushed her.

Shoving against him did nothing. She glared at the stone tower in front of her. Her own heartbeat rose to rival his as they stood there, in darkness, pressed tight. They were still as statues, yet with every nerve alive and pulsing.

There had been lovers in the past. Not many, but

enough that she wasn't ignorant of a man's body and the contrast of masculine skin and muscle against her. This moment penetrated deeper than any of those encounters. She was fully clothed, standing upright, in a strange room, yet a sudden desire overwhelmed her. She could feel each rise of his chest. Hear each inhale and exhale. She was tempted to slip her fingers into the front of Cheng's robe and find out if his skin was as hot as she imagined. Or was it just her, burning like this?

It was the danger of being caught, she reasoned. That was why her mouth had gone dry and her knees soft. And she was certain her heart had never done this little lurch before. Cheng moved his hands around to the small of her back. He didn't look amused anymore. In fact, he was bent so close that she could no longer make out his expression. He was nothing but hard contours, heat, and pulse. His fingers tightened against her, urging her hips ever so slightly closer.

Another scraping sound brought her out of the haze.

"Let's go. Good wine is being poured without us," the voice declared.

They went still and waited as the two men departed. Their footsteps and voices receded into the night. Cheng was still pressed to her, his chest rising and falling steadily.

"Bastard!"

She shoved him away to the sound of his low laughter. Yet her skin was still flushed and tingling with anticipation. He let her go without a fight, which was oddly disappointing.

"There was something hidden here." Cheng moved to a spot in the centre of the room and slid his foot along the floor. "Bring the light."

He'd stowed the candle inside the wardrobe. Jia had to fumble around to reach it. She brought it to him and it took several moments for Cheng to strike the flint to light it. He handed the candle back to her. Together they knelt to examine the floorboards.

Cheng tested the boards with his hands, tapping against the surface to listen to the echo. One of them appeared loose and he wedged his fingertips beneath it to lift it away. Jia crowded close until they were shoulder to shoulder. Her breath caught as she peered into the hollow below.

The candlelight flickered over strings of cash and other papers. Nestled near the top was a journal with a jade-green cover. An elegant inscription graced the front: *Thoughts from a thousand evenings.*

She reached for the book and Cheng did the same. Their hands collided, but Cheng was faster. He plucked the book from its hiding place and she was left to trail after him as he stood.

"Give it back," she demanded.

"I'm just looking to see if this is it."

She wasn't accepting any explanations. Xue Lin's precious poetry was within her grasp. The stubborn ox of a man tried to turn his back to her, but she lunged for the book.

"Careful! Don't tear it," he protested.

He took hold of her wrists as she tried to grab at the journal. It dropped to the floor in their wrestling bout.

The pages fell open before them. Jia stopped struggling. Beside her, Cheng's grasp slackened and his hands fell away. She stared at the brushwork, cocked her head, leaned closer. The candle holder had been abandoned on the floor and the halo of light now encompassed the book.

The same elegant script danced over the entire page on the left side, but that wasn't what caught her attention. A drawing of a young woman reclined on the right-hand page. Her head was thrown back, eyes closed. Her robe fell open in front to reveal the tantalizing curve of her breast. A lover in scholar's robes leaned over her.

Jia knelt before the journal. The boards creaked as Cheng lowered himself beside her. She reached out and righted the pages so she no longer had to stare sideways.

The signs of desire, the inscription read. *As desire heightens, her nipples grow hard. Sweat forms upon her brow. She is ready to take a lover inside her.* The woman's nipples were exposed and tipped in pink. Her lover was poised to enter her as the lines instructed.

Jia swallowed forcibly. Apparently Xue Lin was not only a poet, but an artist, as well. An accomplished artist. Jia could sense the flush of the woman's skin and the tension of her limbs. Entranced, she turned the page.

Soon her mouth goes dry, all words stolen and sound lost. Her lover can move deeply within her as the pleasure rises. Her own throat went dry and she ran her tongue absently over the back of her teeth. It was a book of chamber technique. The woman's back arched and her eyes closed with desire. Her lips were open and inviting. The scholar's gaze was fixed intently on her. Jia felt her skin flushing at the sensuality of the image. Her body grew damp down below.

A shadow fell over the page. Cheng let out a slow exhalation of breath. She'd almost forgotten he was there. She turned her head slightly to find him staring at the painting, his gaze intent. Then he turned to her to focus all that intensity on her. She was lost.

His arm circled her waist and fitted his palm to the small of her back to guide her body against his. They were still kneeling when his mouth closed over hers.

The hardness of the floor dissipated. The awkwardness of the position was forgotten as he angled her until they were hip to hip, her breasts pressed tight against his chest. His tongue took her in a slow, gentle exploration. His breath became her breath and her knees collapsed. He caught her in both arms. His mouth released her for a precarious second.

"It's the book," she gasped.

His gaze locked onto hers, piercing deep into her until she could feel it as sure as his touch. "It's not the book," he muttered, before he was kissing her again.

He was wonderfully rough about the kissing. Her nipples rose to painful sensitivity against her silk bodice. She wanted his hands over her breasts like the lover in the picture. Only his touch could ease this yearning. Nothing else would serve. Her arms curved about his neck to pull him even closer. At any moment, Cheng was going to lower her completely to the floor. To her shock, Jia realized she wanted him to.

She tore away. "We need to go."

She tried to reach for the courtesan's journal, but Cheng flattened his hand over the pages in a commanding gesture to pin the book in place.

His voice stroked over her, low and sensual. "You're not entirely indifferent to me."

"Not entirely," she replied wickedly.

No use in denying it when she was flushed and breathless. She was still kneeling on the floor, looking up at him. He was breathing hard, his chest heaving. The bruise she'd inadvertently caused marred his cheek. It lent him a dangerous appeal.

"Come back to my room," he said simply.

His eyes smouldered with heat. He'd direct all of that focus into making love to her. The sureness of his touch promised that much. Untold pleasure. They could read through the pillow book together, page by page. She had a feeling Cheng would be an exquisite lover, a careful student. She was so very tempted, but this wasn't freedom. Desire had clouded her mind and weakened her. This was surrender.

She rose and took his face in her hands with renewed purpose. She traced her fingertips along the firm line of his jaw and pressed her lips to his, exploring gently until his eyes closed. With a groan, his arms wrapped around her. There was something both comforting and arousing in his embrace. She let herself linger in it, taking her time to run her fingers down over his chest, lower to his abdomen. He shuddered as her hand trailed gradually lower…to the journal on the floor, which she snatched up and tucked securely behind her back.

His mouth left hers to curve into a smile. The candlelight glittered in his eyes. "Clever."

She lifted her chin to him in triumph. "Of course."

"I like crafty women."

His touch remained lightly possessive over her hips. He was unassailable.

"The book is mine," she declared. "I'm going now."

She slipped away from him and was almost disappointed that he didn't pursue her. She had to unfold herself from the floor and smooth her robe back in place. It wasn't until she reached the door that Cheng spoke. His reply came in a low rumble that warmed her skin.

"But you'll come back," he said.

She didn't turn. She tried not to pause, but she could feel his eyes on her as she slipped out of the room and into the night.

Chapter Three

Jia took a sedan to the next ward over early the next morning. The minister's residence was located in a quiet neighbourhood, separated from the main avenues of commerce. He was a minor official, which still meant his mansion engulfed the musicians' quarters in size.

The servants politely asked her to wait in the garden. Peony trees grew within his courtyard, carefully tended by more than one caretaker. A small pond filled with golden carp graced one corner. She stood listening to the trickle of flowing water in her best evening gown with her hands clasped about the pillow book. In the tranquil setting, the bright robe made her feel like a squawking parrot.

An attendant came to let her know that the master of the house would see her and she was led through the courtyard to a study. An elderly gentleman waited behind a great wooden desk. He stood to greet her and beckoned her into a seat across from him. Jia smoothed her skirt over her knees and stared at the grand bookshelf behind the minister as he called for tea.

This was a lower-ranking minister. Someone who had likely passed the imperial exams in the third ranking. Yet he lived in a state of opulence that she could only imagine. This was the sort of life Cheng would have once he passed the exams. A passing mark immediately earned respect and opportunity.

"So you're a musician, young miss?"

She jumped when he addressed her. "Yes, honourable sir."

"And what do you play?" He was looking at her pleasantly, courteous in the way of the elite.

"The pipa, sir."

She felt small beside the minister, though he wasn't a man of great stature. His hair was graying and there were wrinkles at the corners of his eyes that spoke of general good humour.

"Ah, the accomplished Xue Lin played the pipa beautifully," he said. "Did you know her?"

"No, sir."

"She was so very talented."

Jia had played before audiences of noblemen and officials, but being here in this man's house seemed as foreign to her as the desert frontier of the Taklimakan. She was afraid to touch anything for fear of breaking it. Her hands tightened on the book.

"Is that it?" The minister's eyes grew bright as he spied the green cover.

She slid the book across the desk, but he didn't open it. Instead, the minister placed his hand reverently over the cover, touching it with just the very tips of his fingers. After a pause, he finally looked inside. A painting of an orchid greeted him. The vibrant lushness of the petals evoked a sense of the feminine and erotic.

Jia squirmed in her seat. She had read through the entire book while she lay in her bed last night. The words had caressed her to sleep, the gentle scholar lover's face replaced with Luo Cheng's broad and masculine features. For a moment, she'd considered keeping the book for herself a little longer. It was so beautiful and full of secrets. The words filled her with the elusive thrill of desire.

But that was just foolish sentiment. Money was money.

She looked away as the minister continued to browse through the pillow book. It wasn't the explicitness of the pictures that embarrassed her now.

It was the longing upon the scholar's face which grew deeper with each page.

He had known the famous courtesan, Jia was certain of it. He must have been one of her many patrons or even a lover. Xue Lin had left the entertainment district to become Governor Wei's hostess. Was the minister not rich enough or powerful enough to keep her to himself?

Jia couldn't help but feel that she was intruding on a very personal moment. There was too much ceremony involved for what should have been a simple business transaction, but she didn't want to seem a beggar by demanding money.

"My beloved."

He spoke the phrase under his breath, sighing softly with the last tone. He closed the book and once again rested his leathered hand over it, as if the spirit inside the words could run up through his veins and return to him what he'd lost.

Finally he reached for a wooden box and pulled out a sheet of rice paper covered in writing. He lifted his jade chop and used it to stamp his mark on it in red ink. The thud of the seal rang with a finality that sent shivers down her spine. *Freedom.*

"Thank you," he said with an unsettling sincerity.

She took the paper with as much grace as she

could. Her hands were nearly shaking as she folded it away. She had never held a bank note before. The amount was so high that it would have been awkward to carry as strings of cash.

The streets blurred around her as she rode back to her ward in the sedan. She should be floating. She could pay off her debts now and belonged to no one but herself. Instead, she wandered aimlessly back to her quarters, thinking of the sadness of the minister's expression. All he had to remind him of Xue Lin were her words. Ink on paper. It seemed so empty and fragile.

When evening came, Jia prepared herself to perform as she did every night. There were no banquets or performances scheduled that evening. She'd have to work the drinking houses. Music and poetry were as much a requisite part of the revelry as wine and food.

She emerged onto the street with hair combed and pinned, lips painted, pipa in hand. Halfway to her favourite drinking house, she realized she didn't have to do anything. Of course, she still had obligations. Freedom meant she'd have to earn her own way. Otherwise, it would be too easy to fall back into debt and servitude.

But tonight was her first night of freedom. She should do something to celebrate. Something extravagant. Maybe she'd go to the finest restaurant in the ward and order the most expensive dish they served. Or she could purchase that jade hairpin she'd looked at twice at the jeweler's.

Instead she found herself standing before Cheng's doorstep, holding his satchel of books. The weight of them reminded her of the differences between their stations in society.

Her pulse skipped as Cheng opened the door.

"Rose." He greeted her with a slow grin. Her toes curled within her slippers at the sound of his voice. No good could come of this.

"These are yours," she said curtly.

She should shove them into his hands and go, but she'd stayed awake half the night thinking of him. Seeing him only brought back how many times he'd undressed her in her mind, all the places she'd let him explore with his lips.

Those lips were smiling at her now. "Come inside," he invited.

She hid her gaze from him as she ducked past. They didn't touch, but it was close enough for her body to remember him. The silk of her robe whispered against her skin as she went to his desk. The weight of his stare followed her.

"You're quiet today," Cheng teased. "The sun

must be rising in the west." The jest hung awkwardly on silence.

Turning her back to him, she settled the pack on the desk with more care than necessary. "Today was a very busy day." She ran a finger absently along a scratch in the wood. "So much to do."

"Indeed. How was your business transaction?"

"Very profitable." She turned and straightened, her hands gripping the desk behind her. "I'm a wealthy woman now."

What was this heaviness in her chest that wouldn't leave her? The weight only increased as she looked at Cheng. She could pretend that he thought of her as something more than a song girl and a servant to rich patrons.

"Then we both have reasons to celebrate," he said.

"You seem in good spirits."

He couldn't hold back. "I presented my writings to the head examiner today. He invited me to sit down for tea and we had a good discussion."

"You presented the essay today?"

"The imperial exams begin tomorrow, after all."

She'd entirely forgotten. She looked to the satchel that contained the precious essay she'd held hostage. "What trouble I must have caused you."

He shrugged, in too good spirits to be cross.

"I rewrote every word and every word was better, bolder. Something must have inspired me." He gave her a pointed look and her skin flushed.

"So you didn't need your books back after all," she said.

"Of course I did. How else would I see you again?"

He held no ill will toward her. For every taunt and attack she flung at him, Cheng deflected and smiled. She couldn't wound him or push him away. He was impervious.

Fear took hold of her. They were more than opposite. Cheng was generous, industrious and sincere. He was meant for greater things.

"Take care, then, Luo Cheng," she said. "I know you'll do well tomorrow."

"Wait."

He blocked her in one smooth motion as she turned to the door. It wasn't difficult considering the size of the chamber.

"I bought wine," he said. "To celebrate. *Xifeng* wine. I had to haggle with the merchant for nearly an hour, so you have to drink it with me."

She laughed. It had been a long time since she laughed. What did she have to fear? For the first time in her life she could choose what she'd do next. Cheng watched her intently. She reached out her hand and rested it against him. Only her fingertips grazed his chest.

Like all of the scholars that streamed in and out of the city, Cheng would be gone soon from the shifting world of the North Hamlet. The same world she wanted to leave behind. They were walking the same path for this one moment in time only. She didn't want to be grey and withered, holding on to a remnant of a memory she'd never pursued.

Her fingers curled into the front of Cheng's tunic to draw him closer. She hadn't really thought him handsome at first. His features were unrefined and rugged, yet in his eyes she could see a depth of humor and a sincerity that compelled her.

"How much did you pay for that wine?" she asked.

His mouth was close. Heated breath caressed her lips when he spoke. "Three coppers. All I had left."

His gaze darkened with the same hunger she'd seen the night before. The same hunger had plagued her all day.

"You made a good bargain," she murmured.

Cheng took her mouth. She let him.

Xue Lin was mistaken about the signs of desire in her pillow book. They all happened at once. Heart pounding, beads of perspiration, throat parched. Heat, so much heat, inside and out.

The room blurred in a swirl of light as her feet left the floor and Cheng swung her into his arms. He set her on the bed, his eyes on her the entire time. She didn't need any wine. She was already dizzy and floating.

"I should recite you something poetic," Cheng said.

"Why?"

"To woo you."

He captured her earlobe in his lips, teeth scraping tenderly. A shiver ran through her and her heart ached.

"Later," she replied.

The sound of his laughter resonated deep to the very core of her. They could be equals in this, at least for a night. She wasn't in a hurry, despite her reply. The heat inside her was a steady burn, cultivated throughout the day. The events of this life were so fleeting in and of themselves. She didn't want to rush this moment.

She curled into his lap. Cheng's arms cradled her close and she bent her head to press her lips against his throat. Every detail about Cheng fascinated her. The contours of his neck and shoulders. The texture of his skin and how his pulse throbbed just beneath it.

He slipped the robe from her shoulders. His

fingers grazed over her throat, sending a shudder down her spine. They were coarse, not pampered scholar's hands at all. She'd imagined them all day. Broad and confident, holding her.

His hands molded themselves to her body, curving down her back. Slowly, as if this exploration was enough. The sweep of his touch pushed the robe down to pool around her waist. The sense of being cared for overwhelmed her. Nothing ill could happen in his embrace.

He'd found the ties at the back of her bodice. Quicker now, as he pulled at the laces that held the silk cloth that covered her breasts. His breathing deepened as she was revealed to him. For a moment, he did nothing but take her in with his eyes. Heat rose up her neck.

Beauty was prized within the entertainment district. She was surrounded by distinguished courtesans—graceful flowers who enchanted all who looked upon them. She always paled against their glory, but Cheng looked at her as if she wasn't gaunt and inelegant. In his eyes, she was soft-curved and golden. Her small breasts and reed-thin limbs became something to treasure.

She reached for his sash. She needed something to do to tame the dangerous pounding of her heart. His robe opened down the centre. The swath of muscled torso made her breath catch. He helped her pull the linen free of his arms and then he was bared before her. Magnificent. She'd had lovers before. She would never be able to remember them from this point forward.

They came together, impatient now. He lowered her to the bed. Or was it she that pulled him over her, needing his pressure and weight above her? The opposites were one and the same.

They shed the rest of their clothing with a rough urgency. Cheng raised himself momentarily to pull away his trousers, and cool air washed over her in his absence. But soon he was back to hold her. She ran her tongue along the edge of his collarbone. She'd never done such a thing. He pressed his face into the curve of her neck, his groan a low rumble of pleasure. His organ grew thick against her hip.

"You're so beautiful," he said. "My Rose."

She cradled her hand over the back of his head and threaded her fingers lightly into his hair. He was burning. For her. Calling her by a name that wasn't even her own.

Without warning, her eyes grew hot and her chest tightened unbearably. The stinging sensation at the bridge of her nose startled her, as did the flood of implacable emotion.

"Rose? Are you all right?"

She'd gone still. She was filled with both hope and sadness, when there should have been nothing but eager desire. Cheng could sense every nuance of her body, pressed as close as they were. He started to raise himself to look at her, but she couldn't allow that. Her face would show too much. She grasped him tighter. Her breasts flattened against his chest.

She kissed him hard, passionately, desperately. Willing him to continue. The tension remained in him, hanging on the unanswered question, but she dug her hands into his back and ground her hips against him.

All hesitation melted away.

This time when he lifted his head, it was to take her breast into his mouth. His tongue circled her nipple, a liquid abrasion, and her back arched in a shock of desire. At the same time, his hand strayed downward to dip gently between her thighs. Roughened fingers against smooth flesh. The ripple of sensation curled her toes until she cried out.

Yes. Let their bodies persuade one another. For a moment, she'd allowed herself to think of the impossible. To yearn for permanence in this floating world. It had frightened her and Cheng had sensed it, without knowing what it was. This room, this moment, were all passing things.

Cheng shifted above her. This was a primal language without words. He was ready. There could be no more waiting. She was ready, too. A moment of anticipation as he placed himself against her. A pause in time, and then it began.

He pushed himself into her, willing her to take him in. So much growing pressure until she couldn't bear it. She swallowed and curved her arms around him, her legs around him, as he moved in her, taking her breath. Taking everything.

He lifted and thrust forward again. Pushing the pleasure so deep that it radiated through every part of her. Amidst the storm, they kissed, his mouth on her mouth, his hand on her breast. Joined completely down below. Touching as much as they could, in every way possible.

She closed her eyes. An image from the pillow book came to her of two lovers clutched together. She became the woman, her entire body lost to ecstasy. Cheng tensed above her. His movements became short and focused. Her body gripped his in fervent pleasure. This moment was fleeting, but this act was eternal.

And then her mind went black, and there was

nothing but heat, urgency, ecstasy. The rest of it had no words. Their coupling seared away everything else.

She clutched Cheng tighter as the climax rushed over her. Then she opened her eyes to watch greedily as Cheng reached his peak.

They lay still, heartbeats gradually slowing. Cheng twined his fingers lazily through hers. Her body still throbbed with the low echoes of their joining and she could hear music playing faintly from outside.

Chapter Four

"Don't you have to wake up early tomorrow for your exams?" Rose asked him.

They faced each other, lying side by side. The bed was too small for them to share it without being intertwined. Her bare leg stretched languidly over his as she pointed her toe to tease his foot. The blankets were in a tangle between them.

Cheng grinned. "There are exams tomorrow?"

He could climb Mount Tai with the energy circling through him.

Rose shifted to meet him eye to eye. Her outer robe fell slightly away, gracing him with the topmost curve of one breast. Just a hint of smooth skin and feminine softness before being hidden again behind maddening folds of silk. She'd draped the garment over her shoulders as the evening chill set in. If he could afford coal to heat the room, he might have convinced her to remain naked beside him. The small luxuries money could buy.

She swatted him lightly across his chest. "Men are so easily distracted."

"But you're particularly distracting."

"Shameless charmer," she accused.

He could see the hint of a smile before she ducked her face into the crook of her arm. There was so much more to her than she revealed. Rose liked his compliments, but refused to admit it. The only time she hadn't hidden behind barbs or insults or a small show of bullying was when they'd made love, though she had bitten his shoulder rather cruelly at one point during their second time. He hadn't minded.

Aimless conversation had taken them into the later stretches of the night. Rose spoke about the exotic trinkets they sold in the East Market and the well-tended parks of Changan. The ponds were filled with fish released from the market. Released from captivity into a larger prison, according to Rose.

He, in turn, told her of his province: the terraced farms with rows of millet and rice. About jade-green dragonflies that hovered over the harvest and how excited young boys would catch and tether them on silk strings. He felt like an excited boy himself beside her. The imperial exam was as far away as the kingdom of Zhao.

"I've seen students rushing to the exam hall with books held open, still reading," she said. "There's nothing left for you to study?"

He ran a hand over the cinch of her waist and down to the rise of her hip. "Nothing more worthwhile than this."

"You're very confident all of a sudden."

"I have reason to be."

She smirked. "Because of one essay?"

He ran his gaze over her face, then slowly down to the very tips of her toes which were painted red. Women held so many pleasant little secrets.

"Because I sense there's nothing the heavens would deny me today."

She snorted.

"Master Sun says, 'Be assured of your success and you will not fail,'" he quoted.

"Modesty is attended with profit, arrogance brings on destruction," she countered.

"Our greatest glory is not in never falling, but in rising every time we fall."

She wound a lock of his hair around her fingers and tugged playfully. "I see you go to your exams properly armed with a hundred proverbs."

"A thousand," he corrected. "And I must have read ten thousand books."

"And traveled ten thousand *li*." Rose laughed as she completed the saying.

As much as Cheng liked her laugh, Old Man Doubt was back upon him. The exchange of proverbs brought back all the sayings and all the books he'd tried to absorb. He couldn't chase the anxiety back with wine, or even with Rose. The favoured sons of noblemen had the leisure of spending years and years taking and retaking the exams. Without a good name or wealth to shelter him, he had nothing to rely on but his own abilities. This was his last chance.

"I must be ready." He rolled onto his back to stare up at the ceiling. "There's nothing left I can do to prepare."

He let his voice fall away, along with his swagger. Fear and uncertainty poured inside in its place. So many others were counting on him. If his name wasn't called out, he'd have no choice but to go home in shame.

Rose leaned over, her expression no longer taunting. "I'm sure you'll pass this time."

He shrugged and made a sound that meant nothing. Such empty encouragement was meant to puff his chest out with pride, but Rose didn't need to stoop to such flattery for him. It wasn't like her.

"No," she insisted. She placed her palm flat against his chest. "You will pass."

Her large eyes held on to him while his heartbeat thudded against her fingertips. He'd hidden so much of himself behind courtesy in an effort to become civilized. At every step, he walked in fear of revealing himself as a rough-mannered country lout. Yet Rose wasn't afraid of anything. She went after what she wanted without doubt and without apology.

She wasn't gracing him with empty words as a courtesan might. She was trying to give him a touch of that same stubborn determination.

He had to kiss her. He had to do something to seal this moment, but he was at a loss. Even a kiss seemed too insignificant.

Slowly his hand closed over hers. "Rose?"

Her voice came out as barely a breath. "Yes?"

"You've never played anything for me."

She frowned, pretty lips pouted together.

"Play something."

"Now? Here?" She looked about the room.

He smiled and went to the corner, returning with Rose's instrument. "A song to inspire me."

"But it's nighttime," she protested.

"Which is the same as daytime in the North Hamlet," he insisted. The apartments around them were likely still empty during the prime drinking hours of the night. Not that it mattered. The entire world was contained within his chamber tonight—everything he could ever need or want.

He placed the instrument into her waiting hands and reclined back on the opposite edge of the bed to watch. Rose took the tortoiseshell pick in hand and settled the pipa across her lap. She cradled the long wooden neck against her palm and positioned her fingers over the silk strings. Her black hair fell in a fan over one shoulder as she bent over the instrument.

Propped on one elbow, Cheng settled in to listen. Rose bestowed him an indulgent look before striking the first notes with the tips of her nails. She chose a song in the lyrical style. Sound flowed from the instrument, at first rapid and bold, then hesitant, like the unpredictable rhythm of falling rain. And just as clean and pure. Just as seductive.

He'd expected Rose to be technically skilled. He recognized her familiarity with the instrument and the thoughtful way she positioned her hands. Each elegant movement had been crafted and perfected, but the unbidden sensuality that emerged stunned him. His pulse absorbed the song and his breathing slowed. The music slipped inside him, swimming warm through his veins like liquor.

He clapped his hands together as the last note faded. "That was wonderful!"

Rose bowed her head slightly, her hair falling over her eyes in a gesture so demure that he was certain she was still performing.

"Another song," he insisted.

Her eyes were deep and mysterious. Her robe parted enticingly to reveal the pale skin of her throat. She shook her head.

"Please."

"You'd have to pay me and I know you have no cash left."

"Once I pass the imperial exams, I'll have you play for me every night."

Rose grew very still all of a sudden. With stiff movements, she turned to place the pipa by the side of the bed, her face purposely angled away.

"Rose?"

"Once you pass, you can host a great celebration banquet and invite any musician you wish." She made a move as if to rise. He had to reach across the bed to take hold of her arm.

"Rose, wait," he implored, as gently as he could.

"It's rather late." Her voice sounded muted.

Rose's back presented an impenetrable wall. He

could make out the rise of her shoulder blades beneath the silk.

"I've said something wrong." What had he done to ruin things? Just moments earlier, they'd been happy together. At least he'd thought so.

"You need to sleep, oh brilliant scholar," she said in a tone that was meant to be light.

"But we haven't even had the wine," he said in a tone that wasn't meant to be desperate.

"Save it to celebrate after the exams."

"Please stay. We'll sleep, just…just stay."

He soothed his hand down her back. Anything to heal the rift. Rose answered by lowering herself back onto the bed, still never looking directly at him. He left her that barrier as he folded himself in behind her. His arm found her waist. Her body only conceded after a pause, curving back to fit against him.

Carefully, he brushed her hair back from her neck, making a place for his head beside hers. They lay together in silence and he could hardly believe that only moments earlier there had been music in the room. And laughter shortly before that.

"I didn't know you could play with such emotion," he said.

His lips caressed the spot behind her ear. He

wanted to show her he wasn't just a country oaf. Rose had become as fragile as a paper doll in his arms.

"There's nothing emotional about it," she said. "I just practise. Practise all the time, until my fingers bleed."

She sounded distant and he didn't want to argue, but he remembered how her song had filled him. It had to move her the same way. Or maybe he was being one of those overly romantic scholars. He could hear Rose laughing at him over that.

Yet he was certain she'd poured herself into that song. There was no bitterness or cynicism there. For a moment she had opened herself up to him. It was hard to imagine that Rose could be fragile beneath her hard exterior. He closed his eyes and held her until she was asleep.

Jia woke with one half of her exposed to chilled air. The other half was pressed up against a large, warm mass of muscle from which an elbow protruded to dig into her side. Her hands were clutched on to the edge of the wool blanket in what was clearly a losing battle.

The dark of the room and the strangeness of the surroundings pressed down on her. The world outside was quiet which meant it was still early. The streets of Changan hadn't yet woken. She lay still, one arm warm and one arm cold, while she listened to the steady rumble of Cheng's breathing.

His presence tempted her. There was peace and comfort here, close enough to touch. Desire, hope, and fulfillment. A hundred more things she couldn't yet know. She closed her eyes and let herself indulge in the fantasy, but that was all it was. Every song girl and courtesan dreamed about having a wealthy patron, but she didn't want to be anyone's servant. Especially not Luo Cheng's after what they had shared.

With a sigh, she surrendered the battle and let go of the blanket. Her pipa was by the bed, her slippers should be somewhere close. She reached over the side and felt along the floor with one hand to locate them. Pulling the edges of her robe together, she started to slide from the bed.

"Hey."

A drowsy murmur startled her. Jia found herself snatched up in strong arms and tumbled back to the centre of the bed. Cheng covered her with the length and breadth of his body, using his elbows to support his weight over her.

"Where are you going?" In several sharp tugs, he'd repositioned the blanket over the both of them to enclose them in warmth.

She blinked up at him as Cheng's broad hands slipped beneath her back, lifting her into the cradle of his embrace. His hair was untied and fell to his shoulders. His eyes squeezed shut as he yawned. Something about it seemed so endearing.

"You have a busy morning," she said.

"Not until the gong for the Snake Hour sounds."

She'd had her one night, why tarnish it by becoming greedy for more? "But you'll have to prepare."

Cheng stubbornly refused to move. He bent his head to kiss an exposed spot on her shoulder. "You have a momentous day ahead, as well."

"What do you mean?"

"What will you do now that you're a wealthy woman?" Cheng asked.

She wasn't truly wealthy, but the paper note tucked away in her purse was enough to pay off all her debts with a little to spare. "I can play with my musicians' troupe if Old Man Han will still allow it. Or I can make arrangements with tea houses on my own. The important thing is that every coin I earn will now be my own."

The plan sounded empty to her own ears. She was like the carp she'd talked about, freed from a vat to remain captive in a larger pond. Odd that she'd planned and plotted for so long and now that her destiny was her own, she was a little lost and dizzy, like a child who'd run in circles for too long.

"Perhaps I'll run a drinking house of my own one day," she added.

"Really?" Cheng looked pleased. "My shrewd businesswoman."

His use of the possessive made her chest squeeze tight. "You're meant for even bigger things, I'm certain," she said.

He laughed, a little nervous. "We'll see how I fare against the exams. The battle wages on for an entire week."

Her dreams for Cheng were somehow more vivid than her own. He would pass his exams and be given a grand position within the imperial government. At night he'd come to visit her, wherever she was playing, but not as a sponsor or patron. They would be lovers. Friends.

"I may end up on the bridge over Wei River," he said.

"Don't say that!" That was a poor joke and she pinched him for it until he winced. Students were known to throw themselves off the bridge in dishonour after being unable to pass. "You'll be moving into the administrative ward," she predicted. "Into a huge mansion built for court officials."

His mouth curved and she grew warm as he

looked down at her. "Only if heaven and earth switched places would I qualify for the imperial court," he said.

He kissed her forehead tenderly and her heart tore, because she knew then that she couldn't allow herself to accept his regard. It was nothing more than a casual, passing affection. Impermanent, like everything else within the district. As time went by, she would inevitably start to long for more.

Her earlier dream continued, growing faded with time. He would still come to her, but their discourse would become cordial. Their vibrant fire would slowly go to ash, until one day, Cheng wouldn't come anymore. She'd wait and wait and then realize that she'd grown old and withered. He'd find some other song girl or courtesan skilled in the arts of pleasing wealthy and distinguished gentlemen.

Cheng continued. "In truth, I hope to return to my province. I'll take a position within the regional offices. It's more than a poor family from a farming village could ever hope for."

She would not let her disappointment show. Even if he were staying in Changan, she'd already decided she'd never see him again, hadn't she? She couldn't continue this affair. Not in servitude. That's all the courtesans and entertainers were.

Servants. No matter how much they held the higher ranks in their thrall.

"Your mother will be very honoured," she said. "And Minister Lo, as well."

His voice grew quiet. "And you?"

"I'll tell everyone that I knew a famous magistrate once—"

"Rose."

It was Cheng scolding her now. She'd made the mistake of sounding too cheerful. Too dismissive. She was already pulling away. She was a practical soul. Hanging on would only leave her devastated.

"Rose," he said again, gentler this time. He stroked his fingers through her hair. His gaze pinned her and dark fire glinted in his eyes. She knew his next touch wouldn't be a tender kiss on her forehead. There would be more. Much, much more.

Her heart thundered and her breath grew shallow. Could she turn him away now? Or if she just let him—if she just let both of them have this last moment, would it be easier to go away afterward? She squeezed her eyes shut and dug her hands into the corded muscle of his arms. Pull him closer or push him away? She didn't know. His weight pressed over her, securing her beneath him, and her body answered for her, turning to liquid silver and heat.

A pounding at the door made them both jump.

Cheng shot to his feet. Jia clutched a hand to the front of her robe. Both of them stared at the door. The pounding came again. With a creak of wood, the door flew open and three armed men strode into the chamber. The insignia on their armour marked them as Golden Eagle guards, as did the swords at their sides. The officer in charge directed two fingers toward Cheng.

"Take him."

"What is this?" Cheng demanded.

The two guardsmen stepped forward only to be shoved back roughly by Cheng. He wore only his trousers, but even disrobed he loomed large and powerful. The guards reached for their weapons and Jia gasped. Only then did the guardsmen pay her any notice.

She fumbled with the sash at her waist as one of the guardsmen came at her. By the time he reached her, she'd managed to close her robe despite her trembling fingers. The young guardsman cast her a warning look and stretched out an arm to keep her back.

Cheng was still arguing with the officer. Her cronies had told of how he'd fought them and she was afraid Cheng would do that now. The Eagle guards patrolled the city. They were the enforcers of Changan and had the authority to imprison and punish.

"He's an imperial scholar," Jia cried out. "Here to take the exams."

The officer looked to Cheng and then to her. In that one glance, he dismissed her as an insignificant singsong girl, but at least he addressed Cheng with an extra grain of respect.

"You're to come with us," he told Cheng. "You've been accused of theft."

Her blood grew cold. The book of poems. Guo had somehow discovered them.

She opened her mouth to speak, but Cheng shot her a look, urging her to stay silent. He snatched his robe from the floor and shoved one arm then the other into it. The two guardsmen secured him by each arm once he was dressed.

The exams. The exams were this morning and Cheng was being arrested.

"Cheng." She reached for him as they dragged him toward the door. She had to do something.

Cheng tried to remain composed. "Get Minister Lo."

She nodded mutely. Cheng kept his gaze fixed on her as long as he could before the guards shoved him past.

* * *

Jia tried. She tried with every breath inside her to get to Minister Lo.

The administrative district was at the north end of the city. Jia left the ward and hurried to the main avenue that cut through the centre of Changan. She managed to hire a sedan, not wasting any time to haggle over the fare. The markets would open within the hour and the streets were already filling with traffic. They'd only pushed past five wards before the gong sounded five times. The Dragon Hour.

Helplessness sank in. She gripped the edge of the carriage window and tried to breathe past the tightness in her chest. Her eyes stung. The next chime would sound the Hour of the Snake. The examination hall doors would swing shut.

Even if she could fly. Even if she could reach the administrative gates before the next double-hour, she had no way to locate Cheng's benefactor. There were thousands of officials within the district. Offices and sub-offices. She knew nothing about Changan outside the confines of her own pond.

Her stomach dropped and her nails bit into the wood frame of the sedan. This was not sentiment, she insisted. This was anger. She expected such

372   *Capturing the Silken Thief*

misfortune to fall on her, but Cheng didn't deserve to be punished. He was a simple scholar who did nothing but sit in his room and study all night, hoping to bring honour to his family. He'd helped her when she'd been nothing to him.

The carriage rolled on and they passed another ward, moving like a winter river clogged with ice. Jia chewed her bottom lip in frustration. Even now she wasn't being fair to Cheng. He wasn't simple. He was good. Luo Cheng didn't have a selfish act in him.

Cheng had looked at her so tenderly in the still hours of the morning. Whispering her name... No, not her name. She hadn't even been true to him in that sense. He'd embraced her, called her beautiful, made her laugh. Made love to her. In return, she'd had him robbed and beaten and now he was in prison. There was nothing good or pure about her.

She knocked frantically on the side of the sedan. "Turn around." She had to shout in order for the driver to hear her. "Quickly!"

Jia pulled the silk pouch from her belt. The paper note crinkled inside. She took it out and unfolded it in her palm. Paper felt so insignificant compared to bronze. Flying money, they called it, as if it would flutter away and disappear.

Looking at the inscription nearly did bring her

to tears, but sentiment had no place in the North Hamlet. She'd allowed herself to indulge for one night instead of going directly to the troupe master, and look what had happened! She'd had plans. She was going to be free of all her debts and worries.

But Cheng had dreams and plans, as well. A dream that was about to be taken away. She didn't know if she could go on, feeling so ruined inside for the rest of her life.

Chapter Five

The door opened to his holding cell. The stern-faced guardsman at the door gave a brusque nod of his head, which Cheng supposed meant he was free to go. Or it could mean that he was to be led outside for a public beating.

He was surprised to see Rose waiting for him outside the head wardsman's office instead of Minister Lo. She had a bag slung over her shoulder and watched anxiously while they removed the chains from his wrists. Despite the mess of the situation, his chest puffed out at seeing Rose flustered over him.

As soon as he was free, she grabbed on to his hand. "Hurry!"

They ran from the building with Rose dragging him along with the force of a tiny storm. Vendors and pedestrians veered aside in her wake. Her robe whipped behind her like the tail of a kite. She was a wonder to behold.

"Wait, how did you get them to release me?" he asked when she stopped at a busy intersection.

"Your landlord claimed he saw you leaving the room." Rose stood on her toes, trying to peer through the crowd. "But that fool Guo didn't have any real evidence against you."

They were off again, swerving around carts, ducking through alleys. The morning air rushed by his ears. His muscles were on fire and his blood pumped in a fierce rhythm that propelled them ever forward. The imperial exams loomed ahead, the minutes waning away, yet all he knew was that Rose's hand was clutched around his. Nothing could stop them.

Soon the examination hall stood ahead. Rose flew up the steps. Even with his longer stride, he could barely hold on. He swore she wanted him to pass more than he did. Near the top, she finally stopped and swung around.

"Here."

She pulled out his scholar's cap from her pack and tried to smooth out the black cloth with her fingers. He bent so she could place it on his head. Her cheeks were tinged with pink and she was breathless from the wild run through the streets.

"Something's not right," he said.

"I know. It's crooked." Rose fussed over the

headdress, trying to straighten it and arrange the tassels of cloth that fell down his back. Every muscle within her remained tense. Her expression was guarded.

"How did you even get in to see the head of the ward?" Cheng asked.

She wouldn't look at him. Instead she fumbled within the bag. "I told you that I know every official in the district."

He realized then what had happened. He reached for her, his voice thick with emotion. "Rose."

She thrust the writing box into his hands. "Go inside before you're late."

"Rose, you bribed them to release me."

The gong rang through the ward, starting the count for the hour. Another student ran into them, head down, book still open in his hands. Rose smiled as the young man apologized and redirected himself around them. She was still smiling when she finally met his eyes. It was a weak attempt to hide the sadness.

"Go," she commanded. Even her commands had lost their sharpness. She brushed her hands briefly over the front of his robe in a show of smoothing out the wrinkles there. "You're going to be late."

His hands tightened over his writing case. If he could get hold of her, he'd never let go.

The gong had sounded four times. Cheng had no choice but to go into the examination hall. He looked back once to see Rose looking after him. Her hands were twined anxiously together. Her wide eyes were full of fear and hope.

The gong sounded again and it was time to find his place.

The examinations went on for over three days. Jia passed by the examination hall at least once on each of those days, though she knew it was completely senseless. Cheng was locked inside, writing commentaries on the five classics and the great poets. She refused to call her behaviour sentimental. It was just curiosity, that was all.

At the end of the week when the scholars gathered at the head of the turtle sculpture to hear the lists of names, she stood at the far end of the plaza, within the shadow of an alleyway. Cheng stood taller than the rest. She could only see him in profile, but she could make out the tilt of his head as he waited with anticipation.

The first rankings were read aloud. Luo Cheng wasn't among them. She dug her nails so hard into her palms they nearly drew blood. The second ranking was read next. She strained to hear each name as the crier announced them one by one from his scroll. When she heard his name, she nearly shouted with joy. She wanted to run to him, but it wouldn't have been proper.

His colleagues gathered around to congratulate him. Then the next names were being read and everyone hushed with attention. Cheng's shoulders lifted with pride now as he listened to the rest of the rankings. Watching him filled her with joy.

She'd fallen in love. The realization took her breath away. Just the sight of Luo Cheng flooded her with yearning. His happiness had become her happiness.

He turned his head then, inexplicably glancing over his shoulder. Jia ducked farther into the alley, her face burning. Her heart beat fearfully and panic set in. She was too far away for him to have possibly seen her, anyway. It would be too awkward if they met.

She retreated from the plaza to return to the far reaches of the North Hamlet to bury her pain. Cheng had an illustrious future ahead of him now. She was just one of the hundreds of entertainers in the imperial capital, playing the same collection of melodies, reciting the same poems. Another tragic song girl who'd fallen in love with a man above her station.

Over the next days, her routine returned to its

familiar pattern. The troupe played at several celebration banquets for those who had passed the exams with high marks. She was hoarding coins again, saving toward paying back her ever-present, ever-growing debt.

The floating world shifted around her as it did every year. She passed by Cheng's apartment and learned that he had moved out. A new student would eventually rent out that room. The cycle would begin again.

She didn't seek him out before he left. There was no point in doing so. Their time together was precious now, locked in her memory.

In a week's time, the celebrations had died down and the ward resumed a more restrained level of revelry. The houses were only half full by evening time. The atmosphere became languid, a slow smoulder in comparison to the crackling fire just a week earlier.

One evening, she received an invitation to play at the Lotus Pavilion.

"The Lotus?" She had to ask the troupe leader twice.

He nodded and waved her away as if she were a gnat. The invitation was for her alone. She dressed in her most elegant robe, trying not to think of how it was the same one she'd worn her night with Cheng. The same robe he'd slipped off of her.

With her pipa in hand, she headed toward the pagoda. It stood like a beacon with its hanging lanterns and layered towers. She knew several songs that would allow her to captivate a room all by herself. She rehearsed in her head as she entered the pavilion through the side doors.

The reception hall was blinding in its opulence, a pink halo of orb lanterns, jade sculptures, wood carvings that spanned four walls. She wandered for a few steps, lost. Fortunately, the hostess intercepted her and directed her to a banquet room at the back of the pavilion.

The entrance was through an interior corridor. She pushed open the door tentatively. The vast banquet hall was empty except for the one man seated at the head of the table. He stood and the air rushed from her.

Everything about Cheng seemed different now. His grey scholar's robe was replaced with a dark blue brocade. His hair was combed and tied back neatly. He even appeared taller. Or maybe it was that her knees wanted to collapse as he came near. Her heart had stopped beating, she was sure of it.

"Your name isn't Rose," he accused lightly.

She thought of a hundred different retorts she

could use, but in the end her elation at seeing him again overwhelmed her. "I started to like how you called me that."

His expression remained inscrutable as he took her in. He had a new detached confidence about him and she yearned for the Cheng she'd known. She no longer knew how to be with him.

"Yang Jia-jing." He pronounced her name slowly, as if tasting it on his tongue. "It took me a long time to find you."

He'd been searching for her. She warmed at the thought.

Sentiment again. She'd make a fool of herself if she wasn't careful. She composed herself. "I saw your name displayed at the examination hall. I'm very happy for you."

And she was—both happy and sad.

Cheng's expression softened. "I thought I'd see you after the exams. You knew where to find me."

She shook her head, unable to answer. All she'd ever brought him was misfortune. He came forward until he stood right before her. She could already see him as an appointed official. He had the stature and bearing for it. She held on to the pipa as a last barrier between them.

He reached into his robe and pulled out an envelope. "I have something for you."

She hesitated, searching his face. Finally she set her instrument aside and took the letter.

"That poem I promised you," he said as she opened it.

"This is no poem," she protested as she unfolded the paper inside to reveal a column of figures. Then she read through the entire letter. She looked up at Cheng to see the corners of his mouth twitching.

She bent her head to inspect the document one more time. "I was wrong," she said, her throat threatening to close up. "It's a beautiful poem."

Cheng had paid off the troupe master. All her debts were cleared.

"I had to do it," he said softly. He took a step closer. "After what you did."

"Please don't mention that." Her face burned with shame. "It was all one mistake after another. I was only trying to set things right."

"I wasn't talking about you bribing the head of the ward." He reached out to stroke his thumb along her cheek. "I meant what you did for me. When I first took the exams, I was afraid of expressing any opinions. I echoed the classics with cold efficiency, afraid of overstepping my bounds. You made me remember what it was to aspire, to risk everything. You showed me how to be fearless."

"Reckless," she corrected him.

He grinned. "That as well." Then his voice lowered, deepening with emotion. "You're why I passed."

"Nonsense," she scoffed, blinking furiously. She looked down to stare at the letter. "But this is very generous. Thank you."

He still hadn't told her what she was hoping to hear: that he'd missed her. That he could think of nothing else. She should have known better than to dream like that. Her freedom was more than enough. The ring of laughter interrupted her thoughts.

"Rose… Jia. Do you think I learned nothing from you? This isn't generosity."

She narrowed her eyes suspiciously at him. "Then what is it?"

"An offer." He slid his arms around her, tugging at her so that she tumbled against him. "A bargain. A bribe."

She steadied her hands against his chest. He felt so good. "What for?" she asked.

His voice lowered and his hold tightened around her. "So you'll agree to be my wife."

"I can't." She struggled against him, but it was only nominal at best. She'd dreamed of being in his arms every night they were apart. "You have a shining future ahead of you. You can have any match you want. A girl from a good family."

"I want a woman who can take on lords and vagabonds alike."

"But—"

Cheng silenced her with a kiss. Her limbs weakened at the possessiveness in his embrace. She fit herself to him and closed her eyes, letting his solid shape and presence surround her. She'd wanted him so much that it was painful to even think of it.

"I can do this until you stop arguing," he threatened. "Forever if I need to."

She started to renew her protest, but Cheng simply kissed her again to deliver on his threat—just as she'd hoped he would.

* * * * *

*If you enjoyed these stories,
you won't want to miss these other great reads
from Jeannie Lin:*

*A DANCE WITH DANGER
THE SWORD DANCER
MY FAIR CONCUBINE
THE DRAGON AND THE PEARL
BUTTERFLY SWORDS*